EAT YOUR
HEART OUT

KELLY DEVOS

RAZORBILL

To my grandmother, Vivian,
who told the best bedtime stories

RAZORBILL

An imprint of Penguin Random House LLC, New York

First published in the United States of America by Razorbill,
an imprint of Penguin Random House LLC, 2021

Copyright © 2021 by Kelly deVos

Visit us online at penguinrandomhouse.com.

Library Of Congress Cataloging-in-Publication Data is available.

ISBN 9780593204825

Manufactured in Canada

1 3 5 7 9 10 8 6 4 2

Design by Samira Iravani

Text set in ITC Clearface Std

AUTHOR'S NOTE

The following pages contain satire! This book is set at a terrible fat camp run by the world's worst scientists, whose behavior and schemes are more extreme versions of what we see in today's diet culture. By villainizing these ideas and the industry as a whole, and by having these courageous, kickbutt campers blow up the system on their own terms, I hope you'll see how damaging fatphobia is to everyone. Because when you create a culture where people can be dehumanized for trivial reasons like body size, everyone's human dignity is in jeopardy. I intend for this read to be inclusive and affirming, and hope you read with care if these topics are ones close to your heart.

Happy reading!

Kelly deVos

What role are you auditioning for today?

Action Girl (aka Final Girl or the Resourceful Heroine)
Odds of survival: 100%
Action Girl is who we all want to be. That fearless butt-kicker. Who we all imagine ourselves to be. We need our Clarice Starlings, Ellen Ripleys, Donna Chamberses, and Laurie Strodes. Action Girl will survive. She has to.

The Basket Case
Odds of survival: 0%
The girl who cries too much or screams too much or feels too much or falls apart too much. The cheerleader. The social media star. Sometimes the main character's best friend. Secretly, the audience is wondering, "Will this chick die already?" The group is typically better off without her.

The Courageous Captain
Odds of survival: 0%
He's the guy who can somehow get everyone to cooperate. He leads everyone to safety. But everything comes at a price. The Captain always goes down with the ship.

The Jock
Odds of survival: 50–75%
This one could go either way. Jocks can be major dicks. If The Jock makes too many boob jokes, expect him to get his head ripped off. The Jock with a Heart of Gold

has a decent shot. He's easy to like and to root for. He might make it.

The Jerk
Odds of survival: 10%
Everyone loves seeing jerks get what they deserve. The Jerk will only survive if he undergoes a huge character transformation. Or if he's portrayed by a big-time A-list actor.

The Nerd
Odds of survival: 50%
Let's face it, Nerds have essential abilities. They hack computers and read maps and pick locks. Every team needs a Nerd. But Nerds might bite it if they're no longer needed. Or if they're especially likeable and their death would tug at the heartstrings.

The Outcast
Odds of survival: unknown
The dark horse. The unpredictable loner. The bookish weirdo. The kid no one knows or understands. Outcasts keep their skills hidden. Their power is that you don't know what they know. They might have the skills to survive.

In the next few hours, one of three things will happen.

1—We'll be rescued (unlikely).

2—We'll freeze to death (maybe).

3—We'll be eaten by thin and athletic zombies (odds: excellent).

I guess it's possible that there will be some kind of a miracle. But if a divine intervention was forthcoming, you'd think it would have happened already. All but five of us are either dead or down below in the mindless, flesh-eating horde.

Oh yeah, and the pregnant girl's about to give birth. So, there's that.

I'm not even sure I deserve to live.

Allie is dead.

Because of me.

How did I get here? How did we end up trapped on the roof of Dr. Frankenstein's creepy laboratory at Camp Featherlite for Overweight Teens during the worst snowstorm that Flagstaff, Arizona, has seen in a hundred years?

I keep thinking about my mom and those four little words.

"Sweetheart, I'm getting married."

FOCUS

VIVIAN ELLENSHAW

My worst nightmare lurked on the welcome mat.

Coach Hanes just would *not* leave, and that was the first clue that something was changing.

Going wrong.

My mom was *busy*. That was the defining characteristic of her personality. She was busy inspecting franchises of Pied Piper Pizza. Busy writing reports. Busy telling Maria, our housekeeper, that the roast was too salty or that the linen napkins needed to be pressed. Busy posting vacation pics on social media to make sure everyone thought her life was perfect.

So when Mom lingered near the red door with Coach, her hand hovering above the crystal knob, giggling, touching her face with her other hand, it was more than gross.

It was a problem.

I tried to tell Mom that there's something weird about a guy who wants to work at an all-girls Catholic high school. But she wouldn't hear it. *Somebody has to work there. It's a job, and somebody has to do it*, she said with one of her Mom looks. A frown and an arched eyebrow and lips pressed flat that, all working together, said, *I know everything, and you know nothing*.

"The van's here," my mom calls from downstairs.

What I *knew* was that Coach Hanes hated fat people in general and hated me specifically. After I was elected captain of the soccer team, he held a secret meeting without me and tried to get the other girls to choose someone "who better represents the school's athletic ideals." Too bad for him that our team is very, very cool.

They took another vote and stuck with me.

And that was seriously the right choice, because, despite what Coach might think, I rule St. Mary's. My soccer team fundraisers keep the protein bars and Gatorade freely flowing and make sure we usually get an air-conditioned bus to the matches—a huge advantage when you live in Phoenix and it's so hot out that you feel like you're running on the surface of the sun. Blue mathlete ribbons cover an entire wall in my room. I hate to brag, but let's just say that it's not a party until I show up. More than that, my body size is none of his business.

Of course, they got married. Coach Hanes moved from his crappy little post-divorce studio apartment into our place. I did a pretty good job pretending the whole thing didn't bother me. When Mom replaced me in the wedding with Coach's skinny sister, it hurt. I told everyone that the wedding was way gauche, that Mom's orange-sherbet color palette was awful, and that I was glad to avoid the horror of being dressed up like an oversize ice cream cone.

I told people I didn't care that Coach made snide comments about my weight and that my mom did nothing to stop it.

But it bothered me.

The whole thing bothered me a lot.

Maria knocks softly on my door, and a second later, the old Polish woman pokes her gray-haired head into my room. She's carrying my favorite red hoodie. "The van's here," she says. She places the sweatshirt on top of the duffel bag nearest to the door.

"Okay," I say.

She gives me a grim smile. "Maybe it will be nice. They say it might snow."

"Maybe."

She frowns, sighs, and her shoulders slump. "She could've had her pick of a million men. She only has one child."

I fake a smile. "It's fine."

The last six months have not been fine.

Maria takes the bag shaped like a giant watermelon slice, and I carry the one covered with unicorns. Together, we march down the stairs.

She stops in front of Mom's collection of artfully arranged vases with her arms held out for a hug. I feel like the Jolly Green Giant's illegitimate daughter towering over the tiny old woman. Her arms can't reach all the way around my back.

"Maybe it will be nice," she says again.

Looking as composed as an Instagram post, Mom waits in the satin upholstered armchair near the door. She snaps her copy of *World Traveler* magazine shut and rises, her velvet robe barely touching the marble tile floor.

"Of course it will be nice," she says with a huge, cheerful smile. "I mean, it should be, for what we're paying. Did you check the brochure? It's a resort. They've got a private lake. An indoor swimming pool. Guided nature walks. Yoga. A vegan dietician. All the movie stars send their kids. The governor sent his own daughter last spring, and she . . ."

Sigh.

Thanks to Coach, I'll be spending my winter break at the world's fanciest fat camp.

How are fat camps still even *a thing*? Don't they belong

8

in a museum with inflatable dart boards, Flowbees, and Thigh-masters?

I open the door, and the cool winter morning air hits my face. I mean, I guess it's morning. It's before six and barely light outside.

Mom keeps talking. "We're lucky the camp had a few cancellations due to the weather. Thankfully I was able to get all the paperwork done in time. *And* this session they're testing a brand-new weight-loss bar. Just think. You could . . ."

I step outside, and the heavy red door swings closed.

It immediately reopens. "Aren't you forgetting something?"

I make my way down the grand walk without turning back to her. "Nope. Maria did all my laundry and got me all packed."

"You know what I mean."

I hear the light pitter of designer slippers behind me. "Uh, hello. Where's my hug?"

Pushing my arms into my hoodie, I say, "My ride's here."

As I approach the white van with the CAMP FEATHERLITE logo splashed on its side, a guy about my age emerges from the driver's door. He jerks his chin in my direction, takes my bags, and moves toward the back of the van. I hold on to my red hoodie.

Mom steps in front of me before I can grab the door handle. "I know you *think* you don't want to go. But Brad's an expert. He's done a ton of research about health and weight issues and self-esteem. You'll be a lot healthier and much happier—"

Someone should research what having Coach antagonize you every morning at breakfast does to your self-esteem.

I fold my arms across my chest. "Coach knows that I come to practice every morning and do the drills the same as every other girl, and I passed my physical with flying colors. I'm happy the way I am. If you really cared about me, you would be happy, too."

The beefcake guy returns and ducks around Mom to open the door himself.

Mom scowls. "For God's sake, Vee. Could you please stop calling him *Coach*? His name is Brad." She glances toward the house. "Wait a sec. He was coming out to say goodbye."

"The van's here," I say in the same singsong voice she used.

I climb inside the open door and basically fall into a seat in the first row.

Mom sighs. "Someday you'll understand that I only want what's best."

I reach out to close the door. "For you and Coach. Have a nice life," I tell her as it slams shut.

The guy in the front seat seems to have a pretty good read on things. I catch a glimpse of his blue eyes in the rearview, and it's like he kind of gets it. Also, he smells like Irish Spring soap. He puts the van in gear and steps on the gas.

I stare straight ahead and don't look at Mom as we leave our house behind.

The scene is over.

For a second, I'm relieved. It's quiet in the van, and I've got some time. To compose myself. To tell myself that I'll enjoy spending my break with a bunch of perfect strangers whose big bodies are also a big inconvenience to their parents.

By the time we get to the next stop, I'll be that cool girl again. The smart one. The funny one. The one who always has a comeback. Not this pathetic, sniffling loser.

In another hour, maybe I will have convinced myself that the whole thing was my idea. Like I decided that I'd rather run my ass off on a treadmill than have cocoa with Coach.

Except I'm not alone in here.

A high-pitched sneeze comes from the back of the van.

I recognize it instantly, but I turn around anyway.

Of course.

It had to be.

In the back seat. Pressed all the way up against the frosted-over window.

Wrapped in a thick black scarf.

Allison DuMonde.

ALLISON DUMONDE

The driver steers away from Vee's perfect house on her perfect street.

I glance over my shoulder to see Mrs. Ellenshaw, in her velvet bathrobe and Ferragamo slippers, nod in her curt, all-business way. Mrs. E is the same as always. Perfect. Like she'd been to the hairdresser before she had her morning latte. Maria hovers in the doorway, clutching the collar of her work shirt, watching the whole scene with disdain. The thought of Maria's homemade Pączki doughnuts makes my mouth water.

It has been a long time since I was inside 21 Pembroke. I know I'm trash, okay? What I did was trash. I tried to apologize. I tried to admit that I'd messed up. It wasn't enough for Vee. There wasn't a way to make her understand. So six months of the silent treatment.

And here we are.

Even though I knew it was coming, I've been dreading this moment for weeks.

Miss Pariah and Miss Popular trapped in a van together.

Vee is in the seat in front of me, and she's the same as always. With her shiny brown hair bouncing up and down. With her designer bags and strawberry lip gloss. Sure, her mom is loaded and Vee will totally fit in with the bougie kids at a place like Camp Featherlite. But we'd been best friends since . . . well . . . since birth. There is no way Vee wanted to get in this van. She is at war with fatphobia. She's wearing a sweatshirt with a knitted dancing cheeseburger, for God's sake.

I take a deep breath and pat the camera I have taped to my belly.

This is the last chance I'm gonna get.

Vivian glances back at me and gives me that look. The way people look at you when they know you're a total fake. She probably didn't put ten seconds of thought into what she threw on this morning, but it's exactly right. It's the careless kind of look that only rich people can ever pull off. They have everything and don't know what anything costs.

Me? Well. I've been going through thrift stores for weeks. Sewing up small holes in my seams using my trusty sewing kit. Meticulously packing. Repacking. I even sketched out my outfits in my journal. *Pathetic.*

I'm wearing the black cashmere sweater that Dorian kicked at me when she was packing, my black jeans with the zippers at the ankles, and a pretty decent knockoff men's Hermés scarf I found on eBay. I was trying to look like I have a closet full of designer clothes and these were the old things I threw on to travel in.

Vee isn't buying it.

No doubt she is also wondering who coughed up the thirty grand for the camp fee.

I have to keep her from finding out.

The hot guy driving the van takes us out of Scottsdale and onto the freeway. From up on the ramp, I get a great view of the sun bursting over the horizon in a stunning show of reds and oranges and golds.

Vivian turns back again. "So," she begins, drawing out the *O* way longer than necessary. "Where's DeeDee?"

Part of me admires the way that Vivian stubbornly refuses to get on board the Dorian Leigh DuMonde celebrity gravy train. "Dorian's making a film in Prague," I say, trying to sound light and casual, "and obviously my sister doesn't belong at fat camp."

"Neither do we," Vee says through her teeth.

But Vivian doesn't live in a tangerine-colored double-wide in a senior citizen trailer park with an old, crappy strip of Christmas lights blinking haphazardly in a palm tree. Vee's window doesn't have a scenic view of a carport full of junk.

We aren't both stuck in that trailer park.

Only I am.

With that pronouncement, she tosses her hair over her shoulder and turns her attention to the driver. In the rearview mirror, I watch her give the guy one of her trademark grins.

Then she does her best terrible British accent.

"'Ello, poppet," she says. "Where we headed?"

STEVE MILLER

I need money.

That's it.

I don't think these girls belong at a fat camp. Nobody does.

Shit. I can't believe that there even *is* such a thing.

I come from four generations of farmers. We work our asses
off. Take pride in putting food on the table. That's what Granddad
always said. These people are paying someone more than we make
some seasons to keep food *away* from them. It just about boggles
my mind.

Plus, it seems pretty harsh to ship your kids off during the
holidays.

Who does that? And why?

But I have a simple problem.

I need cash.

It's slightly more complicated than that. My parents are involved in some kind of bullshit lawsuit with Monsanto, and until
it's over there's no money for anything extra but paying the lawyer. Keeping food on our own table means all hands in the field.

My dad thought I'd sure as shit get some kind of a football
scholarship.

The scouts had come and gone.

I was good.

But not good enough.

Luckily, I always did okay in school and got accepted to U of A
based on grades. I tried out for the Wildcats and landed a spot as a

walk-on. The coach talked about putting me on the regular roster. Coach said a scholarship was still a possibility. Things like that happened from time to time. There was Brandon Bulsworth. He was a walk-on and played for the Colts. And . . . well . . . there was . . . well . . . Bulsworth is the only one I could think of. But it happened.

The coach kept talking about future options.

In the meantime, my tuition payments are due in three weeks.

So . . .

No money, no school.

No school, no . . . well, no future.

Mom is seriously pissed that I'll be gone right before Christmas, and I know all the gift cards Grandma sends in the mail will be picked over by the time I get home. That's what happens when you're smack in the middle of four sisters. But I'm eighteen, so Mom had to let me go. Dad promised he'd square it for me.

What choice did I really have? The whackjobs at Camp Featherlite are willing to shell out $5,000 a week—*for two weeks*—for nothing really. Basically, me being a butler to a bunch of . . . uh . . . *tycoons of tomorrow*, as my recruiter described the camp kids. I can't for the life of me figure out why they want to pay so much.

A lady in a long white lab coat interviewed me last week in a gray office in Tucson. Said they'd had an employee leave them in the lurch. They needed people like me, she said. Kept referring to me as a *championship athlete*, which I guess is true. Our *team* won the championship. Of course, I didn't tell her that I'd been passed over by every college football scout because there were a million guys out there exactly like me.

I squint and try to focus on the road. It's hard to stop thinking about that woman. Not because she was hot. I mean, maybe she was. For an older lady.

Not even because she was really fucking creepy. Stiff and shiny and robotic. Blonde. Like the androids that will be replacing us all after the apocalypse.

No. It was because she had a private security guard. Two, actually. One guy outside the strip mall office and one on the inside. They had shiny silver crests on their black suits and stood at attention like secret service agents at a political rally.

I keep thinking.

What kind of a doctor needs military-grade security?

I push those thoughts down. I mean, c'est la vie. The cash will make my spring tuition payment in full and buy me some time to get on the full roster.

So Dr. Barbie gave me a bunch of khaki slacks and baby blue sweatshirts, directions to the camp, and assigned me a Pod. Featherlite's super-dumb way of referring to the kids I was supposed to herd from place to place. Make sure they got their meals and their exercise.

Bonus: they let me use the van until camp started.

So here I am. Driving from Phoenix to Flagstaff with two rich girls in the back.

Well. Make that one trailer park girl who looks like a movie star and one rich girl.

I glance in the rearview mirror at Vivian Ellenshaw.

Keep your eyes on the road, buddy.

"We have one more pickup. In Flagstaff," I tell her. "And then we'll meet the rest of our Pod when we get to camp."

"Our Pod?" Vivian repeats, smacking her glossy lips and making the same expression I wanted to make when the CreepBot5000 gave this intel to me.

"It's how they organize you—er—us. Into groups of six that they call Pods. Five campers and a Facilitator," I say in a tone that I hope at least mimicked something professional.

"You're the . . . uh . . . Facilitator, I guess," Vivian says with a grin. She reaches forward. I get a little warm when she taps the cheesy gold name tag they gave me to wear. "You *Fly like an Eagle*, eh, poppet?"

I chuckle. "You're a classic music fan?"

"I'm semi-ironically into 1970s vinyl," she says with a wry smile.

From the back seat, the girl from the trailer park coughs. "Who's *they*?" she calls out.

I stare at her in the rearview. My pickup sheet says that this is Allison DuMonde. She's dressed from head to toe in clothes that look like they belong in *Seventeen* (as I said, I have four sisters). She's a bigger version of that actress in all those teen vampire movies. *Stake My Heart*. And . . . uh . . . *Frostbitten*. Shit. I hate to admit that I've seen them all.

"Uh. What?" I ask.

Her shoulders slump. "You said *they* organize us into Pods."

"Oh. Yeah. MetabaCorp. The company that runs the camp."

"What do you know about them?" Vivian asks.

I steer the van onto I-17. It's getting light. Becoming a bright Saturday morning.

"Nothing." I shrug.

It hits me right then. I hadn't really bothered to find out

anything about MetabaCorp. Or where we're going. Or what we might find when we get there.

Vivian leans back in her seat. A second later, she's got her phone in front of her face.

I sit there trying to think of ways to impress her.

For some reason, I really want to impress her.

Right then, the snow starts coming down.

Not in flakes. In thick mounds that splatter against the windshield like egg yolks.

Another thought hits me.

We should turn around.

Snow continues to fall, and we speed toward Flagstaff, passing a couple of freeway exits.

I can't shake that feeling.

I should turn the van around.

PAUL FANNON

Pickup is late.

It's probably the snow.

Heavy clumps of ice fall from the sky.

Which is unusual. For Flagstaff. For December.

Any kind of weather brings the entire state of Arizona to a standstill.

A single drop of rain can cause traffic jams for hours.

About 9:15, the van finally shows up, and I, once again, regret my decision not to drive myself. The camp is, at most, an hour from our place. I could make it in forty-five in my Porsche. But if I ever want to convince my parents that I am the future head of FannonPharma, I have to fully commit.

Mom comes out of her home office and hands me a blue bag that looks like an oversize lunch box. "I packed you some food. Just in case. I spoke with Dr. Volstead. She said the chef serves normal meals in the employee mess hall. They'll give you an access pass to the restricted area after you arrive." She shoves the bag into my hands. "But you can never be too prepared. So I packed you some of the Snapple you like . . . some Payday bars . . ."

I tune the rest of her grocery list lecture out and grab the duffel bags stacked next to the umbrella stand. We stop together near the door, and even though I was expecting it, the sound of the gate's buzzer still makes me jump.

I press the intercom button. "Be right there," I say, imitating my father's brusque tone.

Mom reaches out to fluff and smooth the collar of my dress shirt. "Are you sure you want to do this? Perhaps we should try calling your father again. I still haven't been able to reach him, and I don't know if he would approve of this plan."

Of course he wouldn't approve of this plan.

You burn down one pool house and you're classified as a screwup forever.

I shake my head. "Mom, I'll be fine."

She gives me what is meant to be a reassuring smile. "I know your father seemed disappointed when Bill's son canceled at the last minute. He was really hoping he'd get an inside view of camp operations. A total picture of how things are working over there. This session especially . . ."

Dad *was* unusually upset when he found out that Dr. Kaiser's son, Carl, had the chicken pox. Upset for Dad, anyway. Which meant that his mouth twitched twice. One of his thick eyebrows traveled up toward his dark hairline. He murmured something about the new investors and drank an extra martini. And he said, "I sometimes question Dr. Kaiser's level of commitment to our project." Which was way harsh criticism from a guy who rarely broke out of his compassionate, caring physician character.

Dad said that they'd come up with a cure for obesity and that he wanted Carl to pose as a camper and give feedback on how the other kids responded to the treatment. I tried to tell myself that Dad wanted to send Carl because he was a little meatier than me and would fit in a bit better at Featherlite. But the truth was probably that he trusted his business partner's son more than he trusted me.

I didn't know what it meant to cure obesity. How do you cure what is essentially a bunch of lazy people eating massive plates of loaded tater tots at the Cheesecake Warehouse?

I guess I'll find out.

"But these new investors . . . well . . . and the storm . . ." Mom's smile fades, and she sort of shivers. The kind of thing you wouldn't even notice if you hadn't been living with someone since birth. Whoever these investors are, they even intimidate my parents.

She forces her face back into typical mom mode. "I'm not sure this is the best idea."

"I'll be fine," I tell her again. "I can fill out these Behavioral Observation Forms as well as Carl Kaiser."

"Be careful," she says.

After kissing Mom on the cheek, I pull up the collar of my coat, head into the cold, and walk past the giant stone fountain that's filling with snow. I have to go slow. For a second, I think about going back inside and putting on my boots. I'm wearing my dress shoes, and they are slippery. But I am halfway down our long drive, and the guy at the gate can already see me.

I'll have to change once we get to camp.

Okay. Let's do this thing.

A generic jock holds the door of a dorky white Sprinter van. I drop my bags at his feet and climb in next to a fat girl who could only be described as a rainbow explosion. Everything about her, from her pink lipstick to her purple Docs, is some bizarre color. Staring at her makes me feel the way I do when I have a hangover. Like everything in the world is too bright.

She tilts her head and opens her mouth. Like she wants to say something but can't quite decide what.

Mr. Meathead hustles back to the driver's scat. He moves quick. He wears boots.

The guy turns around and points to the girl next to me. "That's Vivian. Allison is in the back. Everybody, this is Paul Lewis."

Of course, he *had* to say my last name. I registered as Paul Lewis, my mother's maiden name, but I feel like a fool calling myself that.

I glance in the direction of the back seat. The girl back there looks like a plus-size model. Her eyes keep darting toward the open van door. As if she'd like nothing better than to make a break for it and run out into the white abyss.

"I'm Steve Miller. Your . . . uh . . . Facilitator," the jock finishes awkwardly.

The fat girl eyes me with suspicion. "What brings you to our Pod, Paul?"

"Same as you, I guess," I say. "Trying to get in shape. Learn to eat right."

She frowns. "I'm already in shape and know how to eat right."

"Right." I have to hand it to the girl though. It takes balls to show up to fat camp dressed in a sparkly hamburger outfit.

Miller drives slow. I don't blame him. He has the defroster on full blast and the windshield wipers going fast, and it is still almost impossible to see out into the morning. We're headed north. Occasionally, I recognize something. The Hotel Monte Vista. The observatory. After a few minutes, we are creeping up Highway 180 through a green blur of Douglas firs and piñon pines.

My phone vibrates in my pocket. I pull it out and check the screen.

*National Weather Service Alert: blizzard warning in **this** area in effect until further notice. Prepare. Avoid travel. **Check** media.*

Next to me, Vivian is also staring at her phone. We've all gotten the same warning.

When we pull up to the camp, I am relieved that Miller is driving. I know I would have sped right by the camp's road sign. I've been here a few times before and usually the place is bustling. But now, everything is quiet. Still.

We barely make the turn from the highway onto the dirt road when something gray streaks in front of us. Fast. A silhouette. Of a person. Maybe a woman.

But.

But it was so fast.

Even graceful.

Nobody could run like that in the snow.

Miller slams on the brakes and barely avoids hitting the thing. Whatever it is.

The sharp stop sends us into a skid. The girl in the back screams. Right in my fucking ear. We slide slowly along the icy road, spinning 180 degrees, until the side of the van hits a tree. I knock hard into Vivian. She makes an *ooof* sound and smashes into the leather-covered door. The van rocks from side to side a couple of times.

A ton of snow from the tree we hit lands hard on the hood.

But it settles. It is quiet again. Only the sound of the snow hitting the metal roof.

I can breathe again.

Everything is okay.

We probably saw a bear. A small one. That has to be it.

Miller will call the camp office, and they'll send somebody for us.

I try to relax.

Then.

There is another scream.

But this time it isn't the girl.

It came from outside the van.

Something is out there.

ALLISON DUMONDE

Fuck. Fuck. Fuck. Fuck. Fuck. Fuck. Fuck. Fuck. Fuck. Fuck.

Fuck.

I can't breathe.

Something is outside.

Some kind of an animal.

And that scream.

And we were in a fucking car accident.

My left arm aches.

I'll have even more bruises now.

Vee is hanging off the edge of her seat with that preppy guy practically on top of her. What the hell is with him, anyway? Who wears a tie to camp?

"What . . . the . . . hell . . . was . . . that?" I say in between pants.

"I think it was a bear," the preppy guy answers. He sounds way too calm.

"Did you see that thing?" Vee asks. She uses her super-high-pitched voice. Like when she was little and used to ask me to keep a night-light on during our slumber parties. I scoot closer toward her. She's scared, too.

"That was no bear," she says.

VIVIAN ELLENSHAW

"Well, what do *you* think it was?"

I push the president of the Young Republicans back into his own seat.

Paul Lewis. Riiiiiiiiiight.

The jerk is actually dressed up in a suit jacket and a skinny tie.

He doesn't recognize me.

My mom has basically dragged me to every pretentious gala *ever* in the history of Scottsdale, and it is impossible to forget the idiot who knocked me into a white-chocolate fountain at a hospital fundraiser last year. A quick search of the internet confirmed that this is, indeed, the latest and greatest model of Paul Fannon, a long line of pampered princes. According to Wikipedia, the first Paul Fannon had been a territorial governor. One was the mayor of Flagstaff. Number three owns FannonPharma, a creepy-AF drug company that makes everything from cosmetic fillers to diet pills.

FannonPharma owns MetabaCorp.

MetabaCorp owns the camp.

I shudder.

But we have bigger problems than Paul Fannon trying to play secret shopper at fat camp.

We all sit there in the van for a minute. I don't know what we're going to do. But I'm sure of one thing. That was no bear. Back before my dad decided he'd prefer life with family number two, he used to take me and Allie hunting. The only kind of bears we even have in Arizona are black bears. I've seen them. The thing we saw was too pale. Too thin.

And anyway. "Bears don't move like that," I say. "I . . . I think it was someone."

"People don't move like that either," Fannon shoots back.

"That scream sounded like a person."

Fannon sticks to his story. "Yeah. A *person* scared shitless by a bear."

Steve Miller continues to face forward, staring at the snow-covered windshield.

I punch him on the shoulder. "Hey! You're not going to get in trouble. We all saw what happened. There was nothing else you could have done."

The hit brings him back to life. He grabs the clipboard on the seat next to him and then turns around to the back seats. "Yeah. Yeah, okay. Well. Is everyone all right back there?" He reads our names off his list.

"Vivian Ellenshaw?"

I roll my eyes. "I'm fine. Obviously."

"Paul Lewis?"

I snort at Fannon's secret agent name.

"Here," he says, smirking and raising his hand.

"Allison DuMonde?"

There's a pause.

I turn around as well to see Allison trying to strategically reposition her scarf. "Allie?"

She nods her head. "Yeah. Yeah. I'm okay."

Miller shimmies around in his seat, and it takes me a second to realize he's digging his phone out of his pocket. He holds the phone up to his ear. Then he dials again. And again.

"Maybe try calling the camp office?" Fannon suggests.

"What do you think I'm doing?" Miller snaps. Probably determined not to lose his temper with the boss's son, he takes a deep breath. "I'm getting a busy signal."

Fannon bites his lower lip. "On which line?"

"All of them," Miller says.

Before I can make much sense of that, Allie taps me on the shoulder. "Vee, what was that thing?"

I tug my red hood over my head and reach for the door handle. With false bravado, I say, "Only one way to know for sure."

"You're not . . . going out there?" Allie shrieks.

I open the door and put one foot into the snow.

STEVE MILLER

I open my door, too. That action shakes a new deposit of snow from the tree.

"She's right," I tell Allison. "I can't get through to the office. Maybe we can flag down another car." I went through all the numbers they gave me in my packet, and all of them were busy. I could try to dial 911, but we're pretty far out. My guess is that it would take a while for anyone to reach us.

Our best option is to get to camp as quickly as possible.

"We're the last of the arrivals," Paul says.

"Well, we have to do something," I say. Anyway, Vivian is moving out of sight. It's already getting hard to spot her red jacket in the gloomy day. "Wait here. I'll check things out and . . ."

I don't get any farther before Allison scrambles out of her seat and toward the door Vivian left open. "Oh, nope. Nope. Nope," she says. "I've seen every teen slasher movie ever made. I am not sitting here waiting for whatever's out there to pick us off one by one." She waves her hand at Paul. "We'll be the first to go."

"Nothing's going to . . ." Paul begins. But then he makes a face. Like he's taken a bite of a lemon. "Wait. Why do you think it would be after *us*?"

Allison pauses in the doorway. "There's always an order to mortality in these things. I'd go first because I . . ." Her face goes bright red.

"You're what?" Paul presses.

She freezes. "I'm The Basket Case. The . . . um . . . expendable loner," she finally finishes. I'm pretty sure this is not what she originally intended to say.

"Then you," she goes on. "You're The Jerk."

"Hey!" Paul says. "You don't know—"

"What about me?" I ask. For some reason, this seems like really critical information. Like she could make or break me.

"Can't tell yet," she replies. "You're either The Jock with a Heart of Gold or The Courageous Captain. If you're The Jock, you've got a shot."

Oh, perfect. Another person who isn't sure I could make it as an athlete.

"So, just to be clear here, you think it's the fat girl who'd make it?" Paul says.

Allison shakes her head. "Stop acting like calling someone fat is the ultimate insult. And you don't know her. She's Action Girl. If anyone can survive, it will be her." She leaves the van and begins calling things like *Hey, Vee!* and *Wait for me!*

I'm left with The Jerk and snow that's falling with an intensity that feels impossible for Arizona.

And then another scream.

VIVIAN ELLENSHAW

Allie has spent way too much time watching her sister's movies.

I check over my shoulder in time to see her almost jump out of the van—no doubt to avoid being left alone with The Jerk and The Jock. According to one of her film studies, that group would be highly unlikely to survive an attack by a maniac in a hockey mask.

It's probably for the best anyway. Someone has to do something. Miller is stuck following some million-step checklist from Camp Creepy, and seriously, guys like Paul Fannon the Fourth typically don't make a habit of sticking their necks out for us girls in plus-size pants.

If anyone is getting us out of this mess it will be me and Allie. I freeze for a second. It shakes me a little bit that I've fallen back into the familiar pattern of thinking of Allie as my best friend. Since the third grade, it had been the two of us against the world.

Now it's only me.

I take a few steps away from the van. After a minute or so I can't see Allie.

Or the van.

Or anything.

Shit.

Wearing my Docs had been a decent choice because I'm not slipping around in the snow, but my hoodie isn't waterproof, so I'm getting soaked. And cold. Colder than cold.

When you're from Phoenix, you really lack the vocabulary to describe the cold.

Just *cold, cold, cold, cold.*

Then the scream.

My blood runs even icier. Dead bodies probably give off more heat.

Oh. Yeah. I'm going to die out here. All I can think of is that when my mom gets the call, I hope she's sitting in her nice comfy chair, drinking a cup of the coffee she ordered from Kona and making gross goo-goo eyes at Coach. With some vapid magazine. Like *Celebrity Private Islands* or something. And she'll know this is what I died for. That she sentenced me to death. Because I wasn't a perfect part of her perfect world.

She'd give me a perfect funeral though.

I force myself to take a step forward.

The toe of my boot hits something firm.

I fight the urge to scream.

No. No. I'm not going to give that prick Fannon Four the satisfaction of listening to me scream my head off. I try hard to remember the two jiujitsu lessons I had that one summer when my mom was desperately trying to help me find a physical activity I could, as she put it, *find a connection to.* Trouble was, I don't think we actually did anything in those lessons other than talk about gym etiquette and run laps. The only fun part was getting boba tea with Allie on the way home.

Footsteps crunch in the snow from somewhere nearby.

From almost every direction. Like I'm surrounded.

Fannon Fucking Four is out of his goddamn mind if he thinks *this* is a bear.

I ball up my fists and brace myself for whatever is coming.

A bright light blinds me, seeming to bounce everywhere across the snow.

I am dead.

And then a voice.

The voice of God.

"You aren't supposed to be out here."

Not only is this not what I imagined God would have to say to me, it is also a human voice.

A businesslike, perfunctory man's voice.

Something moves in front of me to block the snow. Again, it takes everything I've got not to scream my goddamn head off. When I can see, the image of a thirty-something man holding up the edge of a green raincoat in front of my face fills my field of view. He carries an industrial flashlight in his other hand and has some kind of radio tucked under his arm. Staticky cross talk erupts from it every few seconds.

"Who are you?" I ask.

He doesn't answer me. "Clear. Situation normal over here," he says into the radio.

Situation normal.

Those words fill me with relief.

But.

Who or what was screaming?

"Roger that," comes the response from the radio.

The official-looking crest on the guy's shirt and jacket catches my eye. A large, silver *S*. He's some kind of park ranger. That seems about right.

I glance down to see my boot butting up against a fallen tree and feel even better about the fact that I didn't lose it. The last thing I need is to ride into camp with a reputation as the girl who got spooked by a log and a guy with a flashlight.

"Who are you? And what are you doing here?" the ranger asks.

"There's . . . someone out there. We heard a bunch of screaming."

"Who's *we*?"

Despite the fact that the guy said things were normal, this interaction doesn't seem normal. I do my best to mimic my mom arriving at the Four Seasons. "I'm Vivian Ellenshaw. Checking into Camp Featherlite."

There's a pause.

"Camp is a half mile up the road. What are you doing *here*?"

"Car accident," I answer. "What are *you* doing here?"

"Show me," he says, ignoring my question again.

"Vee! Vee?" Allie calls out.

"That's Allison," I say. "She's . . ." If we are no longer friends, what *is* Allie to me? "One of the campers too," I finish.

The ranger takes off his raincoat and holds it up over the two of us like a makeshift tent. I pretty much run into Allie and Miller as I try to retrace my steps. He sets a much more confident pace toward the van than I used to get away from it, and in a matter of seconds, we are all back inside, crowded into the middle row, with the ranger outside leaning in.

More conversation breaks out from his radio. A frantic, desperate voice. "It's a real shitshow over here by the lake. We need—" The ranger turns it off and tucks it in his inside jacket pocket before we can hear what they need.

"I told you they would send help," Fannon Four says. The moron has the audacity to paste a smug grin on his face.

No one from camp even knows we are out here.

The rangers were looking for . . . that thing.

And that voice on the radio made it sound like they found it.

"What's out there?" I ask.

Fannon groans. "I told you. It's a bear."

The ranger nods. "Don't worry, miss. We'll catch it."

"What. Is. It?" I ask through clenched teeth.

The ranger's gaze travels across our faces, and then he turns his head to glance out into the snow. "The best thing to do is for you to get to camp. It's straight up the road. You'll be safe there. This snow should lighten up. You can make it in twenty if you set a good pace."

This gets Fannon's attention. "You want us to walk?"

"We'll be soaked," Allie adds.

"We should take the van," Fannon says. "I'm sure it still works."

"Are you volunteering to drive?" Miller asks. He's gone very pale. The accident has shaken him.

"He's right," I say. "The snow is even worse now than it was before."

"And that's a good reason for us to *walk*?" Fannon's voice grows high-pitched.

Allie hugs herself. "At least we won't crash into another tree."

"You can make it in twenty," the ranger repeats. He pounds his fist on the top of the door a couple of times to signal that he's done talking with us and turns to go.

Twenty minutes alone in the snow.

I lean through the open door, poking my head out. The ranger is already several paces away. "Hey! Hey! What's out there?" I call after him.

He doesn't look back, and a few seconds later he's gone.

PAUL FANNON

Walk.

To.

Camp.

Not taking the Porsche was a mistake.

Not changing my shoes was a mistake.

I fall on my ass.

Twice.

I think the fat girl even laughs at me.

It's pretty fucking galling when she asks me if I need help with my bag. And even worse, she is having no trouble with those stupid giant watermelon and unicorn-patterned bags of her own.

Miller keeps checking his watch, and all three of them have to stop every few minutes to make sure I'm keeping up.

I'm not keeping up.

And I can't stop thinking about the . . . the bear.

After about fifteen minutes, we arrive at the camp entrance. The fake-rustic wooden sign created by some artist in South Dakota that my dad paid a fortune for is completely covered in snow.

The instant we pass through Featherlite's wide entry, the un-natural quiet is broken by the sound of a motor roaring to life. Allison flinches.

Behind us, the huge electric-powered wrought iron gate starts to creak to a close.

A large man who sort of looks like a retired professional wrestler exits the small guard shack. "It's about goddamn time," he says. "And you just got *real* lucky. I have orders to close the gate in two minutes."

The blonde girl's teeth chatter. "You . . . you . . . were going to . . . to . . . to lock the gate and leave us out there?"

The guard shoves his hands in his pockets. "You're late. That's on you."

"We were in a car accident," the fat girl says indignantly.

Some of the guard's anger leaves his face. He turns to Miller. "You're the Facilitator, I guess?" Without waiting for an answer, he goes on. "Well, you've pretty much missed orientation. You better get to the Lodge and see what they want you to do."

Miller nods and turns toward camp. He clearly wants to get going.

"Is Dr. Volstead in the Lodge?" I ask.

The guard eyes me with suspicion. "How the hell would I know? The camp director isn't gonna call down here and report her whereabouts to me, now is she?"

Vivian rolls her eyes, and I feel my face heat up.

"Why are you closing the gate?" she asks.

The guard snorts. "There's a damn blizzard. Or maybe you haven't noticed?"

Vivian gives Allison a look. They aren't buying this.

I can almost make out the Lodge building in the distance. Cheerful light pours out of the large windows. "At least we've still got power," I say. Maybe these girls are going to panic, but I plan to stay positive.

The guard is already on his way back to the tiny shack. "For now," he says over his shoulder. "Main power went out about an hour ago. We're running on backup. The generators will keep us sitting pretty for the next twenty-four hours or so. And then . . ." He trails off.

An uneasy feeling comes over me as the iron gate slams fully shut.

It's quiet again.

Allison leans a little closer to Vivian.

I watch the guard through the open shack door.

He chews his cheek as he stares at the camp.

He glances one last time in our direction and reaches out to close the door.

ALLISON DUMONDE

For a camp that costs thirty grand, so far Featherlite brutally sucks.

Our fucking Pod or whatever makes it to the Lodge, half-frozen, half-soaked.

I have to admit that the building is beautiful. It's like someone took a Starbucks and a ski resort and smooshed them together. Everything is wood and green and charming and rustic in that way that's designed to make rich people feel like they're roughing it. There are groups of tables on each side of the huge building and clusters of plush suede sofas in the center.

The room's Tiffany chandeliers are all off, but the scattered floor lamps are bright enough to fight off the gray gloom outside the large windows. And like at Starbucks, I can't spot an electrical outlet to charge my phone. This might be the only chance I have to get a few still pics of the Lodge and, of course, the battery icon on my phone's screen glows red.

We drop our bags in front of the door.

The Lodge is deserted.

Well, almost deserted.

All the way on the far side of the room, two people sit at a table closest to the side door. A girl and a guy. Campers. Maybe. The girl stares out into space almost like she's in a coma, and the guy taps rapidly on a laptop on the table. They're wearing baby blue sweats and navy blue cardigans. Like a uniform.

God. I pray that's not the camp uniform. Shooting hours of

footage of people running around in those getups would make it seem like I'd failed Wardrobe 101.

The two of them ignore us.

Not only that, our Facilitator doesn't know anything more than I do. We stand around like morons on the doormat for a few minutes before Vivian says, "One of us should go figure out who's in charge around here."

Steve Miller is in trouble. I'm still reserving judgment, but so far, I placed him in The Courageous Captain category. Like the kind of guy who'd march into certain death on the orders of some off-screen character. Miller nods, and a few seconds later, he's gone.

Somewhere out there is that . . . that thing.

I shiver.

Vivian glances at me. Luckily, she thinks I'm cold and not a total coward who's busy imagining monsters and says, "Let's go stand by the fire."

I hadn't even noticed the fire until she pointed it out. But there it is. Covering a large part of the wall opposite the other campers. A massive fireplace made of large river rocks. As we step closer, I try to relax in the warmth and sound of pops and crackles.

Vivian seems so calm. She stands up straight. She takes off her red hoodie and holds it close to the fire. The Jerk is calm too. But you'd expect that. People like him . . . well . . . nothing bad has ever happened to them. They think they're immortal. Invincible.

But Vee. She's smart. I saw her face when that gate slammed. She knew.

They were closing the gate because of that *thing*.

And she knew.

I'm not sure how long we're standing there. Long enough for the tension and awkwardness to become almost unbearable. But short enough that I hiccup in surprise when a curly-haired blond stranger appears in my peripheral vision.

A couple minutes later, a guy who could be a linebacker on whatever football team Miller plays on stands before us. He has a name tag.

THEODORE

That is his name.

He carries several plastic bags. "Welcome to Camp Featherlite. I'm Theo, and I'll be handling your orientation." He gives us a wide smile. But there's something off about it. "Sorry for the lack of a proper welcome, but you're late—"

Vee interrupts him. "We were in a—"

"Car accident," Theo finishes, still smiling. "Yes. Your Facilitator briefed me."

Paul steps forward. "Is Dr. Volstead here?"

Theo's smile fades. "Dr. Volstead? Here? Now? I'm afraid not."

At that moment, I'm desperate to be alone with Vee. She always understands things. She always knows what's going on. But then I remember. We aren't friends anymore. Vee would avoid me if she could. Like she's been doing for the past six months.

Theo starts talking again. He hands each of us one of the blue plastic bags. "*Of course* we're all relieved you made it safely."

I peek in my bag. *Of course* it's one of the god-awful baby blue tracksuits.

Ugh. I guess people *are* always saying that you have to suffer for your art.

The blond guy gestures toward two doors in the corner of

the lodge. "Locker rooms are right over there. Go ahead and get changed and then head back out. I'll introduce you to the rest of your Pod and get you all set up to make the most of your time at Camp Featherlite."

Vee turns to go to the door. Like she's doing what we're all thinking and making a run for it.

Theo seems to guess her real plan. "Oh no. Just leave your bag there. Your camp kit contains everything you'll need for now. Bag up your wet clothes and put them in the laundry chute. They'll be cleaned and delivered to your bungalow."

For a second, defiance crosses Vee's face, and it's like she might pick up her bag anyway. But Vivian sighs and follows the directions. I trail after her into the girls' locker room.

The lights are out, and neither of us wants to bother to figure out how to turn them on, so we make our way around in the dim glow provided by narrow windows near the ceiling. My guess is that the walls are a shade of green similar to the trim out in the main room of the lodge.

Tall, skinny lockers line the perimeter with rows of benches in front of them.

I keep going.

I don't want Vee to see me change.

First, because of the tiny camera I have taped to my belly. I didn't make it through most of that boring camp manual, but I did check their image policy.

No pictures. No video. All photo equipment will be confiscated.

I don't know what worries me more: the camp finding out about my plan to make a documentary about the children of the superrich who've been sentenced to spend the holidays trying to choke down kale juice smoothies, or Vee's opinion of me using the camera she gave me for my birthday to do it.

The second reason I don't want her to see me is because of. Well.

Because.

I find the bathroom stalls and lock myself inside one. The bag doesn't include a cardigan sweater like the ones those other kids are wearing. The sleeves of the tee are too short.

"Vivian?" I call out. I can hear her changing near the lockers.

"Yeah?" she yells back.

"Did you get a sweater?"

"They're hanging up out here," she says. "The shoes are out here too."

She sounds normal.

Like when we would hang out in her room. Like when we would make our own movies. Like I could talk to her. Tell her everything. Tell her why I am really here.

Tell her the only thing I really want is to be friends again.

I sit there on the toilet. I can't talk to Vee. Not right now. I have to focus. I have a plan, and step one is to get out of the locker room. I think about asking Vee to bring me a sweater, but that would just attract her attention. I can move fast. Grab a sweater before she notices.

Vee stands in front of a rack of sweaters, pushing them from side to side, checking them out. I pull the first one I can get my fingers on off the hanger and push one arm through the sleeve. Of course it's cashmere.

Vivian turns to look at me.

And she sees. Even in this light she can see.

"Oh. Oh God. Allie. What happened? Don't tell me DeeDee hit you with a block of Velveeta again?"

Her face is frozen in a mask of horror.

"It's nothing." I have the sweater on. "Can you pass me a pair of size nines?" I ask, gesturing to the rows of sheepskin slip-on shoes.

She doesn't move. "Allie. Seriously. What the—"

I reach in front of her and pick up the shoes myself. As fast as I can, I stuff the shoes on my feet and go to the laundry chute. I find a mug full of Sharpies, write my name on my blue bag, shove my wet clothes inside, and drop it through the metal door.

"Wait! Wait!" Vivian calls after me.

I don't know what's worse.

The fact that I just dumped the only decent clothes I own down that chute.

Or the way that Vivian looked at me.

Like I was the most pathetic thing she'd ever seen.

PAUL FANNON

I pace around in front of the girls' locker room.

Waiting.

My camp shoes squeak on the tile floor.

In the opposite corner, Trevor or Tate or Theodore or whoever is setting some stuff up on the table where the other two kids are sitting. A girl with red hair holds a book close in front of her face.

He tells me to round up the rest of the Pod and meet them at the table.

The blonde girl. Allison. She comes out of the locker room. Moving fast. Her baggy blue cardigan swings from side to side. They had racks and racks of the things in the locker room. Was it too difficult to find one that fits correctly?

She brushes right by me. Like she doesn't even see me.

That's okay.

That leaves the other one. Vivian.

She pushes the locker room door open, and I start to mumble something.

Vivian moves close to my face and cuts me off. "You don't remember me, do you?"

I freeze with my mouth open.

I knew a bunch of rich kids came to this camp, but it hadn't occurred to me that they'd be rich kids that *I knew*. This whole thing will be over before it starts if someone recognizes me. Everyone will treat me like a VIP, and I'll get no good intel to take back to my dad.

This whole thing. It'll be one more thing I failed at.

The fat girl *must not* recognize me.

"From the Fannon Foundation gala?" Vivian demands.

Okay. She recognizes me.

"You pushed me into the fondue fountain," she says in a dark tone.

I vaguely remember that party. I'd stolen a bottle of gin from the bar, and there had been this group of models from Ford Robert Black, and . . . Dad grounded me for a month.

I bet Carl Kaiser doesn't go around falling into fondue fountains.

He'll be the future of FannonPharma if I don't stop messing up.

So I need to make my plan work.

Vivian clears her throat.

"Oh yeah . . . um . . ." I try to smile. Try to be charming. Like my dad.

But I didn't inherit his brains. Or charisma. So Vivian scowls at me.

"Sorry about that. See . . . I . . . ah—" That's how far I get.

"I won't tell anyone that you're Dr. Fannon's son," she says.

I straighten my sweater. "Really?"

She squints at me. "Your secret's safe with me."

My dad does this sometimes too. To size me up. See what I have in me.

"For now," she adds.

She moves to step around me but pauses. "If it were me though, I'd stop name-dropping the camp director to every person I meet. That's not really smart behavior for someone trying to fly under the radar."

Great.

She's probably right.

She leaves me here.

A couple minutes later, I take a seat at the long white table, in between Vivian and Allison, facing the two new kids. The red-haired girl and a large guy with greasy brown hair and oversize black glasses.

Theo hands plastic lunch boxes to each of us. He has a clipboard with him now, and he makes a mark on a sheet of paper each time he passes out a box. "Unfortunately, we'll have to go through things pretty quickly. And I'm sure you're all starving."

I open my box to find half a ham sandwich, a side salad, some mixed nuts, and a small bottle of water. Nerd and Red-Haired Girl dig right into their food. They've clearly been waiting a while. Next to me, Vivian fiddles with a pack of trail mix. Allison unwraps her sandwich and pokes at it a couple of times. Theo drops a thick manual on the table near my elbow. The cover reads *Camp Featherlite Field Guide*.

"Okay," Theo says with fake cheer. "How about we go around the table and introduce ourselves? Maybe say our names, where we're from, and why we came to Camp Featherlite? I'm Theo Havers. I'm originally from Chicago, and I'm a senior in the nursing program at NAU. I'm here because I have a passion for helping people learn more about healthy living."

He gestures at Red-Haired Girl.

Red-Haired Girl: "I'm . . . uh . . . I'm Rachel. Rachel Benedict. From Flagstaff. Piñon Pines High. Um. I'm a junior. And I'm here because I gained some weight . . . over the last few months . . . well . . . I want to lose it."

Allison: "I'm Allison DuMonde from . . . Scottsdale. I'm a junior at St. Mary's. My sister is an actress, and she thinks she can get me a part in her next film if I drop some weight."

Theo makes an impressed *ooooohhhh* sound.

Vivian (with an indignant snort): "Wait. You want to *act* in a movie now? Your dream was to *make* your own films."

Theo: "Miss Ellenshaw, let's keep our opinions of other people's goals to ourselves."

Vivian (after a pause): "Vivian Ellenshaw. Junior. St. Mary's. I was told Camp Featherlite is the winter home of the Sasquatch. I'm here to prove Bigfoot is real."

Theo's smile morphs into a confused frown.

Glasses Guy: "Sheldon Smentkowski. From Saint Paul. I'm a senior at Humboldt High. My dad's working over the holidays investigating some big industrial accident. It was either come here or visit my uncle Lloyd in Minnetonka. At least here, you've got ping-pong."

Me: "Paul . . . ah . . . Lewis. I'm also from Flag. Junior. Lowell High."

"And why are you here?" Theo prompts.

Everyone stares at me. "Oh . . . ah . . . you know . . . healthy eating. That kind of thing."

Camp Counselor Ken Doll gets up and goes to the wall. He opens a wooden panel, revealing a big-screen TV and an old-fashioned phone mounted to the wall. Grabbing a remote control, he says, "Uh . . . yeah . . . well. So that's your Pod. And without further ado, here we go."

The camp logo appears on the screen.

And then some crappy New Age music.

Vivian holds up her own copy of the camp manual. "It says here that our Facilitator should be handling our orientation."

Theo's face goes red. "Yes. Usually that's what happens. But because you were—"

I'm sure he intends to say *late* but is stopped by Vivian's scowl.

He clears his throat. "Because of timing issues, Mr. Miller has to have team member orientation now."

Then Dad's voice.

I have a simple question for you. Are you living a life you love?

The logo is replaced by my father's face on the screen. *Good morning. I'm Dr. Paul Fannon, and it's my pleasure to welcome you to Camp Featherlite for Overweight Teens.*

I wonder for the millionth time why I can't be more like my dad. Why I don't have that Fannon look. I know I'm not bad. But I'm nothing like my father. Dad is tall with jet-black hair that always has the perfect amount of wave and skin that is always the perfect amount of tan. Instead, I'm going through life a few inches shorter with the same basic brown hair that every white guy seems to have and skin that goes way too pale in the winter.

"Thanks for the warm welcome," Vivian shoots across the table at Red-Haired Girl and Nerd.

This camp was founded on the idea that learning about healthful living at a young age can lead to lifelong happiness . . .

"They told us we had to remain seated," Red-Haired Girl answers, watching the snow fall outside the window. "And you kept us waiting for two hours."

Dad's voice drones on in the background . . . *which found*

*that genetics are a major contributing factor in weight manage-
ment and weight control issues . . .*

Nerd glares at Theo, who is still standing near the TV and
staring at his clipboard. "Going two weeks without a laptop or
a phone is almost a death sentence. I have to make the most of
the time I have left with my electronics." He pats the curled-up
white earbuds that almost blend in with the table. "It mostly sucks
though. There's only so much you can do without Wi-Fi or a cell
signal."

*. . . while many of the factors that lead to excess pounds
may not be your fault, that doesn't mean you're powerless to
change your destiny . . .*

Nerd has my attention now. "What do you mean? Why won't
you have a phone?"

"Didn't you read the handbook?" Red-Haired Girl asks. "Page
three says—"

"That campers must surrender all electronics upon check-in,"
Vivian reads off the page. "As well as any contraband." She looks
right at me. "What's contraband?"

"I thought it was only cameras," Allison says. She opens her
bottle of water.

*Here at Camp Featherlite, we've developed an innovative,
sustainable, lifelong system for success, incorporating dietary
management, efficient exercise, and . . .*

I shake my head. But I notice our bags. All in a neat row
against the wall. My eyes follow the line to another table. I hadn't
seen it before. A couple of iPads, the candy bars my mom packed,
and a bottle of cheap rum are in a clear plastic bin.

That dick Theo has been through our bags.

And taken our stuff.

. . . your Facilitator will work hard to help you make smart food choices, to connect you with physical activities you enjoy, and to help you develop coping mechanisms that . . .

Lack of privacy. I'll be noting that in my report to Dad for sure.

"You're saying they're going to take our phones?" I ask. It sounds too high-pitched. Almost wimpy. "That we won't be able to . . . tweet . . . or text . . . or . . ."

"It wouldn't matter anyway," Nerd says flatly. "There's no signal."

Vivian turns another page in her manual. "The storm won't last forever. The snow has to let up eventually."

On the screen, an animated periodic table of elements bounces and glows.

"It wouldn't matter," Nerd repeats. He points to a small black box mounted to the wall near the ceiling. "There are cell signal disruptors in every building I've been in so far. There's RF signal–blocking film on all the windows. And I'd bet my Steam Controller that they've used EMF-shielding paint. Nothing's getting in or out of this place."

. . . to achieve the best result, avoid skipping meals and eat your full portion of the metabolically balanced cuisine prepared by . . .

"Where is everyone else?" Vivian asks, suddenly looking worried.

"Lockdown," Nerd answers. He stares at his screen while he speaks. But there's something off about him.

Something nervous.

"Lockdown?" I repeat.

Red-Haired Girl leans forward and whispers, "Right after the snow *really* started coming down, they came in and said that someone got lost down by the lake."

Where those rangers were headed.

Fuck.

"All the counselors were running all around. They sent everyone to their bungalows."

"Except us. Because they're really fucking militant about all this Pod shit," Nerd adds.

. . . including hiking, watersports, yoga, Pilates, and . . .

Theo sighs and turns off the TV in the middle of Dad's description of camp activities. "You get the general idea. And yes. I do need to collect all your electronic devices at this point." He opens a drawer underneath the television console and approaches us with a handful of bags made from aluminum foil.

"What gives you the right to take our phones?" Vivian asks.

"Your parents," Theo snaps. "They had to sign a waiver with your paperwork."

Vivian's face changes. Becomes red. She is maybe . . . embarrassed.

We fork over our phones, and Theo shoves each one in its own silver bag, writing our names on the foil with a Sharpie. When that's done, he goes over to the other table and adds the bags to the plastic bin.

The instant Theo clicks the lid closed, the wall phone rings.

Kind of an odd, old-timey ring.

Theo freezes.

After the second ring, Vivian says. "Phone's ringing, dude."

He walks slowly over to the phone and presses it to his ear. After a few seconds, he says, "How is that even possible?"

A pause.

"But I— What about these kids? . . . Okay. Okay. I'm coming back now." Theo holds the phone in the air for a few seconds before returning it carefully to the wall. "I have to . . . um . . . Wait here for your Facilitator. They're sending him in . . . and . . . ah . . . wait here."

He grabs the plastic bin and heads off in the direction of the locker rooms, ducking into a door labeled EMPLOYEES ONLY.

"Why is he so nervous?" Red-Haired Girl asks.

I frown. "Why would they put *everybody* in lockdown because one kid got lost?"

"Why did they put our phones in Faraday bags?" Nerd replies.

"What's a Faraday bag?" I ask.

"It's a bag that stops a cell phone from getting a signal," Vivian says. When Nerd eyes her with interest, she adds, "My dad's a lawyer."

"Right," Nerd agrees. "They use them to protect evidence."

"*Where* is Miller?" Allison asks.

Vivian turns to the window and watches the snow fall. "Something's wrong. And that guy Theo knows what it is."

STEVE MILLER

I've been standing in an almost dark hallway in the employees-only area for about fifteen minutes, pacing outside a door with DR. D. VOLSTEAD, CAMP DIRECTOR etched on the glass. I listen as a frazzled voice inside the office makes a series of phone calls.

Most of the lights in the building are off.

This doesn't seem right.

Finally, a pretty blonde girl, barely older than me, wearing a white lab coat, opens the door and waves me inside. Her ponytail swings as she slides behind the desk. She motions for me to sit in the orange plastic chair across from her. The office must have been decorated by IKEA. Everything is small and white and low to the ground. I'm almost too big for the chair. It's a tight fit.

"You're Dr. Volstead?" I ask.

She shakes her head. "I'm Zanna. Volstead's PA."

Zanna reminds me a lot of my sister Meagan.

She whirls around in her chair on wheels, pushes herself over to a bookshelf, and returns with a big stack of manuals. "We have to make this quick." She dumps them on the desk in front of me. "I'm sure you went through most of this during your staff training, but there's a reference set of manuals if you need them."

I don't know if I should mention that I didn't have any training.

So I say, "Where's Dr. Volstead?"

That is wrong.

My new buddy Zanna glares at me with the fire of a thousand suns. "She's out dealing with an emergency. But I'm perfectly capable of doing a basic Facilitator check-in."

This is also the kind of attitude I could expect from my sister.

Zanna reaches into a drawer and adds a bunch of file folders to my stack of books. "Okay. So those are the briefs on your campers. Your group is a little unbalanced. You've got a couple of *real* characters in there. You'll see what I mean when you read the files. But you'll just have to deal with it." She gives the manila folders a couple of pats.

It's probably a hundred pages of reading.

I read slower than a herd of turtles. It would take me a week to get through this pile.

She tosses me a single key on a red strap. "There are a couple of things that are new this session that they probably didn't cover in training. First, Dr. Fannon and Dr. Kaiser are testing the Metabolize-A bar. So, very important. The bars are in a locked cabinet in your room in the bungalow. Make sure your campers eat their bars after each meal. *Each meal.* Record the side effects. We're not doing formal interviews with the campers, but—"

"Side effects? What side effects?" I ask.

There's a staticky click and then a man's voice. "Zanna? You on the radio?"

She draws a clunky black radio from her lab coat pocket. "Zanna here."

Zanna also pulls one of the folders from my stack and puts it on the top. She opens it and points to the bold print that says METABOLIZE-A EVALUATIONS. It's a really fucking long checklist with symptoms ranging from dry mouth to seizures.

It does not make me want to force-feed those bars to Vivian and Allison.

I'm fine with giving them to Paul though.

"We've got the gates closed and the perimeter secure. Patrols are set up," the voice says.

"Copy that," Zanna answers. "Now *find* Volstead."

There's a pause.

"The only place she could possibly be is down by the lake."

"Send a patrol over there," Zanna says through clenched teeth.

"We . . . we still haven't heard back from the rangers who went down there," the man says.

Zanna brushes past me. "Wait here for a sec," she tells me.

She goes into the hall, but the glass does little to shield her loud radio conversation. "So? We have to find Volstead. Send everything you've got down to the lake."

Another awkward pause.

The voice on the radio is tense. "What we've got is four shotguns, five boxes of shells, and a bunch of teenagers who were hired more for their looks than their brains. Security went down there looking for that missing girl. They haven't come back."

Fuck.

What the fuck is happening?

I think about leaving then. Just saying *screw it* and getting out.

But.

No car. No working phone. No idea how to get to town. And anyway, I couldn't walk there during a blizzard. And I still need the money.

Plus, there is Vivian.

I have to suck it up and roll with it.

Outside the door, Zanna and radio guy continue to argue about going down to the lake.

I glance at the books and manuals. One of them is called *Camp Featherlite Field Guide*. That seems like as good a place as any to start. I flip it open to a page that shows a happy graphic with one of those megaphones like cheerleaders use. It says STAY STRONG. And then below.

S   *Stay with your Pod*

T   *Treat all campers with kindness and courtesy*

R   *Respect your Facilitator*

O   *Only consume foods issued by the camp team*

N   *No leaving camp grounds for any reason*

G   *Give all assigned activities your best try*

Real cute.

Outside the door, Zanna's voice is getting more frantic. "I don't think *you* understand. Fannon isn't here. No one's seen Kaiser for days. The mainframe that controls the central power system is infected with some kind of virus. No one knows how to fix the computer, so we're running on the backup generators. Volstead took the main phones offline and turned on the cell signal disruption. We can't turn it off. If we don't find Volstead, by this time tomorrow, we'll have no one in charge, no power, and no way to call outside camp. Find her. Send everyone you've got."

Pause. "Copy that. Roger out."

I can barely make sense of most of that conversation, but the words *mortal peril* come to mind.

With a huff, Zanna opens the door and comes back to the desk. She picks up a white phone real similar to the one Grandma has at her place. She must not be getting an answer, because she murmurs, "What on earth is taking Theo so long?" She hangs up the phone.

And then: "Time to get going," she says with a curt nod.

Great.

I have no idea where to go. Or what to do when I get there.

"We're in lockdown. Keep your Pod in the bungalow until dinner." Zanna stands, places the manuals and folders in my arms, and leads me into the hall.

I have a million questions. Like where is the bungalow? What else is new this session? What the hell am I supposed to tell Vivian and Paul? They're smarter than me any day of the week and twice on Sunday.

I open my mouth to say one of these things, but Zanna shakes her head.

She's done with me, and another guy is already coming up the hall.

He has to be Theo.

I've never seen anyone look so fucking terrified in my whole life.

Zanna waves me off. "Watch out for Ellenshaw and Smentkowski," she says. "They're Pod destabilizers. And believe me. Now is not the time for campers to go rogue."

RACHEL BENEDICT

I have always been the good girl.

The camper across from me, Vivian, asked why I didn't say anything when they came in. Because they told us to stay in our seats and be quiet, and I always follow directions. That's why. I always do what I am told. That's why.

The one time I didn't do as I was told is ruining my life.

"That movie was ridiculous," Vivian says.

I don't answer, but of course she is right. The explanation for how fat is expelled from the body when a person loses weight is totally ridiculous. Only someone who'd failed tenth-grade chemistry would make a cartoon of a fat cell burning up and disappearing. Three words: Conservation. Of. Matter.

It's the five of us alone in the huge Lodge building. Sheldon and I have been waiting for hours, and now we are waiting some more for our Facilitator to come back.

The baby delivers a sharp kick right behind my belly button and then another and another. I hope he is okay. Actually, I don't even know if he *is* a he. I haven't been to the doctor since I found an excuse to drive to Phoenix and go to Planned Parenthood. I'd never even driven on a freeway before, and there I was trying not to panic in a hundred lanes of heavy traffic. I was supposed to be volunteering at a food distribution center. Instead, I was using a fake ID at the place my father calls the Killing Cabal. I didn't have a choice though. Flagstaff only has four OB-GYN offices, and three of the doctors go to our church.

That was when the baby was at fifteen weeks. The doctor did an ultrasound and said that the fetus was developing normally. But fifteen weeks was too soon to know the gender. Whoever is kicking me right now could be a he or a she.

"What happened before we got here?" the blonde girl asks. There is something so familiar about her. Like she's a friend who's ghosted me. Allison is her name. She is going to be a movie star. She looks like a movie star.

Sheldon shrugs. "They served lunch to everyone except us. Which kind of pissed me off, TBH. Like, so we're a Pod. We're not conjoined twins. Then . . ." he trails off.

The two of us have been at this table together for so long that we are kindred spirits. I pick up the rest of his story. "Then they made a weird announcement about some kid missing at the lake and not to leave your bungalow without your Pod Facilitator. And everyone left."

"Except us," Sheldon adds.

"What do we do now?" Pretty Boy asks.

"We wait for Miller," Vivian answers, her head still in her book. Since I mentioned the manual, she has been reading, determined to catch up.

"Our Facilitator," Allison says.

"Yeah. Of course we have to wait for him. I mean, maybe we'd like to go unpack. Maybe take a nap. Well, tough tomatoes, I guess. It's totally bizarre to randomly assign people to a group and then expect us to act like we're part of a hive mind or something . . ." Sheldon trails off.

"It's not random," I say before I can stop myself.

Vivian's eyes snap up. "What do you mean?"

I feel my face grow warm, and I am sure Pretty Boy is staring at my belly. Fluffing up my cardigan around my stomach, I try to sound casual. "It seems like they profiled us." I sigh. I will probably never see these people again after camp, so who cares what they think of me. "They've given us an objective, specifically to lose weight. Theoretically, we'll be more successful as part of a stable group. According to group dynamics, small groups of mixed personality types are best. They can get the most accomplished. There are six of us, which is considered an almost ideal group size. My guess is that they divided us up using the Big Five personality traits theory. There are five traits: openness, conscientiousness, extroversion, agreeableness, and emotional stability. The idea is to balance the composition. Like if you have a group made up only of extroverts, they compete with each other."

Vivian nods. "But if they're all agreeable, they don't challenge each other."

"Right," I say. I'm not used to having anyone to discuss this kind of thing with.

"You some kind of science geek?" Pretty Boy asks.

"No," I snap. Everyone stares at me. Again, I go for casual. "I'm . . . ah . . . hoping to be a doctor." In our house, medicine is the only acceptable kind of science. I'm sure my parents are disappointed that I'm not dreaming of marrying a minister. "But . . . um . . . my dad is a pastor. He makes me do the cabin assignments every year at church camp. We use this system so we don't have three hundred miserable, homesick kids."

It is so quiet in the Lodge. I've been to church camp every year since I could walk. There are always people everywhere and kids yelling and talking. And no matter what, there is always someone eating glue and a bunch of those crafty googly eyes dropped all over the place. Featherlite feels more like visiting a sick relative in the hospital.

The lights flicker.

Vivian and Allison exchange a look that seems to mean something.

Sheldon gestures to the two of them. "You guys go to the same school? You already know each other?"

Vivian nods.

Sheldon turns to me. "What does your theory of group dynamics say about that?"

I should say, *Nothing*. Or *I don't know*. I should lie. Instead I say, "That it's not a good idea. That it creates an imbalance in the group." And it's true. We never put two kids from the same school in a cabin. Either they fight or they exclude the other kids.

Allison's face falls into a frown. She is holding on to the arms of her chair with all her might, her fingers turning red and white.

The door on the opposite side of the Lodge opens, and another blond-haired, blue-eyed guy approaches our table. I can't help but notice that all the employees have the same look. That, too, cannot be random. This has to be Steve Miller. He is pale and has beads of sweat forming at his hairline.

"We need to get to our bungalow," he says. "Let's go."

SHELDON SMENTKOWSKI

Well. I've done it.

I hadn't planned on no Wi-Fi or internet access.

But I'd done enough research. Back in Minnetonka, I spent a week checking out the camp. A couple ex-employees posted stuff on social media about the ultra-modern industrial electrical grid and the mainframe computer system that the people from FannonPharma had installed at Featherlite. It was the kind of thing that theme parks or office complexes normally used to distribute power to various locations, and there were a bunch of subreddits full of electrical engineers who loved to argue about how the systems should work. The whole thing was overkill, in my opinion. I mean, how energy efficient did *a camp* really need to be?

But also.

Why would a pharmaceutical company bother building a kids' camp?

I put together a piece of malware that would infect the power grid and shut it down. Like I always say, a company's biggest security vulnerability is its own employees. And Featherlite had all the contact info for their crew on the camp website. It took a couple of tries, but I was able to spearfish a guy who worked as some kind of nutritionist and loved to click on quick recipe videos. "How to make your own red velvet churros" installed the malware. All I had to do was activate the program once I arrived at camp. I found an Ethernet port in the corner of the Lodge that was being used by a smart TV, plugged in my laptop, and my virus took down the grid. The lights flickered for a couple of minutes and then the backup generator came on.

In twenty-four hours, Camp Featherlite for Overweight Teens would be in total darkness.

The FannonPharma techs would probably still be trouble-shooting their system in a week.

The management would never let a bunch of rich kids really rough it without hot showers and gourmet dinners and fresh-squeezed smoothies. They would have to send us home.

In twenty-four hours, we'd all be back in the vans headed to the airport.

For a minute there, I was proud. Screw my dad and his lectures about my lack of practical skills. I *told* him that I wouldn't be staying at this damn camp. By the time Theo took my laptop, I'd already unleashed a can of digital whoop-ass on Featherlite.

But.

What I thought was just a bunch of stupid jocks rushing around trying to make sure bougie kids didn't have to carry their own luggage or smuggle in their phones turned out to be a real emergency.

Someone had gone missing.

Plus, this tiny little snowstorm that everyone was calling a blizzard and completely freaking out about was causing real problems. They told us the rest of our fucking Pod was stuck in the snow.

And I had a little knot in the pit of my stomach. An uncomfortable feeling that was getting stronger. Like that time I swallowed a chewing gum wrapper.

Someone else had screwed with the phones.

I overheard one of the android Facilitators telling another that they couldn't call out and no one could call in.

The girl with me. Rachel. She didn't say much. For a while she read some old book with a grinning dog on the cover. Then she stared out the window.

Every time she glanced in my direction, I felt . . .

Guilty.

I tried to reassure myself.

Someone in this place *must* have a working phone. I tried not to think too much about them being down. What kind of person would want to stop us from making calls home? But then. What kind of person would want to take out the power?

Oh, for crying out loud. Everything will be fine.

This is Arizona. How bad could the weather get?

The power will go out. We'll be sent home.

End of.

I still can't understand why the camp is restricting Wi-Fi and cell service. Outside of a government building or a military base, I've never heard of anyone putting so much effort into suppressing comm. Whatever's happening here, they don't want us telling anyone about it.

Except what the fuck *is* happening here?

As best as I can tell, they're going to feed us fatties lettuce and make us take nature walks around the lake. Basically the same shit my candy-ass stepmom paid a personal trainer a hundred bucks an hour to do for me back home.

I suspect Rachel is right about the group dynamics thing.

But I can't verify it.

And I can't pull any reporting. Normally, by the time I've

been sitting at a table with somebody for more than two minutes, I have their basics—full name, address, phone numbers, and social media handles. After five minutes, I have their parents' credit reports. Right now, I have nothing.

I'm flying blind.

I'm not the only one.

Miller is a dumbass.

But because he looks like he popped off a page of *Sports Illustrated*, of course, no one minds.

He keeps almost dropping his stack of file folders and books. The sum of his knowledge is how to get to the door of the Lodge, where he freezes like a robot at the end of his programming.

Files. The idiot has files.

About us.

"What are those?" I ask, pointing to the stack.

Miller doesn't answer. "So . . . we're going to our bungalow," he says, staring at the ceiling. After a weirdly long amount of time, he opens the Lodge door.

Vivian reaches out and stops him. "We're supposed to put on wellies before we go out into the weather."

I have to hand it to her. She's quick. She probably memorized most of the important stuff in the handbook in the time it took us to watch that stupid movie and wait for Miller. Vivian pushes on a sleek wood panel that opens to reveal racks of gardening boots.

Rachel has a really hard time getting into her boots.

Really hard.

Really.

Like huffing and puffing and having trouble bending over to the point where Miller suggests that she sit down. The two of them go to one of the tables, where the jock kneels down like

Prince Fucking Charming and shoves the boots on her feet for her. Had it been any other girl, I would have been suspicious. Like it's some kind of routine designed to help Rachel flirt with Mr. Captain of the Football Team.

But her face. Jesus. It's red and arranged like a piece of abstract art. One eyebrow up, the other down, her mouth puckered, her nostril flaring in and out. It's not an act. She can't get her damn boots on by herself.

When Miller finishes, we are all back at the door.

"Well, we're in Goldwater," he says. He pulls the camp manual to the top of his stack, almost dropping everything yet again, and turns to the map page. "So . . . I guess we go right."

"Left," Vivian corrects.

Oh, Miller is a dope. You betcha. And yet people always put the meatheads in charge.

Vivian tugs the door open and goes into the snow.

Everyone else follows behind her.

Rachel stays on the mat.

"What?" I ask.

"Once we leave here," she starts. Outside, everyone else is staring at us through the open door. "You ever have that feeling, like when you leave a room, that you're putting something in the past? You're going forward on a certain trajectory, and you can't change it. When we leave here, we're committed to this."

"To what?" I ask.

"Whatever this is."

I should tell them that I turned off the power.

Instead, I say, "Don't worry. We're in this together."

Whatever this is.

ALLISON DUMONDE

The snow shows no sign of letting up, but the sun is starting to go down, transforming the landscape from a light gray blur to a dark gray blur.

It's quiet outside on the campground. But every once in a while, faces pop into windows in the other bungalows. One girl waves. It's reassuring.

We aren't totally alone.

They put us on the westernmost edge of camp, with our bungalow on the verge of being swallowed up by the tall pines. It's already dark here. The wide, wooden Goldwater cabin rests in the shadows of the powder-covered trees.

But on the bright side, we are as far as possible from the lake.

That's something.

In the Lodge, no one bought my "actress on the verge of a casting" story. It wasn't totally a lie. DeeDee *did* say she'd help me. Mom made my sister promise to put me in touch with the producers at the film studio that makes all her slasher flicks. Of course, DeeDee's promises always came with strings attached. She told me to drop some weight first. She said that Hollywood hated fatties. Even *behind* the camera.

I'd let myself believe that talent could be a ticket out of the trailer park. But DeeDee was the one who'd gotten out, and it was because she's a size two and looks perfect in a tiny plaid skirt, not because she can run lines like Meryl Streep.

The truth is that dropping a few pounds at Featherlite won't be a bad thing.

But that isn't why I'm here.

While we walk across camp, I glance over at Vivian.

She keeps doing that thing that she always does. Opening her mouth and then closing it. Like she wants to say something. I can tell she's dying to know who put up the big bucks for my camp fee.

If there is any hope of fixing our friendship, I have to keep her from finding out.

The Goldwater is basically one great big room with bunk beds for kids whose parents struggle to decide which Mercedes to drive to the country club. The beds are huge and covered with massive, fluffy pillows. There's a grouping of leather furniture in the center of the room. Some interior designer was probably paid a fortune to make the place feel like it was home to a fabulous and fun wilderness family. Stacks of board games rest on a heavy wooden coffee table in the center of the room. Bookcases line the walls, and they're full of classic adventure novels and brightly colored gear. Neon yellow flashlights. Red plastic flasks. Coils of green cord. Jars of waterproof matches. Bundles of new field notebooks. Blue raincoats hang from hooks on the wall.

I'm strangely at home here.

Because.

Because it is . . .

A set.

This should be reassuring.

I've been an assistant on tons of local indie films and have been doing behind-the-scenes stuff for school plays since I was a kid. I grew up on sets. This place has great natural light and pops of color in all the right places. Perfect for filming.

Great . . . except.

My original idea was to do a documentary. Part eat-the-rich-style exposé. Part social commentary on how weight-loss culture craps on us all—even the elite and privileged. I planned to get a bunch of good clips of boneheaded camp counselors saying crappy things about fat people. Cut in some shots of rich kids having their butlers smuggle in designer slippers and hundred-dollar bottles of whiskey. Add in footage of Vee's one-liners skewering both groups, and boom! I've got the next *Tiger King* with Vivian Ellenshaw as the hero we all deserve.

She would see it, and we would be friends again.

I hadn't counted on the fact that we would be spending so much time in these fucking . . . Pods. My group really doesn't lend itself to sensationalized narratives. Of course, Vivian is Action Girl. And sure, she hates her mom's pretentious fatphobia and can always be counted on to let the world know it.

But Rachel and Smentkowski are too sympathetic. Miller isn't rich. And Paul? If I look up *underachiever* in the dictionary, I'll probably find his picture there. If *he* is the future of the American aristocracy, the class war might actually be winnable. Anyway, a story of six people who mostly get along and chat about the snow won't get my doc picked up by Netflix.

I need a new plan.

Featherlite feels more like a reality TV show. I have a group of lovable characters living in forced proximity in a totally artificial environment.

We could grow and change and mature. In controlled ways.

And I can get it all on film.

We need character arcs.

Vivian's character sheet is the easiest to do. I mean, obviously.

She's out there kicking ass and taking names. But she could learn to chill out a little bit. Stop and smell the roses. Maybe realize that living with Coach Hanes isn't the end of the world. That if your dad takes you skiing in Zurich because he feels guilty about the divorce, you'll live. That there are worse things in life than your mom being late for dinner at the Cork & Cleaver on Friday nights.

My shoulder throbs.

I ignore the pain.

There are worse things.

This might work for me too. Right now, I'm the useless Basket Case, the trailer park girl banging out scripts on a second-hand laptop while my sister is off being famous. I'm the shitty friend who slept with my best friend's crush. The filmmaker who's never made a good movie. I am a loser.

I planned to stay off camera. There's something self-indulgent about a filmmaker who appears on screen. But sometimes it works. Banksy put himself in *Exit Through the Gift Shop*. What if I give myself a redemption arc? What if the real story here is about six strangers from different worlds who become friends? What if I win Vee back with a film about how much I want her back?

This will work.

And it kind of makes sense. I'd already been thinking about my old horror archetypes. I could start with that and work up some storylines for our Pod.

What about *The Friends of Featherlite*? No. That's too dorky. I'll think about it.

So, okay. Miller. Well, I can't quite decide about him. Maybe he's becoming The Courageous Captain. But I can't say for sure, so I decide to give the guy the benefit of the doubt and go with

The Jock with a Heart of Gold. Better to be a dumb but good guy in over his head than the brave captain of a sinking ship.

That leaves Paul, The Jerk, the privileged prince in pursuit of the world's approval. The Nerd, Smentkowski, better with machines than mortals. And Rachel. I have no idea what her deal is. Maybe she is too much like me. A Basket Case.

Maybe Basket Cases can't really relate to each other.

For now, I'll label Rachel as The Outcast. Subject to revision.

We each have a small closet labeled with our names. I dump my bag on the floor by the bunk closest to the ALLISON closet. I try to appear confident as I slide the paneled door open. But I do this slowly. Truthfully, I'm still on edge from the morning. From thoughts of that thing in the snow. Of the missing camper.

I step back like I'm waiting for a monster to jump out.

The closet is free of monsters. Only camp uniforms are inside.

Sweaters. Pants. Shirts. Shoes. They all look like they fit. The world, and especially my sister, loves to tell me that I'm fat. But my size is *supposed* to be the national average. So why is it so hard to find a pair of jeans that fit on the rack at Target?

Even though I haven't been around for a while, Mrs. Ellenshaw remembered my sizes.

I feel a little better.

Miller is the only one of us who has his own room. It's on the other side of a shared bathroom, and we can hear him in there banging on something metal and cursing. For a minute, it looks like Vivian might go and help him, but she doesn't. Instead, she chooses a bed on the opposite side of the bungalow.

Facing the closet, I slowly peel back the duct tape on my stomach and remove the small HD camera. I sit down, slip into

74

the darkness of a bottom bunk, pile a bunch of pillows on my lap, and power the camera on. Concealed between the pillows, the camera captures my first shot.

FADE IN

INT. GOLDWATER BUNGALOW

The new campers arrive in the bungalow. It's been designed for people who want to pretend to enjoy the outdoors. It's filled with reminders that adventure is "out there" for people who would much rather stay "in here." ACTION GIRL has her knees bent and is about to flop back onto her chosen bunk. THE NERD sits at the desk against the wall, hunched over like someone using a computer. Except no computer. So he rifles through a weathered copy of *The Mysterious Island*. THE JOCK WITH A HEART OF GOLD is next door in his own room, making a lot of noise that the campers ignore.

THE NERD
(to ACTION GIRL)
I am not sleeping on a top bunk.

THE OUTCAST
(fiddles with a strand of her red hair)
Me either.

ACTION GIRL opens her mouth. THE JERK looks on. Like he is wondering what side to take in this fight. THE BASKET CASE films everything, waiting for a confrontation, a money shot.

THE OUTCAST
Please.

> There is something so pathetic about the way THE OUT-CAST says *please*. It pops ACTION GIRL like a balloon.

ACTION GIRL
> (picks up her bag, crosses the room, and drops it beside the ladder near THE BASKET CASE's bed)

Fine.

> A second later, ACTION GIRL's legs dangle in front of the camera held by THE BASKET CASE. Her Doc Martens come in and out of focus. THE JERK climbs up the ladder of the bunk on the opposite wall, without arguing or complaining. This surprises THE BASKET CASE. A banging noise can be heard from THE JOCK WITH A HEART OF GOLD's room.

ACTION GIRL
> (in a horrible accent)

You okay in there, poppet?

> No answer from THE JOCK WITH A HEART OF GOLD. THE BASKET CASE is about to suggest that someone go in there after him when he comes into the campers' room with a ziplock bag full of tinfoil and a stack of files.

THE JOCK WITH A HEART OF GOLD
> (red-faced and out of breath)

Cabinet . . . stuck . . . couldn't . . . and now . . . I guess . . . we . . . let's get started.

ACTION GIRL

(there is an edge to her voice)

With what?

THE JOCK WITH A HEART OF GOLD

(smooths his dark blue polo and tries to take charge)

Camp Featherlite is testing a special weight-loss bar this session. I will distribute the Metabolize-A bars now. At various intervals, I will be conducting short interviews designed to get your feedback on this exciting new innovation. The most common side effects—

THE OUTCAST

Side effects?

THE JOCK WITH A HEART OF GOLD

—are dry mouth and nausea. But please report any other issues you—

I hustle to put the camera down as Miller heads in my direction. He opens up the plastic bag and drops a foil-wrapped square in my palm. It isn't marked in any way. Grandma could have made this in the kitchen of our trailer.

I unwrap it and squeeze it between my fingers. The bar is spongy and a little bit like a Rice Krispies treat. But the color. It is a weird green with black stripes running across it—almost like veins. It reminds me of our one family vacation. To Gatlinburg, where we went to an aquarium. I couldn't stop staring at this small fish in one of the freshwater tanks.

A green discus.

That's what a Metabolize-A bar looks like.

Miller is determined to get through his reading. "—to me at once so I can document—"

Above me, Vivian is saying, "You expect me to put this in my mouth? It's . . ."

"Unnatural," Smentkowski finishes.

Rachel fluffs up the pillows on her bunk and arranges them strategically behind her back. "They're not even properly labeled. Where's the list of ingredients? If this is a pharmaceutical product, where are the drug facts and warning labels?"

Miller sighs and finishes in a defeated tone. "Please be sure to eat your full portion. I will dispense bars after every camp meal." The leather of the sofa crunches as he takes a seat near our bunk. His stack of papers fans across his lap.

He has files with each of our names on them.

Miller might not know who coughed up thirty grand to send me to camp. But that little piece of intel is probably in my file. Someday, when we're friends again, I'll have to tell Vee that her mom sent me to Featherlite. First, I need to earn her trust back. Then, I can confess that Mrs. Ellenshaw hopes I will help Vivian "recalibrate her attitude toward Brad."

Like that's even possible. Mrs. E should know better than anyone that the only person who can change Vee's mind is Vee.

Focus. I'll worry about all of that later.

I have a film to make.

Moving back in my bunk, I turn the camera on again.

MATCH CUT

INT. GOLDWATER BUNGALOW

The campers have been discussing the Metabolize-A bars, a weight-loss product being tested this session. They have taken note of the bars' odd appearance and packaging. THE BASKET CASE has noticed that THE JOCK WITH A HEART OF GOLD has a file for each camper.

THE OUTCAST

(holds the bar close to her face)

What could possibly be giving it this iridescent coloring?

THE BASKET CASE

(stares at the manila folders)

Maybe fish scales?

THE OUTCAST

(pauses and thinks for a second)

Maybe, but you wouldn't expect it to have this kind of look after you'd ground up the—

I look away from the camera's screen. Maybe I've gotten Rachel Benedict wrong. Maybe she is The Nerd and not The Outcast. If so, I'll have to make some adjustments later on. Get more footage of her saying science-y stuff and fewer shots of her startled-looking stares. I let the camera continue to roll.

"They can make stuff like that," Vivian comments. "I've got a whole collection of unicorn-colored eyeshadows that looks exactly like this."

"Yeah, but that's done with ingredients like mica. And titanium dioxide. And technically you can put that in food, but . . ." Rachel holds her bar close to her face again and picks at it with one finger. "This thing isn't coated or frosted. Whatever it's made of *is* this color."

I tear my own bar in half. She's right. The greenish, pearlized color and the black stripes run all the way through the bar. Like this thing *is* a discus and not something that looks like one.

Rachel continues to inspect her own square. "So they didn't give you any information on these bars? Maybe show you MSDS? All the counselors at church camp were trained to access them in case of an emergency."

It takes us all a minute to realize that she is talking to Miller.

His face turns red. "No."

"What's MSDS?" Paul asks.

Vivian's legs swing back and forth. "Did they give you any training at all?"

Miller's face is as red as Grandma's cheap lipstick now. But he says, "Yes. Obviously. MSDS are material safety data sheets. They contain information about chemicals and how to handle them safely. We have to keep them on file on the farm for . . . you know . . . pesticides . . . uh . . . animal vaccines . . ." He lets out a deep exhale. I think he's relieved. Like he is thrilled to finally have an answer to a question. "Okay. You all need to eat your bars, and then we need to get your files set up."

"Files?" Paul's eyes travel to the stack of manila folders.

In fact, Rachel and Smentkowski are looking too.

Perfect. Everyone knows about the files.

Miller takes this to mean that everyone is interested in what we need to do. He goes on with more authority. "I need to take your starting weight and measurements." He is again reading from his sheet. "Then I'll keep a record of your progress—"

Vee ignores all this. "Did they say anything about the camper who went missing?"

Everything in the room stops. Rachel quits fluffing pillows. Smentkowski puts down the book. Vee's legs stop moving. Paul's hands fall into his lap.

We all wait for an answer.

"Um . . . well . . . yeah . . . they said something . . ."

"What did they say?" Vee asks.

Miller clears his throat. "Look, how about you eat your bars and then we—"

Vee tosses her bar, which she's molded into a foil-wrapped sphere, kind of like a hostile moon, onto the sofa next to Miller. "I'm not eating this."

Smentkowski drops his bar as well. "Me either."

Miller glances at me.

I say nothing.

Rachel speaks slowly. "I don't think we should eat them either. For now. Until we can at least have a chance to ask some questions." She's a people pleaser. Like me. She is holding out the hope that we'll cooperate later on. "I'll talk to the camp director at dinner and get some answers. If we're all satisfied, then we'll eat them."

"I'm not eating anything I don't want to eat," Vivian says.

Rachel sinks back, pushing herself farther into her bunk so that her face is out of view.

Paul comes to her defense. "She said we won't eat it if we're not satisfied with the answers we get. If you don't like what you hear, don't eat it." He immediately looks like he regrets saying this. "But . . . ah . . . we could eat them . . . if you want . . ."

"I don't want."

"Fine," Miller says. Although the thin white line of his mouth indicates that it is not fine. "So let's get started with the files."

I can almost hear the whir of Vee's brain.

But Miller has a preemptive strike. "Here's the deal. You guys help me get the info I need for the files, and I'll tell you what they said about the missing camper."

"You should tell us anyway," Smentkowski says. "Information access is in everyone's best interest."

"Maybe. But getting paid for this job is in *my* best interest. So you make the call."

Miller wins this battle.

I make a mental note to set up the camera somewhere before the next weigh-in. Those kinds of shots might come in handy in the editing room.

We all take our turn on the scale. I tell him I'm too cold to take off my sweater, and he doesn't make a big deal out of it. There is also a brief and stupid series of questions about how much exercise we do. Vee is the only one of us who does any daily exercise at all.

Then we're back in Goldwater's main room.

This time Vee sits in one of the leather chairs while the rest of us go back to our bunks. Even Smentkowski heads to his own bed. There is something about that gesture. Like Vee has effectively established herself as an equal to Miller.

They exchange the kind of look that I wish I caught on camera.

"Okay . . ." she prompts.

For a minute, it almost seems like Miller has decided not to tell us. I think he realizes that he still needs us to eat those bars. And that he'll be trapped in this bungalow with the five of us for the next two weeks.

"The missing camper is a girl. She disappeared down by the lake," Miller says.

"We already know that," Smentkowski answers in a surly tone.

Miller scowls at him. "They sent a team of rangers down there to look for her. And they haven't come back."

Uncertainty flickers across Miller's face.

"There's something else, isn't there?" Vee asks.

Miller doesn't answer right away.

"Steve. What is it?"

I think that's what does it. The *Steve*.

"They said that the camp director went down there too," he says. He speaks in a monotone and stares out the window into the growing darkness.

"Dr. Volstead?" Paul asks.

Miller nods. "She's missing. And they said if they can't find her, we're screwed."

We're all quiet for a minute, but the whole thing bothers me. "Are you saying . . ." I start and then trail off. It's hard for me to put what I want to say into words. "Do you mean . . . if the rangers are out there looking for a girl, does that mean the thing we saw was . . . it was a girl?"

"That's not possible," Paul says.

"What did you see?" Rachel asks. She scoots forward so she is on the edge of the bunk.

Vee tries to describe what we saw, but I don't want to hear it.

Like Miller, I watch the snowy night.

"Oh, I am not staying here," Smentkowski says. He gets up off his bunk and moves toward his closet. "I am out of here."

I expect Miller to have more of a reaction, but he says, "Good luck. All the phones are down, and they've closed and locked the camp gates. The only way out would be the lake. But hey, maybe you'll find Dr. Volstead while you're down there."

Smentkowski freezes.

There's a heavy thud against the wall on the far side of the bungalow.

I scream.

And then I almost throw myself back against the wall. Trying to hide from whatever's out there. Miller gets up and stands alongside me. "It's okay. It's okay." He pats my arm. "Someone's knocking on the door."

I'm panting. Trying to catch my breath. Unable to catch my breath. Vivian joins Miller at my bunk, eyeing me with concern. After another knock, she goes to the door.

"Where is your Facilitator?" a gruff voice asks.

Vee holds the door open.

An older Black man wearing a uniform that matches Miller's steps into the bungalow. His name tag reads ROGER. He's carrying a stack of takeout containers. "What exactly is going on in here?" he asks.

"You scared the hell out of Allison, that's what," Smentkowski tells him.

The man's gaze travels around the room. My rational brain begins to work again. The guy had been knocking on the door to

Miller's room. Probably hoping to speak in private.

Miller isn't paying any attention. "Allison. Breathe. Just breathe."

I fight to suck in a breath. My lungs feel like they're full of campfire ash.

Roger grimaces and addresses himself to Vee. "We're keeping the lockdown in effect until morning and calling lights-out *now*. Get your battery-powered lanterns and use them strategically. Here's your dinner." He passes Vivian the containers. "We'll reconvene at oh eight hundred in the commissary."

Before she can ask any follow-up questions, Roger slams the door.

He's gone.

Vee puts the food down on the coffee table.

"Are you okay?" she asks me, her face scrunched up in concern.

"Yeah. Yeah," I mumble. For a second, we're the old us again.

Her worry fades away. "It's nice to have someone care about your feelings, isn't it?"

She turns away before I can say anything. Before I can apologize for the millionth time for screwing Evan. I stay on my bunk as everyone else moves around.

Smentkowski closes his closet door.

Vee and Paul go around the room taking an inventory of how many lanterns we have.

Rachel opens up the takeout containers and sets up our dinner.

Miller turns off all the lights.

I stare out the window until there's total darkness.

Until there's nothing left to see.

Guillermo del Toro once said, "When you see something or experience something extraordinary, you can't go back to normal."

I don't know what we saw streaking across the snow this morning. But part of me knows, as much as I want to pretend otherwise, that I will never be able to go back to normal.

PAUL FANNON

It's a long night.

We have six camping lanterns but only four with working batteries.

By the time we put one in the bathroom, that leaves three for the rest of the bungalow, and this means a lot of fighting over who gets them and where they'll be placed.

And then. Lights out.

And then. The kind of dark that scares small children.

Every bit of snow that falls onto the roof, every sway of the pine trees seems designed to menace us.

I lie awake for a long time, and I think everyone else is awake, too.

Except Smentkowski, who snores loudly.

But then, he hasn't seen . . . that thing.

Despite everything, the next day begins normally.

A little before eight, Miller pretty much makes us get dressed in new uniforms. He leaves right after that, mumbling about a staff meeting and leaving the five of us to make our way to the commissary on our own.

It isn't too bad. The commissary is actually the only building to the west of us, and we aren't far from it.

I have to admit that the camp uniform makes getting ready really simple. The only sucky thing is that the uniforms really weren't designed for this weather. It is rarely *this* cold for *this* long in Flagstaff.

I'm freezing.

But at least it stops snowing.

We go slowly along the packed, slippery ice. As we walk, we get a bit of a better look at each other. Vivian is out in front and is the only one of us fighting to retain a bit of individuality. She has candy-colored bracelets stacked on her wrists, on the outside of her camp cardigan. The rest of us blend in.

Which is fine, I guess.

I'm supposed to be blending in.

But.

There's always Rachel.

She's odd, and I can't quite figure her out. She looks like a potato. With legs. Her pants hang off them, and her cuffs have come unfolded, dragging behind their owner.

We're silent as we travel across camp. I try to look around for anything Dad might want to know. But everything is unremarkable. We pass kids lingering underneath trees and near picnic tables, drinking coffee from the custom-made camp ceramic mugs. Facilitators call out names, taking roll of their campers. The snow-covered trees are straight out of the pages of the Thomas Kinkade calendars our family sends out each Christmas. A couple of guys run past us, splashing snow onto my pant leg. Pods make their way toward the smell of maple syrup, laughing and giggling.

Things are normal.

Like a whole team of rangers hadn't been chasing some monster down by the lake.

In the commissary, we linger near the door. It's a huge room. Kind of like an enormous pancake house. Camp staffers run back and forth across the place, refilling drinks, smiling, and answering questions.

All night, I'd been thinking about the bars. I screwed up. Yet again. I should have encouraged everyone to eat them. That's what my father would have expected.

Why can't I ever seem to do what my father expects?

The whole point was to see how the camp operated. How the bars worked. If the investors would be happy with the Featherlite operation. Instead, I was in a car accident, chased into camp by some . . . *thing*, outwitted by a fat girl, and part of a potential Pod rebellion.

Typical.

A couple of Facilitators streak by us. They seem kind of stressed. But for some reason that reassures me. That, too, seems normal. Having dozens of people shout you down for more orange juice must be a source of pressure.

The campers, on the other hand.

They are positively giddy.

Smiling at each other. Moving from table to table, chatting. Maybe they know something we don't. Or maybe they *don't* know that Volstead and that girl are missing.

Next to me, Vivian must be thinking along the same lines because she leans over and asks, "You see Volstead anywhere around here?"

I've been looking since we came in. I shake my head.

"You sure you'd recognize her?" she asks.

"Yep," I answer.

Yes. I'm absolutely sure I would recognize the woman I caught in bed with my father last summer at our place in Tahoe.

A buffet is set up on one side of the room, where staffers are handing out breakfast boxes. "Let's go get in line," I suggest, eager to cut off any more questions.

I'm kind of surprised when the rest of the Pod follows me to the chow line.

Maybe they're hungry.

The instant I pick up a blue paper plate, a fat blonde girl whirls around. She has a wide smile on her face. "So how did you do?" she asks.

The girl rolls her eyes at our blank stares. "How much weight did you lose?"

I stammer *oh* and *um* a few times before Vivian takes pity on me.

"How much weight did *you* lose?" she asks the new girl.

"Thirty-one point two pounds," the girl says.

"Since when?" Smentkowski demands.

"Camp just started yesterday," Allison adds. As usual, it's barely above a whisper.

"I know! More than thirty pounds in one day," the girl almost yells. Pretty much right in my ear. She's euphoric. Bouncing up and down. Grinning bigger and bigger. "I did the best in my cabin, but even Marlene lost eighteen pounds."

Vivian yanks a paper plate off the top of the stack. She doesn't bother to ask who Marlene is. "You're saying you lost over thirty pounds? Since yesterday? That's not even possible."

I fight off a sense of excitement. "Maybe it is."

Here is something that would please the investors. *Here* is something I could tell Dad.

"No. She's right," Rachel says. "Assuming that there are

approximately 3,500 calories in a pound, you would need to expend around 105,000 calories more than you took in."

A guy farther up in line says, "Tell us more, Dr. Science."

Rachel's face flushes red, and Vivian glares at the guy.

"So?" the girl asks.

"So?" Rachel repeats. But she goes on with less conviction than before. "That can't happen. Even Olympic athletes don't burn those kinds of calories."

"That's true," Vivian says, with a forceful glare that stops any more sarcastic responses.

The line moves forward, and I pick up a small container of scrambled eggs that has been left on a stainless steel rack. There is a cheerful yellow sign overhead that reads ONE CONTAINER PER CAMPER. After breakfast, I'll have to hit the employee area that Mom mentioned and search for some real food.

Vivian ducks around me, watching the girl who is pulling on the waistband of her camp sweatpants. I notice for the first time how baggy they are. She holds the drawstring out for me to see. She's knotted it several times to keep her pants up. "All I can say is that these sweats fit me perfectly yesterday. They were even kind of tight. Ask anyone in my Pod."

"Maybe I will," Vivian says.

"Okay. Well. I weighed in yesterday right after orientation and then first thing this morning. Everyone saw. The scale doesn't lie."

"Good."

"Fine."

Vivian turns her attention to the line, adding small premeasured portions of eggs, bacon, and melon to her own plate.

Rachel does the same, moving like a robot, lost in her own thoughts.

Right then it's clear why everyone is so happy.

They're tugging on their clothes, showing off how baggy their pants and cardigans are. And all I can think of is one thing.

We are going to make a lot of money.

If Kaiser and my dad have really figured out how to help people get skinny overnight, we are going to make some serious money.

A total fuckton of money.

Money. Money. Money.

Sure. We're already rich. But FannonPharma isn't one of the big boys. We are the kind of rich where you have a couple summer homes and a Cessna Citation. An invention like this would make us a big-time player. Make us Richard Branson rich. The kind of rich where your children's children would have titles like *philanthropist* or *noted industrialist*.

I get a glimpse of a future that includes me sitting at a glossy mahogany table. Chairman of the board of the world's biggest drugmaker. With a supermodel wife and a private island and a collection of Lambos in my twenty-car garage. A bunch of kids off at some prep school. I'd see them on the holidays.

If I wasn't flying around in my personal space rocket.

I'd be a success. I'd be taken seriously.

The tables in the commissary are labeled with the bungalow names. We take our seats at Goldwater, which is all the way against the wall, in a corner by itself.

Miller cruises by and drops off some bottles of water and sugar-free juice at the table, knocking them over twice before finally pushing them into the center. "So . . . uh . . . after breakfast, we're supposed to head outside for our first camp activity. Um . . . it's a brisk snowshoe walk."

"We're not going to the lake, are we?" Allison asks.

"Did they give you any more information about the bars?" Rachel says.

He shakes his head. "No. Just from one end of camp to the other. Then you get free time until lunch. There's . . . uh . . . ping-pong . . . racquetball . . . some classic arcade games . . ."

"Craft stations set up in Babbit Hall, a book club meeting at ten thirty in the Poston Lounge," Vivian finishes for him.

Miller gives her a thin smile and can't get away from us fast enough. "Right. See you outside after you're finished."

Then we're alone.

And he hasn't answered Rachel's question.

Vivian turns to Rachel. "Does this make any sense to you? Thirty pounds in one night? How could that even be possible?"

It strikes me that they are already a team. That they are working together.

Allison stares at the blonde girl, who is happily chatting with another group at a table on the other side of the room. "*Is it possible?*"

"We need a computer," Smentkowski says, shifting his weight from side to side. This is his answer to everything.

"It shouldn't be possible," Rachel says. "But . . ." She trails off.

"But what?" Vivian says.

But what if it is possible?

Fame. Money. Success. Women. More money.

Still, something about our Facilitator was a bit off. "Did Miller seem nervous to you?"

I'm surprised when Allison answers. "We're the only people in here who didn't eat those bars. He's probably worried about getting into trouble."

Somehow, I don't think that's it.

Vivian pokes at her eggs with her fork a couple of times and then shoves her plate into the center of the table.

Apparently, breakfast is over.

Outside, a light snowfall has begun, but the camp counselors are making us do the walk anyway. I guess this makes sense. According to the schedule, every day is supposed to begin with some cardio.

Miller comes back with five pairs of snowshoes in a basket and passes them out.

Smentkowski is the only one of us from a cold state, and he has to show us all how to put them on. After a couple of minutes, he has a little queue going of people who need help adjusting the leather straps to fit their Wellingtons. The whole time he's saying things like *Oh, for the love of Pete* and *Are you serious?* under his breath.

It takes all of us to get Rachel's shoes on her feet. That girl *really* has a balance problem. We can barely keep her from falling over in the snow. Eventually, Allison and Vivian hold her up while Smentkowski and I handle the straps.

Miller is waiting for us.

"Okay," he says, clapping his hands once, mustering as much enthusiasm as he has. "We're going from one end of camp to the other. Along the way, we've hidden Easter eggs." He gives the basket to Vivian. "There are prizes for collecting the most eggs and for finding specially marked golden eggs."

"Specially marked, eh, poppet?" Vivian says. "What are the prizes?"

At least she still has her sense of humor.

"You'll have to collect the eggs to find out," he says, trying to match her tone.

"How long is the walk?" Smentkowski asks.

Miller smiles. "Two miles across camp."

Rachel sighs like she's already exhausted.

Vivian frowns. "And then back again."

"Great," Smentkowski says.

We get started, and it's basically an Easter egg hunt in slow motion, with campers fanning out along the path. Walking carefully on the ice. Heading east in clusters. Smentkowski is competitive. He sets a fast pace for our group to try to get to the eggs on the east side before anyone else.

By the time we pass the last bungalow and come to the end of the wide path, we have seven brightly colored eggs.

"But no gold ones," Miller says with another odd smile.

Rachel stands at the very edge of the path, where it branches off into several small trails. One goes down to the lake. The others disappear into the thick forest.

I'm about to go stand by her, but something catches my eye.

A fleck of gold glints in the sun.

"I found one," I call out. I'm not really even sure who I'm talking to.

The sparkle comes from the base of a tall ponderosa. A pine cone crunches underneath my boot as I make my way over there. I kneel down.

Too late I realize.

It's not an Easter egg.

A part of a gold bracelet is exposed by the snow.

Only.

It's still connected to a fucking wrist.

A few fingers jut out from the ice.

One has been bitten off.

By something.

Savage.

What am I looking at? What am I actually seeing?

Iced-over blood. Ragged torn skin.

A broken-off bone with the chunk from the knuckle up gone.

Behind me, I'm aware of voices.

"I said, what did you find?"

A voice. Maybe Vivian.

I stay there. Frozen.

Footsteps grow louder.

It takes everything I have not to throw up.

The chunks of scrambled eggs rise in my throat.

They taste like gasoline.

My eyes find a few strands of blonde hair. Caked with blood.

Allison screams.

Under a light layer of melting snow.

A face.

Another scream.

It's Volstead.

VIVIAN ELLENSHAW

For the next hour or so, everything is in total chaos. People running everywhere. People screaming. Everyone slipping around on the ice. Crowds pushing into camp. And a few stragglers, moving against the masses, trying to get a look at Volstead.

What's left of her.

Eventually, the Facilitators get everyone inside their bungalows.

They never tell us what the prizes are.

For some reason, I get stuck on that fact.

Miller shuts us in and goes right back out again. They have to dig the camp director out of the snow. They carry her, wrapped in a blue tarp, all the way from the east side of camp, past our bungalow window, and toward the employees-only area.

At first, we keep ourselves busy getting out of our boots and into clean, dry uniforms. Fannon paces around. I think I'm the only one who has put it together that he actually knew Volstead. Or noticed that he's taking the news hard.

We have to do something. Fannon and Smentkowski play cards. I get Allie to help me inventory the supplies. In addition to the lanterns and canteens that are out in plain view, there is a large closet that contains several thermal coats, some sleeping bags, a tent, and a first aid kit. It kind of feels like old times. Like we're working on a school project or something.

Rachel goes through all of the documents they've given us, looking for information about emergency procedures. Or anything more about the bars. She doesn't find much of anything.

Eventually, I pick up an old copy of *Robinson Crusoe* and curl up in my bunk.

Miller comes back a little after lunchtime. He's different. White as the snow. He comes in, first to his own room and then into the main part of the bungalow. He drops a bunch of boxed meals on the table, disrupting the card game.

"Who went through my stuff?" he asks.

He turns and stares right at me when he asks this.

My face heats up and my pulse flutters under the intensity of his gaze.

"What are you talking about?" I ask.

Miller runs his fingers through his hair, trying to contain his frustration. "Someone was in my room. The files are missing. And so are some of the bars."

"You think *I* did it?"

He stands in front of my bunk. "Did you?"

He's so close that it's hard to concentrate. "I . . . uh . . . no!"

Fannon glances up from his cards. "None of us wanted to eat the bars. And Smentkowski was the one who was so interested in the files."

Smentkowski pushes the lunches out of the way and lays down a straight on the table. "You're a sore loser, you know. Anyway, I've been sitting here with you since we came in." He points in my direction. "It was the two of them who were going around inspecting every nook and cranny."

"I haven't left this room and you know it," I tell him.

"She did though," Rachel says, her head ducked into one of the manuals.

It takes me a minute to register that the *she* is Allie.

Why would Allie want the files? If anyone needs them, it's Fannon. Those files probably contain his real name and address.

"She was in the bathroom with the door locked for, like, ever," Rachel continues.

"Oh, so going to the bathroom is suspicious now?" Allie demands. "If so, you're the most suspicious person here. I think you went in there like twenty times last night."

Rachel drops the book, her face bright red. "I'm . . . I'm sorry. You're right. I shouldn't have said that."

A familiar expression creeps over Allie's face. Like when she's filming and she figures out the exact right way to get a shot. She has an idea. "Maybe you're the one who took them," she says slowly, "so that no one will know that . . ."

Rachel's eyes widen in terror.

"So that no one will know what?" Miller presses.

Allie thinks for a second. And then she speaks. "So that no one will know that Rachel isn't serious about losing weight."

Fannon rolls his eyes and deals out a new hand of cards.

"Okay. So that's it, then?" Miller asks. "I've been cool with you guys from the very beginning, and you're gonna screw me over like this? I'm gonna get fired—"

I hop down from my bunk. Miller is on the verge of losing it. "Steve! For the love of God, pull yourself together. I don't know what happened to the files. But someone's been murdered. Do you seriously think you'll be let go for incomplete paperwork?"

"What makes you think it was murder?" Smentkowski asks.

Fannon puts down his cards. "Volstead was thirty-two. They found her buried in the snow without all her fingers. What do you think she died of? Heart disease?"

Miller lowers himself into one of the leather chairs. "We couldn't even find all her body parts," he says tonelessly. "She was missing her left arm and a foot below the ankle."

I shudder.

I catch Fannon's eye.

We both know.

It was that thing.

When Miller doesn't say anything else, I move to sit in the chair next to him and pat him on the shoulder. "What's really happening?"

There is a long silence, but eventually he answers. "They want to evacuate the camp. Something weird's going on with the power, and they haven't been able to make contact with anyone from town."

Smentkowski perks up at the mention of the power systems but says nothing.

Miller goes on in a gloomy voice. "They're sending a truck out in an hour. And they . . . they put me on the patrol schedule. Up by the north gate. I have to go . . . out there . . ."

Out there. With that thing.

The thought is there. Unspoken.

"You don't *have* to do anything," Fannon says.

It's an interesting thing for him to say. Our options are narrowing down. Our list of choices is becoming smaller.

Miller chews on his lower lip. "I'm supposed to refuse to go, when other people are out there protecting the camp?"

I stand up. "I'm going with you."

This seems to snap Miller out of his gloom. "Like hell you are. Campers aren't allowed. It's bad enough that I have to go out there. There's no way you're going too."

I'm terrified. I think my legs might give out and I'll be stuck here on the wooden bungalow floor forever. But what scares me most of all is the feeling that things are getting away from me. The idea that my destiny is slipping out of my control. I've been driven to this camp by Coach Hanes. By my mom's unrelenting perfectionism. But I'm going out. If that thing is going to get me, I'll at least decide when and where.

There is a sense of urgency to these feelings. They have a beat, keeping time with the race of my pulse. The thud of my heart. And the only thing that will make me halfway normal again is to put myself in motion. "I'm going." I get up and put my Wellingtons on.

Allie's on her bunk, hugging her knees. Part of me wants to ask her to come too. To be a team again. It would be like that summer we spent hiking around the Kaibab forest, trying to find Bigfoot. We thought we could do anything. As long as we had each other. But the one time I had really tried to talk to her about my problems with Coach, she basically told me that I was a pampered, unappreciative whiner.

There's no *I* in *team*. There's no Allie either.

This is stupid. I should apologize or . . . say something . . . or do something . . . and we could be friends again. I hesitate for a minute. But there isn't time for that. When we get home, I'll fix things.

I go to the large closet, find a puffy coat in my size, and pack a bag with a couple of flashlights, the first aid kit, and a few other supplies. "If you don't let me go with you, I'll wait for you to leave and go by myself."

Smentkowski nods. "There's strength in numbers. I'm going too."

"Put some water in some of those canteens," I tell him.

Miller shakes his head and mutters things like *This is a bad idea* a couple of times, but I can tell that he's relieved.

Fannon stares at me like I'm a fool when I insist on taking the yellow plastic oar.

There isn't anything else that can be used as a weapon.

We leave a few minutes later. In our waterproof jackets and boots, we are almost prepared for the weather. Smentkowski insists that we wear the snowshoes. They make my calves burn as I walk. But we aren't slipping and sliding.

Miller has a shitty sense of direction.

If it weren't for me, he'd have ended up down by the lake.

I did pack the compass, but I've spent enough time staring at the camp map that I don't need it. Not right now, anyway. I know that all we need to do is go to the center of the camp and then walk through the employees-only area to the north gate.

A chain-link fence and a row of tall pine trees separate the main part of camp from the staff area. There is a narrow gate, thrown open, and a small guard shack. In better times, there is probably someone making sure campers don't enter.

But the shack is empty.

When we move from one side to the other, I can understand the need for the trees. The camp's charming décor stops abruptly at the fence. On one side of the wide path, there are groups of portable trailers, and on the other, a series of gray concrete-block buildings. Bright red signs mark metal doors.

We pass FOOD OVERFLOW, DRY STORAGE, RESEARCH, DATA

PROCESSING, and, at the very end of one of the last buildings, KAISER. Off in the distance is an even larger, more generic, grayer building. A barbed-wire-topped fence, with RESTRICTED AREA signs every few feet, sits behind the camp buildings. That place isn't on our map. The whole thing screams *Go away*. Whoever is in charge doesn't want anyone to get near that big, creepy, hulking structure.

I find myself falling back behind Smentkowski, trying to imitate his walk. He's obviously spent a lot of time in the snow, and his movements are efficient. He's able to take step after step without sinking into the powder. He's a big guy, but there is something light about him. Something weightless.

"Do you hear that?" Smentkowski asks, pausing for us to catch up.

"No," I say, almost dropping the oar. I crane my neck in every direction.

Looking for *the thing*.

Smentkowski frowns in concern. "That crackling sound?" he clarifies. "Almost like tissue paper crumpling?" He points to the restricted building. "That fencing must be electrified. The snow has caused some kind of short."

"Electrified fencing?" I ask. My shoulders slump a bit as I relax. I glance at Miller. Supposedly the power has been out since yesterday. How in the hell is the camp keeping miles of electrified fencing going?

Smentkowski rolls his eyes. "You guys can stop giving each other *very significant looks*. Even though they're trying to pretend it's business as usual back at camp, I know that the main power is out." Without waiting for me to ask how he knows this, he goes on. "The generator system that they're using can't consistently crank out sixty hertz. That's why the lights keep flickering."

I should have realized that he'd guess the significance of that better than any of the rest of us. "When we arrived yesterday, the guard let it slip that they are running on backup power." I pause. But it seems prudent to give all the info we have to Smentkowski. He's probably the only one who knows what to do with it.

"The guy said he thought the generators would only make it until . . . well . . . this afternoon."

He nods, but he seems nervous. A little off. But we are all nervous. If I had a mirror, it would probably show a shocked face that matched Smentkowski's.

"That'd make sense," he says. "They can't get *that* much inclement weather in a place like this. A twenty-four-hour backup would be more than enough for most circumstances."

"Yeah," Miller agrees. "Only too bad no one told that to *this* blizzard."

"The cell phone suppression is a bigger issue," Smentkowski says. "It's a problem that we can't call out for help."

We keep walking.

A cluster of Pod Facilitators linger in front of the final building, right under the KAISER sign. They recognize Miller.

"Steve! Good," a blonde girl says. I can tell she's the kind of girl who is usually neat as a pin, but right now she's a mess. Frizzy hairs escape from her ponytail, falling onto the collar of her coat. She has a long smudge of dirt across her cheek.

"Hey, Zanna," Miller says. He glances from me to Smentkowski, his lips puckering and eyes narrowing. He's worried. And I understand. This is his boss.

And campers are supposed to be confined to the bungalows.

But if Zanna is surprised to see us, she doesn't let it show. She hands Miller a walkie-talkie-style radio. "We haven't been able to charge these, so most don't have a lot of battery power left. Keep it off except in case of an emergency. We're using channel two."

She turns to the group of ten or so Facilitators. Whoever did the recruiting must have really had a thing for blonds, because they all have hair ranging from white to yellowish brown. In their matching blue coats and khaki pants, they look more like they are gathering for a team photo than forming a posse of people capable of protecting the camp.

"Okay," Zanna says. "Louise, Phillip, and Aven, you're with me. The rest of you have your patrol assignments. Miller, you and, uh . . . them . . ." she says with a disapproving nod in my direction, "are taking over for Roger at the gate. Follow me."

The *rest* of the Facilitators, the ones going on patrol, are turning various shades of green and moving very slowly across the snow in all directions. Miller follows his boss, and I follow Miller.

After we've gone a few feet, Smentkowski is in the lead again.

We keep walking until the trees are again tall enough to block the view of the hissing electric fence and the standoffish building. We come to the gate, much like the one we passed through when we arrived, where a line of four vehicles is parked, ready to leave camp. The two trucks and two SUVs are stuffed full of supplies and people.

Zanna isn't sending out for help.

She's abandoning camp.

Smentkowski's face goes red with fury. He steps in front of Zanna. "The town is what? Two hours away? And you're taking twenty people and more supplies than Lewis and Clark had on the Oregon Trail?"

"We don't know what we're going to encounter out there," Zanna says. She tries to sidestep Smentkowski, but he mirrors her movements.

"They're taking all the guns too," Miller adds.

I notice that each of the vehicles has someone in it who is holding a shotgun. If Miller is right, that means the whole camp has a grand total of four weapons. And they are all leaving with the escape crew.

"What you're gonna encounter is that when you get a mile or so outside of camp, you'll have full access to your cell phones," Miller says. "You'll be able to call for help, and we'll be stuck here in the dark." He's shouting at Zanna. People are moving around inside the cars, craning to get a view of the fight.

"We don't know that," Zanna says through clenched teeth.

"What we do know is that you're supposed to be in charge around here," Miller says. "And you're just leaving?"

"You are such a fucking coward," Smentkowski says.

"You don't understand. Fannon is gone. Volstead is dead. Kaiser is missing. I'm going for help," Zanna says, almost pleading with Miller. "And I'm taking as many people as I think I need to make it."

Smentkowski mutters something that sounds like "Fuck that."

Her big blue eyes are almost circles. It occurs to me.

She knows more than she's saying.

"What is that thing?" I ask. "What's out there?"

I'm almost out of breath as I wait for the answer. It's almost like the weight of the thing is already on my chest.

She bites her lower lip. "Something . . . I don't understand . . . I don't know how . . ."

I'm not sure if Zanna would have gone on to say anything more helpful.

We'll never get to find out because the massive iron gate begins to creak open. Slowly.

We all fall silent.

Watching it open the safety of the camp to whatever is out there.

My fingers are sore. I'm gripping the yellow oar so tightly that my fingers are turning white and starting to throb in pain.

The ice crackles under my feet as I shift my weight from one foot to the other.

Miller releases a long, loud exhale.

The man from earlier, Roger, comes out of the small guard shack.

He moves like Smentkowski.

Efficient.

He, too, is used to the snow.

"Roger, we need to get a move on it," Zanna calls out to him.

He nods but goes to the first truck in the line, emerging with one of the shotguns and something in his hand. Roger is the only person I've seen so far not wearing the dumb Featherlite uniform. He has a thick green coat with a waterproof hood casting a shadow across his weathered face and large black snow boots.

Roger moves toward us, passing Zanna on the way. "They're right," he tells her. "We need to leave 'em one of the guns."

He reaches Miller. "You know how to use one of these, son?"

"Yes, sir," Miller replies. He takes the gun and what I realize is a box of ammo from Roger's hand.

The gate is halfway open. Smentkowski is frozen. Watching.

"Don't let anything through that gate," Roger says.

"Yes, sir," Miller says again. He adds the ammo to his left pocket. His right one already bulges with the radio. His face gives nothing away.

Roger stares right at me. "I know how this looks. But believe me. We're going for help. We *will* be back."

A couple of car doors slam shut as Zanna and her crew shove their way into the already-crowded vehicles.

"The large red button closes the gate. Press it the second we're out," Roger says before walking fast to the first vehicle and sliding behind the wheel.

One by one, the car engines roar to life.

It is somehow too loud. Too much of a disruption of the gray afternoon.

Miller and I stand there in the center of the wide path, watching them go.

Smentkowski has the sense to make his way over to the guard shack.

Roger's truck takes off smoothly with the other vehicles trailing behind. The SUVs slide around in the snow, the drivers not able to manage the icy road conditions quite as well as the lead vehicle.

The instant the rear tires of the last green SUV pass through the gate, Smentkowski hits the red button and the iron begins to creak again. Closing.

Closing even more slowly than it opened.

For a minute, we watch the line of cars disappear down the white road and wait for them to be swallowed by the trees.

But.

The scream.

Like the one we heard the morning we arrived.

Primal.

Bouncing off the pine tree trunks.

The gray thing. The monster.

It comes into the open.

I can't breathe.

It's coming.

For us.

RACHEL BENEDICT

Everything is falling apart.

Someone has been murdered, and Vivian, Sheldon, and Steve have gone out there.

And it is snowing again. And the other girl, Allison, knows I am pregnant. And our personal files are missing, so God only knows what information about me is in there and who has it now. And the baby is doing gymnastics in my belly. And I am no closer to having a plan than I was a week ago or a month ago or eight months ago.

In four weeks, I am going to have this baby.

He is coming.

And then what?

Paul and Allison try to keep the card game going, but she is terrible at poker. A few minutes later, he says he is going to take a shower and goes into the bathroom.

I want to do something useful. I search all the manuals one more time for any mention of the Metabolize-A bars. For why we are taking them or who has made them or what they are made of. I find nothing.

Steve left his paperwork behind, but that isn't much help either. Featherlite hasn't given him any more information than they've given us. He basically only has standard survey forms for clinical trials. Typical medical stuff. But you'd expect that, considering the camp is the brainchild of a couple of doctors.

I grab a few pillows, hit the couch, and pretend to read a book.

When we hear the shower water running, Allison comes over and sits in the leather chair next to me. "I've seen every teen pregnancy movie, like, ever. So . . . you're, what? Seven months pregnant?"

I am thirty-six weeks.

"Geez," Allison continues, shaking her head. "And your parents sent you to fat camp? Even when we *have* to gain weight because it's, like, medically necessary, the world makes us feel like crap about how we look."

"My parents. They didn't send me. I . . . I . . . I sent myself. You . . . you wouldn't understand." I force my eyes onto the pages of *Frankenstein*.

"Try me," she says gently. Her brown eyes are kind of golden, and something tells me that she might get it.

I give it a try. "My father is a minister. He's the head of the largest church in Flagstaff. If he knew, if he . . . if anyone found out I was pregnant, I don't know what would happen."

"You mean your parents haven't noticed?" she asks with even wider eyes.

"I've been really careful. Wearing baggy clothes. And I've been eating more, so I think they assumed I was gaining weight. And my parents are very involved with the church." This all comes out in a rush. In a breath of relief.

Allison nods. "So they're distracted. But how did you end up here?"

I shrug. "One of the deacons is on the Featherlite board of directors. I asked him if he could get me a spot here. I figured it would give me some time to figure stuff out."

"Have you?" she asks.

I shake my head.

"It's hard to be one kind of person when your parents want you to be another," she says.

She doesn't understand me. I hug one of the pillows tight. "I'm not the kind of person who's pregnant at seventeen. I'm a straight-A student. I practically run New Horizon's youth program. Sometimes this all feels like a bad dream."

A preacher's daughter. You ever do anything just for fun?

I should have said no to that question.

Allison gives me a small smile. "I understand. You're the good girl. But that's not what I'm talking about. You're totally some kind of geek and you're in a world where people like to act like science doesn't exist. Even if you weren't pregnant, you'd still have a problem."

She does understand me. She understands the trap that my life has become.

Maybe even better than I understand myself.

I can't help it. Small tears run out from the corners of my eyes. I swipe at them with my sleeve, hoping Allison won't see.

She scoots forward on her chair and reaches for my hand. "It's okay. You can cry. What you're going through. It's a lot."

I can't stop the tears. For the past eight months, I have been keeping my secret. Hiding everything from everyone. Avoiding my friends.

Allison squeezes my fingers. "The father. What does he think?"

It occurs to me how much I want to avoid *the father*. "He doesn't know. I want to keep it that way."

I hate the father.

She nods. "You ever wish you could run away somewhere? Escape?"

"All the time." Except there is nowhere to run. I still have the fake ID and might be able to show it and check into a hospital. I used the computers at the public library to google Arizona's newborn safe harbor law. I can drop off the baby at any fire station within seventy-two hours and be okay. In eight months, this is the only plan I've been able to come up with. But would everything be okay? Would I be able to go in and lie to everyone at the clinic and then walk out of there with a baby that I planned to abandon? Could I go back to church and turn to Hymn 152 in my book and smile and sing the same way I did every other Sunday?

When I in awesome wonder
Consider all the worlds Thy hand hath made.

Will my little guy be okay? Will I?

I see the stars, I hear the rolling thunder,
Thy power throughout the universe displayed.

I shudder. I'm never going to be okay.

"It'll be okay," Allison says, more quietly. I realize the shower has stopped running.

"You're not going to tell anyone, are you?" I ask her. I am already putting my face back into its calm mask.

"No," she says. I can tell she is telling the truth. My secret is safe.

I want to change the subject. "Do you think Paul stole the files?"

Her face goes blank. "I don't know. He does kind of seem like the type."

Paul comes out of the bathroom then, smelling of the camp's fancy juniper-and-sage shampoo. He glances around from bunk to bunk and then goes over to stand in front of the large window. "They're still out there?"

"Yes," Allison says, reaching up for a strand of her long blonde hair. There really is something about her. About her very pale white skin and the handful of freckles on her straight nose. She also is not particularly fat. She is more like the average-size person Hollywood would cast to play a fat person opposite a size-zero model.

I can't help myself. "You know, you really do seem so familiar."

That is wrong.

Her shoulders drop, and the corners of her mouth turn downward. When she speaks, it is with the air of someone forced to make a terrible confession. "I look a lot like my sister. Dorian Leigh DuMonde. She's been in a bunch of those vampire movies."

Around our house, the only movies we went to were ones about dogs who could perform miracles or kids suffering from horrible diseases. So the name is only vaguely familiar.

Paul sits in the leather chair on my other side. "No way! She's fucking hot. I mean, that scene in *Stake My Heart* where she was crawling through those catacombs in that Catholic schoolgirl outfit . . ."

Allison is stricken. This is why she understands me. We are the same. Our lives are cages we want to bust free from.

I interrupt Paul. "We need to talk about what we're going to do."

He stops in the middle of a sentence about Dorian Leigh DuMonde's mile-long legs. "Do? Do? About what?"

I roll my eyes. "About what's going on around here. Aren't you the slightest bit curious about what happened to Dr. Volstead? Or about these magic bars that supposedly made someone lose thirty pounds in one day? Or the fact that Sheldon said they're using the same security technology around here that the NSA uses at Fort Meade?"

Allison nods along vigorously. I am gaining steam. Building up momentum. Maybe I don't know what is going to happen to my baby or to me, but here is a problem I can do something about. I can figure out what is happening at Camp Featherlite.

The baby gives me a little kick to egg me on.

"Of course I am, Rachel," Paul says. "But I don't see what we can do about any of that right now."

A thought strikes me suddenly and possesses me totally. Vivian went out there. She got her gear together and went out. We could, too. I move over to the closet and pull out a coat like she did.

Allison's mouth falls open in horror as I force my arms into the coat sleeves and go around the room gathering up supplies. "Rachel. We can't go out there."

I know more than I have ever known anything in my life that not only could we go out there, we have to. "Miller said that all the remaining Facilitators would be on patrol."

"Aren't you the least bit concerned about whatever they are patrolling *for*?" Allie says.

Paul smirks. "Allie has a theory that we'll all be killed in a specific order based on our personality types."

I return to the couch in time to see Allison's face turning bright red. "Not according to personality types. It's based on . . . archetypes," she says.

"You mean like Jung?" I ask, stopping my search for a canteen.

Paul's smile widens. "No, like *Friday the 13th*. Like I am The Jerk, so I get it first."

Allison shakes her head. "I told you. It's The Basket Case who gets whacked first."

I freeze. I am not sure if she is talking about me or herself.

But that will have to wait.

There is another yellow plastic canteen on the bookshelf near Vivian's bunk. I take a couple of steps in that direction. I am already tired. But I have to keep going.

"What am I?" I ask to distract myself more than anything.

"Not sure. Either The Outcast or The Nerd," Allison says after a pause. "You might live."

I head to the bathroom for some water. Also because I have to go to the bathroom.

Again.

When I come out, Paul hovers near the door.

"We're *all* going to live," I say with as much force as I can muster. "Like I said, all the Facilitators are out on patrol. That means there won't be anyone in the camp offices. Someone around here must have more information about what's happening. I say we find it."

I expect Paul to argue and am surprised when he goes over to the closet and returns wearing a coat. Part of his collar stays up while the other half flops down. He is effortlessly cool. A James Dean in real life and in color.

"What if Vee and Miller come back?" Allison asks in a high-pitched voice.

She does not want to go. Who am I to make her?

"Why don't you stay here?" I suggest.

She is breathing hard and fast, and when she speaks she is shrill. "You want to separate? You want to leave me here alone?"

"That's another no-no," Paul says, tossing a jacket onto Allison's lap. "We'd be leaving her here for the monster."

"There's no such thing as monsters."

"You hope," Allison says. But she is settling down. Her breathing is normal again. She stands up and puts on the jacket.

"We're all going." Paul is now the leader of our little expedition. He checks his watch. "If we haven't found anything in an hour, we'll come back." He turns to Allison. "Whatever is out there, we'll face it together."

I smile. I might not have a plan. But I have something. I have friends.

Paul scribbles down a note addressed to Sheldon, and we head out into the snow.

SHELDON SMENTKOWSKI

I know it's a big cliché, but after the scream, everything goes in slow motion.

Miller is pumping shells into the gun, and Vivian has the oar held up like a baseball bat.

Finally, I'm afraid.

Up until now, I had managed to convince myself that everything was complete bullshit. That there *had* to be a more logical explanation for what happened to that camp director than a bunch of supernatural monsters running around in the snow.

Okay. Shit just got real.

You betcha.

What does it is the fact that Vivian and Miller are expecting something to happen. They're getting ready. They are fucking terrified, and they think three people and a twelve-gauge shotgun won't be enough.

I'm feeling the way I did the last time I put together a computer and tried to disassemble a power supply without letting the capacitors fully discharge. I'm shocked. Electrified. Like my blood has become coffee and all my organs are getting one hell of a jolt.

The gate is about fifteen feet tall and made of iron, and sturdy fencing surrounds the rest of the camp. The system is probably designed to keep out large bears or maybe mountain lions. Once the gate closes we'll be relatively safe.

It is closing at an unbelievably slow pace.

We can still see the vehicles out on the road ahead. I have to say, I understand the scope of the situation.

I have to say, I understand how fucked we are if those jugheads don't make it to town.

The metal bars of the gate are spaced about six inches apart. It hits me that the bars aren't casting much of a shadow. Dark clouds drift over the sun.

In a few hours it will be night.

I stand a couple of paces from the guard shack.

Another scream.

And then a gray streak clears the gate, swiping the rolling part as it passes.

It is so fast.

And graceful across the snow. Like late-night Animal Planet videos of the arctic fox.

Vivian screams as the thing slides through the open gate onto our side of camp.

It is almost human. But somehow more than human. Its chest is wider, its waist slim, and it has exaggerated, too-defined abs and pecs.

It's almost beautiful.

Up close, the thing's skin is actually made up of small, shiny, and iridescent scales. Every once in a while, bright, phosphorescent patches of red, green, and blue disrupt the gray. It's like an exotic bird or a fish.

And it is strong.

Those muscles aren't just for show. The thing easily knocks Miller back, sending the shotgun sliding along the snow.

What the fuck is that thing? An animal? An alien? A monster?

I do the only thing I can think of.

I run.

Into the guard shack.

Which I quickly realize is not only cowardly but also really damn stupid.

My commotion attracts the monster's attention.

It follows me.

And the shack provides next to no security.

I barely make it inside when the monster is practically on top of me.

Even worse, as the thing comes at me it pounds everything in sight. Its large fists hit the green button on the console.

Vivian screams again, and through the shack's small window, I can see the progress made so far reverse itself and the gate begin to open instead.

The monster lifts a hand above its head and smashes it into the console, breaking the wood and bending the metal, crunching it into the circuit board below. Those controls are now useless.

I fall back onto the wooden wall of the shack. The thing's hot, foul breath hits my neck. It smells so goddamn bad. Like it has been out all night eating roadkill skunks. It gnashes its sharp white teeth at me.

It watches me with its big pitch-black eyes.

I am going to die.

This.

Is.

It.

My last moment on earth.

The thing is going to rip my jugular out with its teeth.

Until Vivian.

She really goes after the fucking thing with the oar. Bashing it with every ounce of strength she's got. And it's working too. The shack is so narrow that the monster has a hard time pivoting, or maybe it can't figure out what to do. Vivian gets eight or ten really good whacks in. Right on the top of the thing's smooth, bald head.

She saves my life.

But the monster has taken as much of a beating as it's going to. It reaches out with each arm and rips away the wood that formed the doorway, basically tearing the shack apart with its bare hands.

As it turns, I notice that the thing has something blue around its neck. Like a necklace or something.

It's the neckband of a blue T-shirt. Exactly like the one I'm wearing.

Maybe the monster killed a camper.

Or.

Or shit.

Maybe it *was* a camper.

I try to get up, but the snowshoes make it hard. It takes me a minute or so to get my feet positioned on the floor and pull myself into a standing position. A small bulb lights up the shack. Or is supposed to. But it accomplishes the odd effect of making everything yellow and dingy and somehow darker than outside.

I feel around for anything I could use as a weapon.

The shack is clean, and I don't find anything, but it doesn't matter.

Leaning over, I peer around the monster to see Vivian

bracing herself, knees bent, with her oar up in the air. I can't stay in the shack and wait for that shit to play out.

I push myself up and away from the wall.

A shot rings out.

Miller has finally come to grips with the shotgun, and he gets a round of ammo off, hitting the monster in the chest. It lets out a horrible, gurgling wail.

When I get myself out of the shack, both Miller and Vivian are going at the thing. It falls onto the snow. Vivian keeps smashing at it with the oar while Miller continues to fire. By the sixth shot the thing is down.

We are safe.

I take a deep breath.

Except something is still wrong with the two of them.

My ears are ringing from the gunfire.

Vivian comes right up to me and screams in my face. "You have to get the fucking gate closed. Now!"

At first, I don't understand what the problem is, but then more shots are fired. Except they aren't from nearby. They aren't from Miller's gun.

Vivian is waving and pointing at the gate, and I turn in that direction. Out there. Through the open gate, I see another one of those things.

And it is charging one of the SUVs.

It picks up a fucking car and overturns it. The red vehicle skids on its roof before crashing into a row of pine trees.

"Smentkowski! You have to do something," Vivian shouts.

All I can think about right then are those words.

You have to do something.

Is it fate?

Those words. They put me on the road to Featherlite.

You have to do something. That's what my dad said when he set up a job interview at his company in the IT department. They needed help, and Dad said I could fill in on evenings and weekends. "You're supposed to be some kind of a genius. Why not put that talent to good use?"

"I'm busy with school," I told him.

"You mean you're busy hacking the school district's mainframe," he corrected. "You clearly have too much free time, and I insist that you fill it with something constructive."

For Dad, the only thing that's constructive is making money.

I'm not sure I could explain, even to myself, exactly why Dad sucks so much. Like, his whole life is about safety. He prevents accidents, stops accidents, investigates accidents, and yet he *is* an accident. Someone needs to tell Dad to investigate his own damn personality. Maybe he could figure out why he had Mom give up her teaching career and move all over for his stupid job and then dumped her when she got breast cancer. Or explain why he treats people like property to be used and then thrown away.

He doesn't like me, or anybody, or anything. He has no joy.

Except maybe when he's screwing the twenty-three-year-old he met after he divorced Mom.

You have to do something.

Dad sent me into Bill Knudsen's office for an interview. Knudsen is to coding what Mariah Carey is to coding.

This was Knudsen's question. "Tell me how you'd design a piece of software that would estimate the number of gas stations in Alaska."

Dickhead managers live for these kinds of stupid questions.

And they never understand anything. They stay up late at night trolling Reddit like script kiddies. They can't code. Not really, anyway.

I could have answered.

I mean, obviously.

I've done my fair share of variants of the gas station problem. I could have written an algorithm in the time it would take to use the john.

Instead, I said, "No."

Knudsen's jaw almost hit his desk. "I'm sorry?"

"No, I will not tell you."

He scowled. "You mean you don't know?"

"I mean I won't tell you."

When I came home that night, Dad stared at me for a minute. "Brittani is right about you. You have no practical skills. You're a punk determined to waste every ounce of your potential."

You have to do something.

That's what he said.

Brittani can go fuck herself.

After that, the two of them decided they'd help me get my life in order.

Featherlite was step one.

You have to do something.

But I decided to do nothing to the very best of my ability.

I decided to hack Featherlite's power systems because I wasn't staying at this camp.

Because fuck them.

But now.

Vivian is right.

I have to do something.

Okay. Okay. Okay. Okay. Okay.

Lucky for me, my dad is wrong. I have plenty of practical skills.

The buttons in the booth are gone, but so what? They are nothing more than radio controls anyway.

I have to find the main control box.

Taking big steps, I go to the far side of the gate. The large black box is mounted to a wooden pole in the shadows of several snow-covered trees. I tear open the panel door.

I'm grateful for how anal these camp people are. When I work on hardware, I never take the time to bust out the label maker. But here, I find neat white stickers that say things like OPEN, CLOSE, STOP, and PROGRAM in raised block letters. I hit stop.

The gate shudders and stops moving.

In the middle of the road, Miller and Vivian are arguing.

"You *can't* go out there," she tells him.

More distant shots sound out from up the road.

"I can't just stand here and do nothing," Miller argues.

I push the close button.

"Steve. They have twenty people and three guns. If they can't handle what's out there . . ."

The iron creaks as it moves a few inches across the snow-covered track.

And then it stops again.

Shit.

I scan the control panel and then the gate.

It only takes me a second to locate the problem.

One of the obstruction sensors is cast downward like a sad face. That *thing* must have hit it. The sensors aren't aligned anymore. The system won't work until the sensors are repaired.

Which could take hours.

"Smentkowski!"

Vivian is screaming at me again. I duck around the pine tree.

Oh fuck.

I see what she's talking about.

There are three of those monsters in the road.

And they are becoming very interested in us.

"Smentkowski!"

Shit. Shit. Shit.

There is really only one thing I can do. Disconnect the sensors.

Disconnect the sensors and hope and pray that this model isn't programmed not to function if the sensors aren't working.

I locate the OPEN AND CLOSE OBSTRUCTION label and pull as hard as I can at the two green cables poking out from underneath, ripping them free from the panel and exposing the ragged internal copper wiring.

"Jesus. Fucking. Christ. Smentkowski!"

I hit the close button again.

There really aren't words to describe how relieved I am to find that it actually works. It's like the clouds open up, revealing the sun, as three choruses of "Hallelujah" play.

The gate is closing.

I join Miller and Vivian in the middle of the path.

Off in the distance, one of the things springs away from the mess of the overturned Jeep.

Running.

Fast.

Right for us.

The gate continues to creep.

When one iron part is about a foot from meeting the other, something else breaks out of the thick row of pines bracketing the road.

The Barbie-girl camp counselor.

Screaming. And with blood all over her shirt.

Help. Help. Help. Please. Please. Miller. Please. Help.

And it is so obvious what is going to happen.

What we will have to witness.

What we are powerless to stop.

The *thing* slows, distracted by a new target, and runs up behind the blonde girl.

The two parts of the gate join together in a solid thud. Five seconds later the girl arrives, closing her small hand around one of the bars, pulling on it frantically, and hanging on like her life depends on it.

Like she isn't already dead.

"Smentkowski. You have to open the gate back up!" It's Miller. He is pumping more rounds into the gun. Behind him, Vivian's eyes bulge. Like any second they might roll out onto the fucking snow.

Opening the gate sounds like one messed-up idea to me, personally.

Three of those creatures are pacing around out there, and so far the fence is high enough and strong enough to keep them out. Those iron bars are the only thing stopping us from becoming monster food.

But I find myself doing it. Forcing myself back over to the control panel. Maybe because someone needs to be in charge and it might as well be Miller, the guy who looks like the hero. Maybe because I can't stand around and watch a girl get slaughtered without at least trying to do something.

At the panel, my finger hovers over the open button.

For a second.

I close my eyes and push.

Nothing happens.

My heart drops into my stomach, and I really fucking hate myself.

I already know, but I push again. And again. And again.

The thing comes for the girl.

She doesn't turn but instead begins to pull on the gate with more force.

Miller gets a few rounds off, but he isn't a particularly good shot and he doesn't even hit the thing until it is already much, much too close. Vivian pushes her oar through the bars, trying to hit the monster with her long, rough stabs.

The most horrible sounds come from over there. The screaming. The boom of the gun. The squishy whack of Vivian's oar. And, in the in-betweens, ripping flesh. And chewing. Like that time I bought a giant turkey leg at the Ren Fair.

The girl is being eaten.

I push the button again.

Miller and Vivian have the monster down on the ground. But dark red blood gushes down the girl's body, soaking her khaki pants and sliding across the ice.

She has maybe a minute to live.

This is all my fault.

Help. Help. Help. Help.

It's a guttural chant. A bark.

"Smentkowski. The gate," Miller calls.

I try the button one more time. I force myself to turn toward what is left of the guard shack. The tiny yellow light bulb has gone out. It has been twenty-four hours since I hacked the camp's power grid. That was the maximum amount of time the backup generators could run.

Shit.

The second monster comes from the other side and charges the iron bars.

The gate holds.

I go back to where Vivian and Miller are standing in the path.

The girl's eyes roll back in her head.

Her breath comes in sharp bursts, and her hand floats away from the bar.

The second monster stares right at us with its horrible, soulless black eyes.

It reaches out and tugs the blonde girl away from the gate, carrying her body the way a toddler would drag an oversize doll, and streaks into the trees.

The third monster lingers in the road for a minute before disappearing into the forest.

Miller whirls around. Like he might attack me. "Why didn't you open the gate? Fuck. Smentkowski. Why didn't you open the fucking gate?"

I shake my head. It's hard to breathe. It's hard to look away from the trail of blood. "I couldn't," I whisper.

But they need to know, so I pull myself together.

"The power's out."

I have turned off the power, and now someone is dead.

ALLISON DUMONDE

Well. I am now shooting a gritty teen horror flick.

First I had to shelve my documentary idea.

Now even my backup plan is dead in the water. How can I make a feel-good friendship story while we're running for our fucking lives?

Part of me wonders if this is all my fault. Like somehow I brought this on us. I kept thinking of the six of us as horror movie archetypes and look what happened. I should have focused on getting shots of weigh-ins. Of poor little rich girls crying into their low-carb omelets because their daddies would rather spend the holidays on the Continent. Of kids poking dolefully at expensive salads.

Instead, I have film of the lights flickering, of people running in the snow. A grainy, super-zoomed-in bit as they carried that body by the window.

The Friends of Featherlite is canceled. *The Fight for Featherlite* got the green light.

And things are gonna get worse. Because you can't have a good horror film without the cast doing a bunch of stupid crap. Pretty girls going into the dark by themselves. Someone insisting on picking up that creepy doll or playing that forbidden video. Two people heading to a secluded spot to make out.

It's getting dark and snowing again. We heard what sounded like gunfire and screaming. So, of course, we're marching off into the restricted section of the camp.

Perfect.

If we are trapped in a horror flick, will I live long enough to finish the film? Will I make it to the end? Will I be able to patch things up with Vee before I fade off screen?

She took off with Miller without even saying goodbye.

It's poetic, in a way. I totally betrayed her with the whole Evan thing, and now she has chosen a guy over me.

Sigh.

I look around. What do I have left? Where will I find my next shot?

I have Smentkowski—The Nerd. Nerds often bite it in films. They are usually too curious for their own good and are always wandering off every time there's a strange noise. But Sheldon has practical intelligence too. I can't see him investigating things alone while something pops out of a bush and eats his face off.

And Rachel. I still can't figure her out. Have I miscast her? Is she really a Basket Case or a Nerd?

She is pregnant, so there's that. But she feels so bad about it. It's eating away at her. Rachel wears her remorse like a heavy coat.

No. She *has* to be The Outcast. And obviously, I'm The Basket Case.

That means Paul and I are goners. Miller and Smentkowski are maybes. Rachel will probably make it. And Vee.

She'll be fine.

I shudder.

I'm surprised that we don't pass anyone else on the way. Or spot any faces in the windows of the bungalows. No one else appears to want to know what's going on.

It's quiet.

Like when we first arrived.

I don't understand exactly what we are doing out here. I consider suggesting that maybe we ought to be walking away from all the gunshots and the screaming. But out here, the noise echoes and bounces off the trees. I have no idea what direction the screaming came from. No idea where we would be safe. Rachel keeps mumbling about *theories* and *additional data*. But this isn't a video game where a bunch of mad scientists have run around dropping notes for us to collect.

Paul says what I'm thinking. "So, what are we looking for?"

We come into the employees-only section of camp. It looks like the trailer park. In fact, I think some of the trailers are even the same model that we have in El Mirage. Paint peels off the white wooden panels. And unlike the area near the bungalows, they haven't decorated the trail with large gray stones here. The edges fray and bulge, forming a ragged, weary path.

Home sweet home.

Meanwhile, Rachel is talking. "They're testing the Metabolize-A bars, right? It's essentially a clinical trial. There has to be someone here who has more information about what they're looking for and is keeping records. I'd be stunned if there wasn't a supervising doctor."

I slow to a stop. "There was a doctor. It was Volstead."

Paul passes me, shaking his head. "Volstead is . . . er . . . *was* the psychologist. Kaiser is the MD."

Rachel stops too. "How do you know that?"

Good. I don't give a damn who this Kaiser guy is. But maybe Rachel will find a new mystery to turn her attention to and we can go back to the bungalow.

"That's what it said in the video," Paul says.

Paul isn't exactly smooth, but maybe he will be someday. His answer conceals something, but it's enough to send Rachel off on a new tangent. All I want to do is go back to the bungalow, see if we can get the fireplace to work, and sit there and massage my ankles. I'm not used to walking in the snow.

I hate walking in the snow.

Rachel starts mumbling *Kaiser* over and over.

"Hey! What if we go back to our room and search for info on Kaiser?" I suggest.

I follow behind the two of them.

Paul and Rachel ignore this idea.

There is no stopping them. We drift past doors that are identical except for neat white signs. FOOD OVERFLOW, DRY STORAGE, RESEARCH. We are coming to the end of the employee building when, almost like magic, we arrive at a door labeled KAISER.

Rachel glances at Paul and then reaches for the metal door handle.

It looks like a fairly sophisticated electronic security system.

My hopes rise a bit. Surely the door will be locked and we will have to go back.

I hold my breath as she gives the door a little push.

It's open.

And the room inside is totally dark.

Rachel flips a light switch near the door. "The power's out."

Because of course it is.

I guess that makes sense. The guard at the entrance told us that the camp could run on backup power for twenty-four hours. And that was twenty-four hours ago.

There's more shouting coming from somewhere outside. Paul pushes me through the door and slams it shut behind us. Except for a sliver of light coming through from the doorframe, we are in total darkness. My breathing, almost panting, fills the space around me. I can't catch my breath, and I can't understand how the two of them are so calm.

Paul has his hand clenched tight on my sore shoulder, and I'm about to slug if off when I realize his grip is the only thing keeping me standing. My knees wobble, and my legs move like they are made of Grandma's banana pudding.

"I guess that's why the door worked," Paul says. "They're set to default to the unlocked position. Um . . . in case of a power outage . . . I . . . uh . . . assume."

"Probably for safety," Rachel agrees.

There is a slight catch in her voice. She is worried too. For some reason, that makes me feel better. Like if she can keep it together, so can I. I stand up straight, and Paul takes his hand off my arm. "I'll get out the flashlights," I say.

I slide my backpack off my shoulders and kneel down on the cold floor, feeling around in the dark for the zipper. I get the pack open and am able to dig one of the flashlights out. I turn it on, and it illuminates a small circle around me. And I remember.

My camera has a night vision mode.

For a second, I get excited.

Maybe I'll get a good shot.

Then I realize. I'm shooting our real lives.

I shudder again.

And turn on the camera.

CROSS CUT

INT. KAISER'S OFFICE

The large room is part boring gray office, part high school biology lab, and part way-nerdy computing commons. THE BASKET CASE stands near a large steel desk with papers and notebooks and candy bar wrappers tossed all over it. Beyond that, there's a series of high tables with microscopes and other equipment and even more papers. The back wall is entirely made up of computers, and to the left of it is another high table with a series of monitors. They are all blank and dark. The place sort of smells. The three teens all get out their flashlights, and with them all on, the room is lit reasonably well.

THE BASKET CASE

(looking down at an overflowing trash can)
Whoever this Kaiser is . . . well . . . he is a terrible slob. It really smells in here.

J CUT

THE OUTCAST slides into the office chair behind the desk and in spite of herself gives a sigh of relief at being able to sit down. She picks up the papers, reads them, and then places them into neat stacks.

THE BASKET CASE

I'm going to look around.

Rachel and Paul stay at the desk near the door. Keeping the camera concealed in my coat, I let it run as I move around the room. My snowshoes make a terrible racket. I consider taking them off, but I don't know how long we'll be here or if we'll need to make a hasty retreat. I'll have to do something about the audio in post.

I open a couple of the cabinets. The first one is stocked with food. The kind of stuff you keep on hand if you never want to leave your office. Trail mix, ramen, instant coffee, protein bars. The next one contains stacks and stacks of the same kind of composition books that are all over the desk.

"This can't be right," Rachel says.

"What?" Paul asks.

I shine my flashlight over the wall of plastic towers. "Why would he need this many computers?"

From behind me, Rachel answers, "Actually, that's pretty common in biomedical research. I went on a tour of the college of medicine at U of A last summer, and they showed us all kinds of stuff like that. You need a lot of processing power for medical data."

"But how much medical data do you need to store at a camp?" I ask.

This is an issue for Smentkowski. Who, of course, isn't here.

Behind me, I hear Rachel continue to sift through papers. "At a normal camp, probably none. But there's something really weird about these notes. I mean, I'd need to go to school for another ten years to be able to even understand most of this stuff. But look here."

I pause for a second and turn to see Paul leaning over Rachel's shoulder.

"Look at this," she says.

I keep moving while Rachel goes on in the background.

"Of course, I can't be totally sure, but it looks like they're using corrective gene therapy. Here. See this."

The next cabinet is stuffed with about a million boxes of blue Bic pens.

"Kaiser thinks they've isolated a series of genes that cause obesity. And they're using CRISPR technology to edit the genes."

"What does that mean?" Paul asks.

I open the next cabinet. It's full of boxes of unopened laptops. For a second, I think of taking one. Or two. I could eBay them for a ton of money.

"I think . . . I think it means that the Metabolize-A bars essentially give people a virus. The goal is to change the subject's DNA. To replace the genes for obesity with ones that provide a more effective metabolism. But what do you make of this? Kaiser is keeping a log in these notebooks. This one is from last week."

I swing open another cabinet door. Reams of copy paper.

"*Fannon told the investors that we've corrected the issues that led to the anomaly. However, it seems clear to me that continued human testing is not only premature but also dangerous*," Rachel reads. "*I've resolved to* . . . Can you make out that last part?"

I almost drop my flashlight.

I stare at them.

Anomaly.

The thing.

Paul takes the notebook from her, "Um . . . *conduct* . . . maybe *contact*. That looks like it says *Richardson*. Is that *CDC*? Doctors always have such shitty handwriting."

"I wonder why he just didn't keep a log on the computer."

"Kaiser is old-school," Paul says.

"What?" Rachel asks.

Hot impatience surges in my blood. Who cares about some weirdo doctor? "Um. Hello? Anyone else think the *anomaly* was the monster we saw on our way into camp?"

"I told you, there's no such thing as monsters," Rachel says.

Paul shifts his weight around.

We both saw that thing. It *was* a monster.

I scowl at them, a wasted effort in the dimly lit room. "What kind of a doctor do you think this *Fannon* guy is anyway?"

"According to this, a geneticist," Rachel says.

Paul sighs. "Let's finish up here and get back to the bungalow. We have all night to debate what may or may not be out in the woods."

My pulse slows, and my heart beats sluggishly. A dull thud.

But he's said the magic words. I want to get out of here.

Rachel pushes aside a messy stack of papers. "This looks like it might be Kaiser's primary laptop."

I come to the end of the cabinets, to a narrow door. Probably a closet. I hesitate for a second before tugging on the handle.

Something heavy must be pressed up against the door on the other side, because the closet opens in a rush.

I scream.

Something.

Some*one* falls on top of me.

Sending both of us crashing to the floor.

STEVE MILLER

Vivian spends about five minutes heaving and puking in the center of the path.

She wanted to go into the trees, but I didn't let her.

I'm sure of one thing.

We have to stay together.

I think I would probably be in the same situation as Vivian except I grew up on a farm. For the first time, I'm relieved at the thought of some of the gross shit I've seen. When you've gotten a good view of your goat kidded with triplets in breech, it takes a lot to make you puke.

When Vivian can stand, we mill around in front of the gate for a few minutes.

Watching for signs of life.

And arguing.

I think we owe it to Zanna and her crew to stick with the patrol. Vivian is already putting together an escape plan and gives us the rundown of every vehicle she's laid eyes on since coming into camp. Smentkowski keeps talking about finding whoever is in charge.

"They must have some kind of plan. They have to," he says.

"*They're* dead, Smentkowski," Vivian snaps at him.

I'm getting the sinking feeling that *I* am in charge. For whatever reason, I'm thinking about Allison. Am I The Courageous Captain? Does that mean I'm going down with the ship? Right now, I have less than zero confidence. I don't know whether that is reassuring.

Or not.

I fiddle with the half-empty box of shells. "I said I'd patrol. I gave Zanna my word."

Vivian rounds on me, rubbing her hand over her lips. Her knuckles are bloody from the fight. She has wet goo in the strands of her reddish-brown hair. "Patrol? The whole point of a patrol is to figure out if something is out there and report back. We *know* those things are out there. We *know* there are at least three of them. We don't need to keep patrolling."

Smentkowski nods. "She's right. And let's imagine we find another one of those *things*. We actually got pretty lucky a few minutes ago. We had plenty of time to prepare. We can't assume that'll happen again, and we probably don't have enough ammo left to take another one out."

I notice for the first time that my fingers are wrapped so tightly around the gun that they've gone numb, and I loosen my grip. I remember my dad then. I wish he were here. Or at the very least that I could talk to him.

He always knows what to do. What would he do?

Do not corner something that you know is meaner than you.

That's what he said.

I take a deep breath. "Okay, look. We'll go back the way we came. Hopefully, we'll see someone in one of the employee buildings. If not, we'll go back to the bungalow."

We retrace our steps. As my adrenaline surge ends, everything starts to ache. My back from hunching over. My pecs from holding Zanna up for as long as I could. And my shoulder. It's been a long time since I've been hunting with my dad, and I'd forgotten how to position the gun to avoid getting hurt by the recoil.

We walk much faster than we did before. I try to convince myself it's because we are getting used to the snow. Getting better at maneuvering. But I know the truth.

We are scared shitless.

And we want to get the hell away from the gate.

Vivian's voice is hoarse from all the puking. "What are those things?"

Smentkowski is in the lead again. "Some kind of a monster."

"I think they're human. Or they used to be. And now . . . they're . . . like . . . zombies."

Smentkowski freezes. "What makes you think they used to be human?"

"The way they moved. And the one at the gate. It kind of looked at me for a minute, and I thought . . . it was like somebody was in there."

Smentkowski accepts this and keeps walking toward our bungalow.

It is going to be left to me to hope that those monsters aren't human. Because if they are, that means that *they* could be *us*. Or *we* could be *them*. I want to scream or collapse or hide somewhere. "I don't know what those things are, but they aren't people, Vivian. Anyway, I'm not sure it really matters what they are."

For a second, Vivian isn't that cool, confident girl who defiantly went into battle with nothing but a plastic oar. She speaks in a faint, scratchy voice. "If something's going to eat my heart out, I'd at least like to know what it is."

We're coming into the employees-only section of camp. I put a bit more effort into my steps and catch up with her, reaching out to place my hand on her upper arm. She really is very pretty.

It's getting dark, and I can't make out the exact color of her eyes.

"I'm not gonna let anything eat you. I promise."

It hits me that this is what Allison's Courageous Captain would say.

My pity party is interrupted by a series of horrible screams coming from one of the buildings. Vivian drops the oar. A second later, she has it again and is moving fast. It has to be another one of those things. We could run or we could try to fight it, and Vee has made the decision for us. She'll be at the door in ten seconds.

"It's Allie," she calls out to me.

Smentkowski stands in front of the door with a KAISER sign on it with his hand hovering above the handle. Like he knows he needs to go in but doesn't want to do it.

Vivian pushes right past him, her oar knocking against the doorframe. Behind her, I load the shotgun and enter the building.

It isn't immediately clear what is happening.

Our snowshoes clank against the concrete floor.

There are a few flashlights on, and they are doing a decent job lighting up what looks like a small lab or a really messy office. The rest of our group from the bungalow is already inside the room. Rachel sits at a desk near the door, frozen in the process of stacking papers. Paul is on the opposite side, standing near a small closet with his mouth open.

I scan around. Those things, the zombies, aren't in here.

The screams are coming from the far side of the room, near the floor. Paul is already moving in that direction. Vivian and I meet him in the corner.

Shit.

Vee is right. It's Allison on the floor screaming bloody murder.

She's squirming underneath the weight of a man in a long white lab coat. As Paul pulls the guy off, it gets even worse.

It's a dead body.

Shit, shit, shit.

I fight the urge to run.

Smentkowski catches up with us, and he tugs Allison off the floor and puts her in an office chair. Vivian leans the oar against the wall and goes over to help.

Rachel joins us. "I guess this is Kaiser."

Paul nods. "I think so." But he sounds oddly certain. Like he *knows* so.

On the other side of the room, Vivian is trying to get Allison to talk. "Allie? Allie? Are you okay?" Vivian is asking. "Allie?"

"You think one of those *things* got him?" Smentkowski asks.

"What things?" Rachel says.

"Allie?" Vivian repeats.

I hesitate. "There's definitely something out there. Some kind of a monster. We killed one. There were three more. They took out the convoy that was trying to make it into town."

"What do you mean *took them out*?" Paul asks.

"They killed them all. Zanna. Roger. All the people in the cars."

Everyone is backing away from the body, and I don't blame them. The smell is god-awful. It's like someone has sprayed a T-bone steak with cheap cologne and then left it to rot out in the open for a week. But I need an answer to Smentkowski's question.

Has this guy been killed by those things?

Covering my mouth and nose with my jacket, I squat down next to the body. Kaiser is . . . or was . . . probably about five foot eight. White. Midforties. Hair turning gray at the temples. A little pudgy. Judging from the fact that the fingernails have fallen off one hand and the skin has split in a few places, the guy has been dead awhile. He's wearing a gray suit jacket underneath the lab coat, and the edges of a brown carnation peek out from where part of the jacket lapel is exposed.

I don't know what killed Kaiser, but his body is intact. It hasn't been ripped to shreds by the creatures.

"We think they used to be human. But are now some kind of a zombie," Smentkowski says. He's trying to show an interest in the stacks of computers that are near the back wall.

"I . . . we . . . might have found something too," Rachel says.

"What?" Smentkowski asks.

"I knew it!" Allison bursts out. "I'm going to die. I knew it! I'm going to die. I'm going to die. That thing is coming for me. For me!"

Vivian shakes her friend by the shoulders. "Allie! You're not going to die!"

The blonde girl pulls herself free. "Like you care! Like you care!"

Rachel goes to one of the cabinets, which, for some reason, are all open. "Here. There's some water and chocolate chip cookies. She'll feel better if she has something in her stomach."

Vivian takes the cookies and opens the bag. "Allie, of course I care. Of course I do."

While the two of them get Allison calmed down, I glance at the open door. It's gotten even darker, and snow is coming down hard. "We can't stay here. Let's get back to the bungalow. Then we can decide what to do next."

"Lucky we found each other," Smentkowski says.

"Not really," Rachel answers. "We were *trying* to find you."

I don't know why it seems so important to get back to the bungalow. We aren't gonna be any safer there. Kaiser's office is probably in a better location. But we need a base of operations. One that is ours.

My idea appears to make sense to everyone. Rachel gathers up a stack of the notebooks from the metal desk. She gives a couple of laptops to Smentkowski. The rest of us gather as much of the food and water as we can carry. We haven't seen any other camp employees. I seriously doubt that meal service will be continued.

When we get into the main part of camp, I'm surprised to find a lot of people milling around outside the bungalows. We're stopped by several groups of campers on the way back to Goldwater.

A girl with long brown braids: "Have you seen Kennedy?"

A guy with chocolate stains on his shirt: "Are they sending dinner to the bungalow?"

A short kid with a buzzcut: "What the hell is going on out there? I heard shots."

An older guy with a deep voice: "We've been waiting for hours. Where's our Facilitator?"

A girl with pink streaks in her hair: "Are they gonna let us use our phones?"

The guy next to her: "Do they know the power is out?"

And then finally: "What happened to you guys?"

And: "Where did you get that gun?"

And: "Is that blood?"

I realize that Smentkowski, Vivian, and I look like total shit.

She has blood splotches all over her. His camp jacket and shirt have long, jagged tears where the zombie clawed at him. Filthy smears of reddish-brown dirt run down both my sleeves.

"Leave most of the food and keep going," I tell the group.

They drop all but one case of water and one box of trail mix at my feet. With Smentkowski out in front, they continue their procession to our bungalow. I add the case of water I'm carrying to the pile and step up onto a rock. A group of about forty campers forms a semicircle around me.

Vivian stays, taking up a position a couple of paces to my left, clutching her oar like she's expecting to have to beat back a mob. But I'm pretty sure that rich kids don't riot.

I'm not a Courageous Captain. But I'm gonna have to act like one.

"Listen. We've discovered some dangerous animals in the area around camp." Murmurs break out at this point.

"What kind of animals?" someone yells out.

"The kind that really want to eat you," Vivian calls back.

It gets quieter. "We've closed all the camp gates." *Possibly a lie.* I have no idea what has become of the patrols sent to the other gates.

"The fencing and gates are adequate at keeping them out." *That too might be a lie.* My experience on the farm has taught me that some animals learn to get around fences.

"Zanna led a group into town to get help." *Obviously, that's a lie.* But I need to say something. To give 'em a reason to stay in their bungalows. "Hopefully, she'll be back soon with a plan to restore power and cell phone access."

"Hopefully?" Pink-Haired Girl repeats.

"Yeah, hopefully," Vivian says through clenched teeth, backing me. "What? You'd prefer to be stuck out here forever?"

"In the meantime, let's divide up this food and water. Stay in your bungalows. Turn on the gas fireplaces so you're warm enough after dark. Each bungalow is stocked with things like flashlights and camping lanterns. Make sure yours are workin', but use them sparingly."

"There's not gonna be any dinner?" someone calls out.

"If you don't change your attitude, you're gonna *be* dinner," Vivian shoots back.

Damn. Being in charge really *is* a thankless job.

"Stay in your bungalows," I say again. "I'll come by as soon as I have news."

More nervous chatter erupts.

Stuff like *No dinner*.

Wait till my father hears about this.

We're stuck out here.

And *Why does he get the gun?*

Vivian has the stance of a comic book superhero and white flecks of snow in her hair like polka dots. "Okay. Let's form two lines. Water on the left. Food on the right."

We give out everything we have, which roughly translates to one bottle of water and one granola bar per person.

And my speech mostly seems to work. By the time we get back to Goldwater, the center of the camp has emptied, with almost everyone back in their own cabins.

In our bungalow, the argument from the lab has resumed.

Paul paces the great room. "That's not possible."

Smentkowski sits on his bunk. "Yes. It is."

"I've read articles where researchers have eliminated obesity in mice by deleting certain enzymes," Rachel says. She is at the bungalow desk reading through the notebooks she's taken from Kaiser's office.

Vivian takes off her coat and snowshoes. I do the same.

"In mice?" Allison asks. She's huddled up in a blanket over by the fireplace, hugging herself. It's like she's shrinking. "That doesn't mean they can do that for people."

"They do medical testing on rats and mice because they're biologically similar to people. But they have short life spans, so doctors can see the effects that stuff has really quickly."

Paul picks up one of the notebooks, opens it, and frowns. "Their life spans probably get even shorter once they get rounded up and sent to the lab."

I can't resist an opening to show that I do know *something*. "It's not like in that movie *The Secret of NIMH*. They don't catch mice or rats. They're actually bred to be genetically identical."

"Really?" Rachel asks, looking up from her reading.

"Yeah. We toured one of the breeding facilities for my Animal Genetics class."

She nods. "That would make sense, actually. You'd want to control as many variables as possible during testing."

Smentkowski grunts. "I'm really glad that you're all so concerned for the fate of the rodents. But as it stands at the present, the rats of Camp Featherlite are doing fine. The human beings, on the other hand, are in mortal fucking peril. We need some kind of a plan."

We have to come up with a better idea than hiding in the bungalow and hoping those creatures don't figure out how to scale the gate.

But I want to put off that moment as long as possible. "What are you guys arguing about, anyway?"

Paul stands in front of the fire, which burns blue at the base of the flames. With his back to me, he answers, "Rachel and Smentkowski think that the Metabolize-A bars are changing people into those . . . well . . . things . . . you guys saw out there."

"How?" I ask. As much as I want to fall into one of the leather chairs, I can't. I have to stay busy. Because I can see where Rachel is going with this.

And if she is right . . .

And I think she *is* right . . .

We are so fucked.

I move over to the desk, standing over her shoulder. I can't make any sense of what she is even looking at. There are notes scribbled in chicken scratch. And math equations. And periodically corrections made with a red pen.

Rachel turns a page. "I think the bars deliver a virus that is trying to essentially edit the gene for obesity. But something is going wrong. Like the virus is causing a mutation."

"That sounds like something out of science fiction," Paul says.

"Well, it's not. Most cancers are the result of genetic mutations in cells, and viruses are known to cause some forms of cancer, like cervical cancer, for example."

"That's what these notebooks say?" I ask.

"I think so," Rachel says.

"You *think* so. You *think* so," Allison repeats.

Rachel drops the notebook onto the desk and rubs her temple. "Yes, Allison. I think so. I mean, I'm a junior who has to read *Nature* with a flashlight after my parents go to bed, and whoever wrote this stuff probably has multiple PhDs in molecular biology and chemistry. So, yeah. *I think so* is as good as it's gonna get."

"Why do you have to read after your parents go to bed?" Paul asks.

Vivian pulls a chair up to the fire. "Rachel's right." She says this with so much conviction that the room falls silent. "That *thing*. The one we killed. It was wearing a camp T-shirt."

Paul turns, a dark silhouette with the fire at his back. "What?"

"Smentkowski saw it too. The thing. The zombie. It used to be a camper."

"And the two of you were planning on mentioning this when?" I ask. I want to get angry at them. To feel something other than the cold terror that is building in the pit of my stomach.

"When we weren't running for our fucking lives," Smentkowski says.

I finally have to sink into one of the leather chairs. "You're telling me that anyone who's eaten one of those bars could potentially become one of those things?"

Vivian stands up. "We need to get out of here. We should go for the van. The keys are still in it, and it works."

"You hope," Paul says.

"And just leave everyone else?" Allison asks.

"Everyone else might eat us, Allison."

"We should at least warn people." Allison's ponytail swings as she shakes her head.

"The point is, we need to get help. We can't figure all this out on our own."

"I agree," Rachel says.

Smentkowski puts the laptop aside and scoots forward on his bunk. "No."

"What do you mean *no*, Smentkowski? You saw those things—"

He gets up and moves to the closet, stuffing things in his pack. "Vivian, even if we make it to the van, *those things* took out four Jeeps. It was no problem for them."

"What?" Paul asks.

Smentkowski disappears into the bathroom for a moment, calling out, "That building we saw when we walked through the employees-only area. The industrial one. Judging from the electric fencing that surrounds it, the place has power and it probably has telephone access too. It's got an entrance within the camp gates, so we might actually make it there. And it looked pretty well fortified."

"I'm not sure if that's such a great idea," Paul says, turning back to the fire.

If he knows something, now would be a great time for him to tell us.

I close my eyes. All I want is to get as far away as possible. "Yeah. But you just said that it's surrounded by an electric fence."

"Exactly. But there are work-arounds. We go there, and after we do, we're much better protected than we are here."

The sound of breaking glass ends Smentkowski's analysis.

Screams spill into the evening from one of the other cabins.

The discussion is over.

We have to move.

VIVIAN ELLENSHAW

Smentkowski bolts across the room.

Before I can make much sense of what's happening, he's busy strapping Rachel's snowshoes over her boots. By the time I get my shoes, jacket, and pack on, he's already in his own gear and is helping Allie.

Allie stays calm by the fire. Almost like she wants to sit there forever.

I grab her hand and tug her toward the door.

Outside, we find a horrible mess.

Two of those things dart through camp, rampaging like the rogue dinosaurs in *Jurassic Park*. One of them tears at a pair of camp sweats hanging from its slim, muscular body, sending scraps of blue into the air. My knees almost give out. These zombies are new. They aren't the same ones from the gate.

There are five of these monsters.

At least.

All through camp, people are running and screaming and falling and sliding in the snow. I try to scream as one of the *things* lifts a girl up and throws her thirty feet or so into the wall of one of the bungalows. But nothing comes out of my mouth. I don't even have any screams left.

Allie's words haunt me.

We should at least warn people.

We should have warned them.

A third monster bursts out of a window of the bungalow

across from ours. As it does, the cabin catches fire, spreading a bright orange glow over this part of camp.

The thing is coming in our direction. I don't have the oar anymore, and anyway, maybe it's better to face what is becoming more and more inevitable.

Dragging Allie behind me, we make it only a couple of feet away from the bungalow before I collapse into the snow. I squeeze her hand hard, but her grip is relaxed.

Like she has accepted everything. Made peace with it.

Miller jumps in front of us and fires the shotgun right into the monster's chest.

Firing right through the thing's baggy blue T-shirt.

The thing. A few minutes ago, *it* was a camper. A person.

Like me.

The shots aren't enough to immediately kill it.

But the bullets do send the thing running off in the opposite direction, back toward the mayhem in the main circle of the camp. Miller helps Allie and me off the ground. Smentkowski tosses the yellow oar at my feet, mumbling, "Here's your melee weapon," as he passes us.

Stupid as it is, I do have more of a sense of control with the oar in hand.

We haven't agreed on Smentkowski's plan, but we are following it anyhow. Allie and I scramble to catch up with him as he disappears into the tall pines behind the bungalow. And I have to admit that he is probably right. The zombies have control of Featherlite. We don't know how many monsters there are or how fast campers can *become* monsters. Trying to make it to the van is not the best of ideas.

The sun has gone down. When Smentkowski reaches a point in the trees where it's quite dark and the sounds of the camp are muffled, he pulls out his flashlight and turns it on, sending the beam bouncing off the tree trunks.

I do the same.

Miller joins Smentkowski at the front of our traveling band. Between the dark trees and the silence punctuated by the occasional scream of someone back at camp and the high-pitched howls of the monsters, I don't know how the two of them can remember where to go.

I have to hold both the oar and the flashlight, so I can't even put my hands in my jacket pockets to keep warm. I have never been so cold. Snow sloshes up to where my boots meet my sweats, giving me an icy ring around my calves.

We come to a point where the pines intersect with the path. Smentkowski blocks the way forward with his arms, stopping us. He kneels down in the snow, and I do the same.

He opens his pack and pulls out something rolled up like a long sheet of paper. When he runs his flashlight over it, I realize that it is the rubber mat from our bathtub. The second thing he takes out is a pair of long yellow rubber gloves—the kind Maria uses when she cleans the kitchen.

"Okay." He scans the trail, checking each way. Searching for the monsters. "It's clear. Here's what we have to do. We'll go over the fence one at a time. The boots will protect our feet. Whoever's climbing wears the gloves. We can put the mat over as many of the fence wires as we can. At most, we'll get a mild electric shock."

"I'm not going to make it," Allie says in a dead voice.

Rachel takes deep, heavy breaths. "Me either. Go on without

me. Leave me here. You'll have a better chance without me."

"A mild electric shock? Are you serious?" Fannon whispers.

The whole plan is beyond hopeless. "What makes you so sure that building has power?" I whisper to Smentkowski. "Usually, when the power goes out in an area, it's out everywhere and—"

"The electric fence we saw earlier had power, so it stands to reason that the building does too. Trust me. The power's on over there," Smentkowski says, unable to keep the frustration out of his voice. And he does sound sure. Like, way too sure. "Anyway, we don't have any other options."

"Yeah, but the—" Fannon says.

"The fence. I know." Miller crouches close to me. He smells like a combination of pine air freshener and exploded fireworks. He puts down his flashlight and makes some kind of gesture that it isn't bright enough to see. "Listen to me. All of you. We're gonna make it. And Smentkowski's right. Electric fences are made to stop animals and maybe deter a few burglars. This isn't the movies. You can't actually go around putting up things that kill people. We'll be fine."

"No, we won't," Fannon says. "I keep trying to tell you. That's a four-thousand-volt stun-lethal fence."

"How do you know that?" Smentkowski asks. When no one answers, he goes on, "It doesn't matter. Rubber doesn't conduct electricity. As long as we don't touch the fence directly, we'll be fine."

Fannon snorts. "If all it takes is a bath mat to beat an electric fence, what would be the point of building them?"

"Do you generally carry a bath mat and rubber gloves in your pocket, Paul?" Smentkowski shoots back. "The point of the fence is that it's a practical deterrent against most people. Not that there's no way to defeat it." He takes off his snowshoes and the rest of us find ourselves following his example.

Miller pushes himself to a standing position. He turns his flashlight back on, tosses all the snowshoes over the fence, and takes the mat and gloves from Smentkowski. Allie and I follow him into the path. "Enough. Paul," he calls. "You go first, and then we'll help Rachel over."

My instinctive reaction is to smack him for his sexism. All of us girls are more capable than Mr. *GQ*. But Miller's flashlight beam crosses Rachel's face. He's right. She is barely able to get off the ground, and she lingers behind us at the tree line, hunching over with her hands on her knees. Smentkowski takes her arm and brings her over to the fence. She nearly trips in the middle of the path.

There is something really wrong with Rachel.

"Are you okay?" I ask her.

"Fine . . . fine," she says in between pants.

This is *not* normal.

I'm about to ask more questions, but Fannon catches my attention. He is making quick time and is already on the opposite side of the fence, almost halfway down. I turn in time to see his climbing method. He balances himself on one of the wires with his feet, sucking in a deep breath, before letting go with his hands and moving the mat to a lower wire. He is then able to grab the lower wire where it is covered by the mat and step downward.

When he's on the ground, he throws the gloves and mat over the fence for Miller to catch.

"You can apologize later," Smentkowski says.

"Don't hold your breath," Fannon answers.

"Steve. Steve, I can't do this," Rachel says.

Miller hands her the gloves. "You can and you will."

With Fannon and Miller working together, they're able to get Rachel up the fence. Miller supports Rachel's back, keeping her steady while she moves the mat. They're making progress. But it's slow. And when she gets to the top, she'll be too far up for Miller to reach.

She'll be up there on her own.

Allison moves close to me. "If I don't make it, I want you to know something."

I stare straight ahead. This is not the time for her to have another meltdown like the one in Kaiser's office. Jesus. Could Rachel go any slower? "You're going to make it. We're all going to make it."

"Listen to me, Vee," she says, putting her hand lightly on mine. "I stole the files."

I loosen my grip on the oar and turn to face her. The moon has risen high into the night sky, illuminating her profile, her skin almost glowing. She is different somehow.

"What are you talking about?" This hardly seems important. "Allie, we're running for our lives from flesh-eating zombies. I don't think Miller will be mad that you took his paperwork."

"You don't understand," she says urgently. "I need you to understand. Your mom paid for me to come to camp. She was hoping we could make up. I wanted us to make up. Mrs. E even paid extra so we could end up in the same cabin. I thought we could make a movie together. Like we always said we would."

Mom. I don't know if I'll ever see her again, but if I do, I'll take turns hugging her and kicking her butt for sending us to this awful camp.

More screaming echoes off the trees.

It's closer than before.

Rachel reaches the top, but she's stopped climbing.

"You got this, Rachel," Miller says.

I want to make up too, but this really isn't the time.

Allie's voice is so calm and sort of singsong. "And so I want you to know, I'm really sorry for what happened. It was total trash. I'm total trash."

"You are not trash." I think about the bruises on her shoulder and all the times she didn't want to go home to that trailer.

"I am," she whispers. "I stole your boyfriend. Fries before guys. That was always us. I broke that. I should have never screwed your boyfriend. I am trash. I am a shitty friend."

"Don't say that," I whisper back. "You are not. And Evan Moorehouse was *not* my boyfriend. He sucks so bad."

The enormity of what I've done hits me right then. I blamed her for everything. Made her take the blame for everything. "I'm the one who's trash. I never cared about Evan. I didn't care that you went to prom with him. That day. When you said . . ."

"Get over yourself. Some people have real problems," she finishes in a lifeless voice. "That was so selfish. You were always there for me. I was a terrible friend."

I sigh. "No. You weren't. You were right about a lot of things. I was so mad all the time. About my mom and dad. About Coach. And I . . ." My voice breaks. I bite down on my lip. I don't want to be out here in a blizzard bawling like a little baby. "I took it out on you. Even worse, I felt good when other people took it out on you too. *I* was a terrible friend."

I watch Paul help Rachel down off the fence. She immediately sits down on the snow, holding her belly. Before I can ask what's wrong, Fannon kneels by her side.

"I'm fine. I'm fine," she tells him.

She is not fine.

Fannon tosses the gloves and the mat over the fence. Miller catches them.

It does generally seem safe on the other side of the fence. For a moment, I let myself believe that we'll be all right. We'll be okay. We'll be rescued, and I'll make someone pay for what has happened at Camp Featherlite. Allie and I will go back to being friends.

"All I wanted was a scapegoat," I mutter.

"All I wanted was to be like you. To be you. To have your confidence," she says.

This makes me so cold. "Allie. Would you forgive me?"

She sucks in a deep breath. "If you forgive me."

I turn to her, wishing there were enough light for me to see her face. "When we get home, I want you to come stay with me. You have to get away from your house. DeeDee is horrible . . . you can't keep . . . Promise me you'll come home with me. Promise me you will."

"I promise." Allie leans in to hug me, and the moonlight catches something silver poking out from the pocket of her sweatpants.

The pants that are baggy and cinched up with a long length of drawstring hanging down the front. She's knotted her camp tee several times to keep it in place.

Oh. God.

Oh. My. Fucking. God.

The tears come.

It's like the ground is falling out from underneath me.

I shake her by the shoulders. Forgetting, for a second, the bruises I saw in the locker room.

"Allie? What did you do?"

Smentkowski turns and gives me the *shh!* gesture.

I ignore him.

"Allie? Allie? What the fuck did you do?"

Smentkowski sticks his elbow into my ribs.

And I see.

About thirty feet ahead on the trail.

A zombie breaks free from the trees.

It shrieks in the twilight.

ALLISON DUMONDE

I ignore Vee. I have to focus on the scene. My last scene. The Jock with a Heart of Gold shoves the rubber gloves toward The Nerd.

The two of them stare at Vee and me. They don't know.

They don't understand.

The Nerd begins to climb the fence.

I pull the camera from the inside pocket of my jacket and turn it on.

Vee won't take the camera. "Why did you eat those things? Allie? Why?"

I don't know how to put it into words that I thought eating the bar would solve all my problems. That I'd look just like Dorian Leigh DuMonde. I'd get out of the trailer park like my sister did. Make movies like she did.

Movies about girls who were really fearless. Like Vee.

The thing screams again. A howl devoid of real life.

The sound of a monster.

"Please. Please," I tell Vivian.

Even as I'm standing here, I can feel myself becoming both heavier and lighter. Like a rock that can somehow float. My own hands are turning into stone, but I can lift them with ease.

"I'm sorry. I'm sorry," she says. She's crying. And she won't hold out her hands. "You have to listen to me. We can still make it. We can all make it. I believe in you."

It's already too late.

"Please," I say again. "This camera, it's all that I have. Take it. You have to take it."

The tears run down her cheeks.

She does. She accepts it.

I reach out and grab the oar. Vee shakes as she lets it go.

And a calm settles inside of me. I face the monster.

SMASH CUT

EXT. CAMP FEATHERLITE—TWILIGHT

The full moon is hidden and only occasionally comes into view through a break in the snow clouds. THE OUTCAST, THE NERD, and THE JERK are on one side of the electric fence. THE BASKET CASE, THE JOCK WITH A HEART OF GOLD, and ACTION GIRL are on the other. About twenty feet ahead, one of the creatures has entered the road, owning it, possessing it the way only an apex predator can. There's no way they will all survive. There isn't enough time.

EXT. CAMP FEATHERLITE—NIGHT

THE BASKET CASE knows what she must do. She's got a look of steely determination. She's stronger than she's ever been. She's no longer cold, which she knows is wrong. Dangerous. Her humanity is slipping away. She grips the plastic oar and takes off at a run. She moves easily through the snow, with an efficiency she never had before.

THE JOCK WITH A HEART OF GOLD
(to THE BASKET CASE)
Hey! What are you doing? Where are you going?
(to ACTION GIRL)
What the fuck is she doing?

ACTION GIRL
(crying)
It's my fault. It's all my fault.

THE JOCK WITH A HEART OF GOLD
What the hell are you talking about?
THE NERD throws the gloves and the rubber mat over the
fence. THE JOCK catches them and tries to give them to
ACTION GIRL. She shakes her head.

ACTION GIRL
You first.

THE JOCK WITH A HEART OF GOLD
What the hell are you talking about? I have to—

ACTION GIRL
(tough, fierce even through tears)
Steve. Get your ass over the fence.
THE JOCK WITH A HEART OF GOLD knows better than
to argue with ACTION GIRL. THE BASKET CASE can hear
the squeal of the rubber mat as THE JOCK starts to climb.
ACTION GIRL stares into the road. THE BASKET CASE

is quite close to the creature now. The thing has fully turned. Every ounce of body fat converted to muscle and marble. She won't be able to kill it. But she can keep it busy for a while.

ACTION GIRL
(crying again)
This is all my fault.
Allie. Allie.

For a minute, I'm Allie again. I remember that summer right after Vee's seventh birthday. Back when her parents were still married and my sister wasn't my family's meal ticket and everything seemed like it might turn out all right.

I went with the Ellenshaws on a road trip. We spent a week in Louisiana. Her parents took a house outside Lake Charles overlooking the Calcasieu River. There were NO SWIMMING signs posted everywhere, and even if there hadn't been, I wouldn't have been tempted to dive into the water, which ran deep brown, like the tree trunks that crept up to the river bank.

Near the house, there was a short wooden pier. Every afternoon, we would sit so that the tips of our toes almost dipped down into the water.

We sat in silence. Not the kind of silence loaded with a million unsaid things or unspoken anger or the awkwardness that happens when people want to talk but somehow can't. It was the kind of silence born from comfort and love, and it created the freedom to listen to the river lap against the pier and watch pieces of clover pushed along by waves and ripples.

I found my reflection on the surface of the water and wondered if someday my hair would stay tied back in a neat ponytail like DeeDee's. If someday I would have cute freckles on the end of my nose and my mom would stop calling me pleasingly plump.

"Even if you do, don't act like DeeDee. She's horrible. I like you the way you are."

She made me hopeful and brave, and I said, "I'm going to make movies."

She nodded. "I believe in you. Will you make movies about us?"

I said that I would.

The last night, Mrs. Ellenshaw helped us set up a tent in the backyard. We hid out there with our flashlights, eating peanut butter and jelly sandwiches and drinking grape juice boxes. Vee had her dad's old Polaroid camera. Even then, she was into old things. She took pictures of us.

"How does it work?" I asked her.

She grinned. "It's magic."

"You believe in magic?"

"I believe people make their own magic," she said with a yawn.

I peeked out of the tent. There were so many stars in the sky. The deep dark blue. The swaying trees. The cool night air. It was for us. Everything was for us.

I was the moon. I was a star. I was magic.

THE BASKET CASE pounds the creature again and again with the oar. When it breaks her arm, the bone twists and snaps, but it doesn't hurt. It isn't even her arm to break anymore. She knows that Vee will wait till the last possible second before finally climbing the fence. When the metal links rattle, THE BASKET CASE knows it's almost over. She exists in a thousand different moments. Her memories flow through her like the chilly green-brown river water. Of yesterday and all the days. She plunges through infinite futures. Destinies and dreams. All at once, she is everything and nothing. Until.

She isn't anything at all.

FADE TO BLACK

PAUL FANNON

There's some seriously messed-up shit going on.

When the monster comes into the road, I am real fucking glad to be on the opposite side of the fence.

Miller got over the fence fast. He's coordinated. I guess it's not for nothing that he is a championship athlete. The instant his feet land on the ground, he shouts at Vivian, who is still on the other side. "You need to climb the fence. You need to do it now. Right now."

Smentkowski is with Rachel, so I stand up. I should do something. There are still two girls on the opposite side of the fence, and for some reason that fact makes me feel like a complete ass. Like they are braver than me. Better than me.

The zombie screams.

I'm ashamed of the hot panic that runs through me.

And even more ashamed of my relief at being relatively safe.

Rachel falls over on her side, kind of moaning and breathing heavy.

Smentkowski does his best to prop her up. "Did you hurt yourself?" he asks. "Are you okay? What's happening?"

She doesn't answer.

"Get up on the fucking fence, Vivian," Miller says.

It's getting darker and darker, and both of the girls have turned off their flashlights. I can't exactly make out what is going on. At first, I think that maybe Vivian is worried that she won't make it. But really, that is pretty stupid.

Vivian is actually crying and repeating, "It's my fault," over and over.

A sliver of moonlight escapes through the storm clouds.

Maybe the storm is nearly over.

Maybe I'm going to be fine.

But then.

The blonde girl. Allison. She's run off in the wrong direction. Toward the thing.

She is trying to save us.

My heart stops.

Miller reaches out and stops me from grabbing the fence. "What the hell are you doing? What the fuck is wrong with everyone?"

Allison approaches the monster. Goes right up on it. Only a few paces away from it when the clouds close again and swallow the scene up in darkness.

I can't process what I'm hearing. Even make sense of it.

"Aww. Man. Fuck, man." I stumble a few paces away from Rachel and throw up into the snow. Chunks of trail mix and stomach acid stay in my mouth.

It's like the sound of my voice does something to Vivian. A second later she's up on the fence, scaling it with almost as much ease as Miller.

When she's on our side, she gets her flashlight out of her pack and points it all over the place.

And then she comes for me.

"You did this! You did this!" she screams.

Before I can figure out what's going on, her fist connects with my face. White spots explode in my vision as I close my eyes.

I put my hands up defensively, but she lands another punch on my upper lip.

Miller drags her off me.

I fall back, lying flat in the snow. The cold comes as a relief.

I can hear them struggling and scuffling and Vivian shrieking.

"Let go of me. Allie's dead. Allie is fucking dead."

"This isn't helping anything," Miller says.

"What are you talking about?" Smentkowski asks.

"What am I talking about?" Vivian laughs. High-pitched. Maniacal. "Oh, I'll tell you. May I please present Paul Fannon the Fourth? Scion of the mad scientist behind Camp Featherlite."

It's silent for a second.

"What?" Miller asks. He has the look of someone who wishes he had a clipboard full of paperwork to consult. "No. That's Paul Lewis."

"No, it isn't," Vivian says through her teeth. "All rich people eventually end up at the same parties. And I've been at one with him!"

"You lied?" Rachel says. "You lied to me?"

I have just let down the only decent person who ever seemed to like me.

"Jesus. Not having my laptop really sucks," Smentkowski mutters.

I sit up. What the fuck would I do if they all decided to leave me here? "I had *no* idea what was going on here," I tell them. "And that girl is dead because she decided to run that *thing* down. I didn't tell her to do that."

Vivian tries to charge me again, but Miller blocks her.

"That girl's *name* is Allison DuMonde. And she decided to

run it down because she'd eaten your dad's evil fucking bars . . . and she knew . . . she knew . . ." Vivian squats down and breaks into sobs.

Rachel reaches out to pat her arm. "She ate the bars?" she says in between pants. "She ate them? Even after we found out what they do?"

Vivian cries even harder. "Yes, yes. Why would she . . ."

Drawing in a deep breath, Rachel says, "The world is so cruel. It makes us think we have to do anything to look like . . ."

"Him," Smentkowski finishes, waving his hand toward Miller.

Vivian rounds on the jock. "Why didn't . . . you shoot . . . the damn thing?" she asks in between sobs.

"It's dark. I only have six rounds of ammo left, and the odds that I would hit *anything*, let alone take down one of those monsters, are nonexistent," Miller tells her. "I'm sorry."

"She was my best friend," Vivian says.

"I'm sorry," he answers in a sad voice, and for some reason this sends her into another round of heaving sobs. "But you'll have to deal with that later."

Miller kneels in front of Rachel, helping her put her snow-shoes back on. "When are you due?"

"What do you mean?" she says.

He waves the beam of his flashlight over her face. "Please. I have four sisters, and I grew up on a farm. When is your due date?"

She hesitates for a second. "Not for four weeks."

Smentkowski says what I'm thinking. "Shit. You're having a baby?"

"Has your water broken?" Miller asks.

"No," she says.

"Wait. You're pregnant? And your parents sent you to a fat camp?" I ask.

No one answers me. They've probably decided I'm a traitor. "Look, I'm sorry I lied, okay! I was supposed to be checking out the camp and reporting back to my father. I thought I'd be writing reports on which yoga instructors campers hated. I didn't think . . . I just wanted to . . ." To prove I'm not a total screwup. Except I am.

They ignore me again. Everyone busy with their snowshoes.

"We can't sit around talking all night. We need to think about getting out of here," Smentkowski says. He shines his flashlight into the road, where the thing is on the move.

Miller stands up. "Rachel, I doubt you need me to tell you that there's absolutely no way we can deliver a baby right now. If you go into full-blown labor, the baby will die and so will you. We need to keep you as absolutely calm as possible. And keep you from doing anything physical. As much as we can."

Miller can be real helpful sometimes. "Sure, Steve," I say. "Sure. It'll be easy to stay calm after that little speech."

"You guys. Seriously. We gotta get a move on . . ."

The creature's howl drowns out the rest of Smentkowski's words.

I hustle off the ground. The monster has come very close.

Close enough that I can smell it. It has the scent of a dirty aquarium.

Miller and Smentkowski hoist Rachel up from the snow. Vivian grabs the other girl's pack and swings it over her own shoulder. I flinch when she takes a step forward, but she doesn't come for me.

I guess Vivian Ellenshaw has decided she'd rather live to fight another day.

Off in the distance, in the opposite direction of the monster, I can hear thick branches break and heavy footsteps growing louder.

Then.

I jump back as a second zombie hits the fence with full force.

A soft hum.

Miller points his flashlight at the monster as it charges the fence again.

This time the fence is supposed to deliver the lethal charge.

The chain links let out a sizzle.

The creature pushes itself back and retreats a few paces, nurturing an injured, bluish-black forearm.

It's hurt.

But not dead.

In what is becoming an annoying pattern, Smentkowski again says what I'm thinking. "So much for stun-lethal."

He and Miller each take one of Rachel's sides.

And together, we run.

SHELDON SMENTKOWSKI

Ope. Paul has his little secret, and I have mine.

I don't know if the fact that Paul Lewis is actually Paul Fannon helps us or hurts us. But I do know that the redbrick building probably has power. Because the power is probably still on *everywhere* outside of camp. The only reason that the electricity is off back at Featherlite is because I flipped the switch. Paul is a liar. But I'm worse.

I put our fucking lives in danger.

Now Paul's secret is out. What if everyone else finds out about mine?

We keep running. Getting to the building is a slog.

Miller and I shoulder as much of Rachel's weight as we can. We are pretty much carrying her, and only once in a while does one of her small feet push into the snow.

Vivian and Paul are a few paces ahead, shining their flashlights, blazing a path. They aren't exactly cooperating, but they aren't trying to kill each other either.

Behind us, we keep hearing the monsters hitting the metal fence. Like they're testing it. And if they are, our problems will get exponentially worse. Because it would mean that those things have superhuman strength and abilities but also some amount of intelligence.

What if they find the section of the fence that has the electrical short?

The closer we get to the building, the more I begin to wonder if this idea of mine is going to work. What from a distance and in the daylight was a cheerful redbrick building is growing darker and gloomier by the second. It becomes larger and more imposing with every step we take.

But we are out of options.

And I am almost out of breath.

"Let's give it a rest for a second," Miller suggests.

I'm grateful for this. But also embarrassed. Miller isn't out of breath.

We place Rachel down on her feet gently. She leaves her hand on Miller's shoulder and continues to use him to brace herself.

"How's your pain?"

"Same . . . as before."

The side of the building we are on doesn't have an entrance. Vivian runs her flashlight up the wall, highlighting brick after brick until she arrives at a series of narrow windows. They are way too high and probably too small for us to use to get in.

"Four!" Vivian calls out in a harsh voice. "Is there any chance you might have some useful information? Like where we might find the fucking door?"

There is a pause, but then Paul answers. "The main door is around the corner. But I'm sure it's locked up pretty tight."

"You'd expect a building of this size to have some security," Miller says.

For a second there, we are all kind of hopeful.

"They have a service. They're supposed to send a patrol a couple times a night. But . . ."

"But," Vivian finishes for him, "nobody in their right mind is going to come out and check on some big creepy building in the middle of the zombie apocalypse."

So we are screwed again.

I don't know why, but right at this moment I'm thinking about my dad. Like, I want to be mad at him. I want to focus on how bad he sucks. On how much it sucks that he left Mom when she was sick. But he isn't always bad. We have our fishing trips in the summer. And I know he cares about me.

I want to hate him.

But the truth is that I just want to see him again.

I want to live long enough to see my father.

Paul's voice breaks through my thoughts. "Oh! But my dad's office is on the other side of the building. On the first floor. And the office has a window."

"All right. We'll try that," Miller says.

Paul comes around to try to take Rachel's other arm, but even though I am tired, I stop him. "No offense, bro, but you're not good in the snow."

Miller is smoother. "You should show us which way to go, anyway."

We head around to the front of the building. The place has oversize reinforced steel doors with a few square windows made from ballistic glass. Paul is right. We'll never get in that way.

But the lights are on inside the foyer.

"Good call, Smentkowski," Miller says. "The place has electricity."

Even though I'm getting pelted in the face with ice, I can't stop myself from grinning. If the building has power, the chances are really fucking good that it also has working phones. Maybe we'll get out of this. Maybe I won't get us all killed.

We keep moving.

"What does your dad do here, anyway?" Vivian asks Paul.

"I'm not totally sure," he says.

She takes an aggressive step in his direction.

"I'm not! I've only ever been here a couple of times, and the inside was totally empty except for some office furniture."

"Right," she says.

"I'm serious!" Paul picks up his pace a bit so that he gets in front of Vivian. "I'm sure this will come as absolutely *no* surprise to *you*, but my father, the great Paul Fannon the Third, thinks I'm the world's biggest screwup. He isn't going to tell me all his secret plans."

Vivian slows down. "And . . . that's why he sent you here? To punish you?"

I can see what she is getting at. If those notes we found from the scientist are real, and people had been warning Dr. Fannon about the bars . . . well, you wouldn't send someone you liked into that kind of a situation.

"He didn't send me at all," Paul answers. "He wanted Carl Kaiser to come. Dr. Kaiser's son." He seems weirdly bitter about the whole thing. I mean, I would be thrilled to give Carl Fucking Kaiser my spot in the zombie apocalypse.

Next to me, Rachel squirms and pants. "You mean . . . the dead guy's . . . son?"

"Uh . . . yeah."

We round the corner. Yellow light from a row of windows casts a dull glow onto the snow. Soon, we'll be inside.

"You think that's some kind of coincidence? That Kaiser is dead? And his son was supposed to be here too?" Vivian asks.

We form a little circle near the first window.

The first thing I find in the light is Paul's confused, haggard face. "It would have to be, right?"

Miller leans Rachel up against the wall and shrugs out of his jacket. He takes the flashlight from Vivian, wraps the coat around it, and before any of us have much of a chance to ask what he's doing, he bashes the window in.

He uses his coat to cover the windowsill. "Give me a boost," he says.

Paul makes a loop with his hands and hoists Miller up. The jock disappears into the building.

Rachel takes a deep breath. "What if it's not?"

"Not what?" Paul asks.

"A coincidence."

"Yeah," Vivian agrees. "I mean, it's not like Kaiser died of old age."

"I don't think my father knew Bill Kaiser was going to be eaten by zombies." Even as Paul says this, he doesn't sound sure.

"Not eaten . . ." Rachel says. She wraps her hands around her stomach. "Did you see his skin? How . . . gray it . . . was? Poisoned. I think he was poisoned. And he'd been dead for . . . several days. Before we came to camp."

Miller leans out the window. "I see a couple of motion sensors in here. My guess is that some kind of alarm is going to sound any second. I need you guys to lift Rachel up. Carefully."

The three of us work together to push Rachel up and into the window. She's very little help. It's clear she is in a lot of pain.

The second Miller has her in the room, I scramble up and land inside a boring gray office with one of those cheesy motivational posters hanging on one wall. It's actually more like a webinar backdrop than a real place where someone might work. Rachel sits behind the desk in the room's lone office chair. I help her out of her snowshoes while Vivian and Paul keep talking outside.

"Will you two cut the chatter?" I say. "We need to find a phone. Those things are out there, and the sooner we can call 911, the better."

They're still down there in the falling snow talking. Like we have all the time in the world to investigate the death of a scientist we've never even met.

"Several days?" Paul repeats. "Before we even arrived at camp? That can't be right. Surely my dad would have noticed that Kaiser was dead."

"Do you hear that?" Vivian asks.

Miller reaches out the window. Determined not to have a repeat of the scene at the fence, he practically drags Vivian into the small room with us.

She immediately gets up and stares out the window. "There's something out there."

Miller follows her gaze and squints.

"Where's the gun?" she asks him.

It's on the floor near the window. He doesn't argue with her. Miller picks it up and pumps in two rounds.

"Four! You better get your ass in here!" Vivian calls out the window.

I strain my ears to listen for the creatures. But it's a pointless activity.

The building alarm wails.

I turn to see if Rachel is okay only to find her face curled up in a horrified scream.

Paul is halfway in the window, and one of the creatures is only a pace or two behind him. Vivian grabs his arm and tries to pull him the rest of the way inside but can't manage it.

I run up to the window to see that *the thing* has a large gray hand wrapped around one of Paul's legs. Miller fires off the first shot. He shouts something at me, but I can't make it out over the alarm.

I'll be honest. I want to run. Run into the building. Run to find a phone. Run to save myself. And maybe Rachel.

I don't know how, but I force my legs to move in the direction of the window. I take Paul's other arm and pull as hard as I can, leaning back with all my weight.

Vivian must be out to win some kind of award for creative weaponry. She rips the COMMITMENT sign off the wall and uses it like a bat, leaning out the window and hitting the zombie again and again.

Miller fires off the next shot.

He is so close that he hits the thing right in the head.

Blood and tissue explode onto the snow, and the creature falls back.

We're able to tug Paul through the window.

Blood runs down his fingers.

Outside, the monster is down. It's dead.

It doesn't move again.

I feel no sense of relief.

The things have defeated the fence.

There isn't much time.

We *have* to find a phone.

Rachel is still in the black chair, but she's rolled it back into the corner and has covered her mouth with her hand.

"Did it get you?" Vivian yells.

"No," Paul screams back. He bends over and feels his own legs. Like he needs to double-check. "It was the glass."

Miller comes up right next to me, and this time I can hear him. "Smentkowski! Do you think you could do something about that fucking alarm?"

RACHEL BENEDICT

Another contraction.

More pain.

My whole abdomen seizes. Like something is tearing me up from the inside out.

God is punishing me.

My father always loves to quote Job.

Man is also chastened with pain on his bed and with unceasing complaint in his bones.

In a blur of motion, everyone pulls off their snowshoes and tosses them aside. I hope we won't need them again later, because it's still really coming down out there. Steve puts his flashlight in his backpack and wheels me along in the office chair into a long gray hallway.

Paul is a couple of paces in front of us and rubbing his bloody hands on his sweats.

Just when I was beginning to trust him, he lied to me. But I can't be mad anymore. We're lucky those creatures didn't kill him.

The siren wails, and there's nothing but blood and gray as far as I can see.

There are only five of us, and everyone seems to have a purpose. They are pointing and planning and yelling at each other. Paul gestures to a door at the end of the hall. Sheldon pushes ahead of us and disappears through it.

And we wait.

For the vengeance of an angry God.

A couple of minutes later, the alarm suddenly stops.

Sheldon is back a second later, shaking his head. "Companies invest a fortune in these high-tech security systems, but then there's always some idiot who leaves his password on a Post-it note stuck to a monitor. It's like I always say, a company's biggest security vulnerability is its own employees."

"Well, thank God for small favors," Steve says.

Sheldon grins. He is way more relieved by our current situation than any of the rest of us. "Thank God for *big* favors. There's a working phone at the security desk. We're gonna get out of here."

I fight off the urge to groan as another spasm hits me. Somehow, I can't share Sheldon's optimism.

The rest of us follow him through the hallway into a large vestibule that is on the other side of the massive entrance doors we passed earlier. It's only lit by dim safety lights, but Sheldon hits the main light switch as we enter. The room becomes bright and falsely cheerful. Beyond a large gray desk, there are several modern neutral-colored sofas and a coffee table covered with magazines.

Sheldon takes the chair behind the desk, and Steve pushes me next to him. The desk is mostly covered by a series of monitors and a keyboard. A few file folders are stacked in one corner, and a standard black desk phone sits on top. Sheldon picks up the receiver, dials 911, and hands the phone to Steve, who hesitates for a second before taking it.

I can hear a woman's voice respond before Steve presses the phone to his ear. "911 operator. What is your emergency?"

Talking on the phone is not Steve's strong suit. "Uh . . .

hi . . . uh . . . this is Steve. Steve Miller. And we're at camp. Camp Featherlite. And there are these things. We think they might be zombies. And uh . . ."

He stops to listen to the woman on the other end of the line.

"No. This isn't a joke . . . you have to send someone . . ."

More listening.

I realize that I am freezing. That we probably all are. The wet of the ice has completely soaked through my sweats. My waterproof jacket has mostly protected my upper body, but as I register my cold, I shiver.

Sharp. Jagged. Pain.

Sheldon's smile fades.

Paul paces around in front of the desk.

Vivian yanks the phone out of Steve's hand. "Listen. This is Vivian Ellenshaw. My mother is Elaine Ellenshaw, the vice president of global strategy for Pied Piper Pizza. I'm here with Paul Fannon the Fourth, son of the owner of FannonPharma. This is *not* a prank call. We're trapped in a facility north of Camp Featherlite, and we have a girl with us who needs immediate medical attention."

I take deep breaths and try to do something to stop or at least slow the inevitable. Steve is right. There is no way I can have my baby here. We'd both die.

My baby. I am going to have a baby.

As Vivian is talking, Sheldon reaches around the desk and turns things on. In a few seconds, he has the computer going, and images fill the various monitors. It is the feed from the security cameras.

A wave of horror washes over me as I take in the images.

This is a manufacturing facility.

In front of me, Vivian's face contorts in rage. "I *know* there's a blizzard. I'm calling you because there's a blizzard. The whole point is that it's snowing like hell around here, and the building is surrounded by these . . . things. We need help. Now!"

Images of conveyor belts and manufacturing equipment flicker onto the screens. And stacks and stacks of boxes of Metabolize-A bars.

The anger falls from Vivian's face. "What do you mean? Are you saying what I think you're saying?" It is replaced by something new.

Fear.

"What? *What are they?* You're asking me?" Vivian's hand is turning white from gripping the phone so hard. "We . . . we think they're people. People who've been genetically modified somehow."

Terror.

"*Yes* it's possible! Lady. Look. I don't have time to workshop this with you. Just send the fucking paramedics, okay?"

A large, empty laboratory fills one of the screens. Then a wide break room with orange chairs and several vending machines.

"Yes, we're inside. But my friend needs to be *inside* the hospital!"

Friend.

I can't say why, but that word does make me feel a little better.

Until my gaze lands on the monitor that is on the far side of the desk.

It displays the door of a smaller brick building lit up by a couple of floodlights. The camera is at kind of an odd angle as it is clearly meant to register anyone coming or going from the building.

"What is that?" I ask, pointing at the screen.

The building's steel door has been torn off its hinges and thrown out of the view of the camera. Through the open door, I catch a glimpse of what looks like a bunch of complicated electrical equipment. The whole place is surrounded by the zombies, and we watch as one moves into the open doorway.

"I think it's . . . basically it's like a giant breaker box," Sheldon mumbles.

"What?" Steve asks.

"The list! What list?" Vivian shouts into the phone.

Sheldon frowns at the image on the screen. "Large buildings use a ton of electricity, so they buy it at a high voltage and then use transformers to convert the power to usable levels." His face freezes in horror. "Oh shit," he says.

The creatures move around on the screen. Fast. Crashing and bending metal.

The lights flicker. And then go out.

The images disappear from the screens. Vivian drops the phone onto the desk, and we sit there in the dark for a minute.

"Are they sending help?" Paul asks hopefully.

"No," Vivian says in a hoarse whisper. "Apparently the zombies have made it into town. They're keeping a list of emergency sites. We're on the list. But it sounds like . . ."

Zombies in town?

"Like they're not sending anyone," Paul finishes.

"Yeah."

Another contraction hits me. "We're all going to die, and it's all my fault."

STEVE MILLER

We are gonna die.

In the meantime, we have to stay busy. I need to take control of things. I have to pull myself together. Maybe I'm a shitty leader. But I'm the only leader our Pod has.

I reach into my pack and get my flashlight back out. "We are not gonna die."

We need a new plan.

Putting the flashlight on the desk, I keep talking. "Rachel, what's happening right now is not your fault." To stop Vivian from jumping in, I add, "It's *none* of our faults. What we need right now is a plan. We're in a reasonably secure building. And they *are* coming for us. Help just might take longer than we want it to."

This speech is met with silence.

My crew is gonna mutiny.

But to my relief, Vivian says, "He's right. We have to hold out as long as we can."

"Okay, what do we do?" Fannon asks.

I have no fucking idea.

Luckily, Smentkowski answers. He's good with logistics. "Okay, we'll stay here until help arrives. This is all a waiting game. We need to search the place for supplies. Quickly but methodically. The priority should be to find weapons. But we need other things too. Food. Water. Dry clothes."

"And medical supplies," Vivian says.

That, too, is good thinking. Hopefully, the paramedics will

show up before the baby, but if they don't, we might find ourselves winging it.

Will I get paid for this?

I don't know why that thought is running through my brain. But it's like I can't fucking believe what is happening. Two days ago, my biggest concerns were registering for summer school and getting my bike fixed. How can I get back to that place? How can I be that guy again?

I should have said something before. I mean, I knew the girl was pregnant. When you have four sisters and have delivered more calves and kids than you can count, you learn to spot these kinds of things. I figured it was her business. Maybe I should have told someone. Maybe I should have tried to get her back to town even if that was dangerous.

What if my decisions might cost her life?

But who the hell am I? Why would anyone expect this kind of shit from me? I'm not Vivian. Or even Smentkowski. Nothing in my past has prepared me for this. Yes, I am an athlete. Sure, I can do stadiums without breaking a sweat. I was my team's best running back, but my yardage wasn't even good enough to put me in the top ten in the state. And anyway, all I did was carry the ball where the quarterback told me to.

Vivian goes through the drawers of the security desk. She has her own flashlight out. "Okay. I have a pair of scissors, a roll of duct tape, and a candy bar."

I smile at her. Try to give off a reassurance I don't feel. "That's a start."

Rachel rests her head on the desk. She's trying hard to control her breathing.

Smentkowski has his light out too. He's leafing through the pages of a white binder that he found on the desk. "Okay . . . here's the employee handbook. Ah. Here we go."

He pulls a sheet of paper out and puts it on the desk in front of me. It's a diagram of the building that is mostly designed to point out all the bathrooms and coffee makers. But it also has all the entrances and exits marked. Smentkowski *is* smart.

"Okay," he says, pointing to a spot on the map. "According to this map, on the second floor there's laboratory space and a security office. Since that seems like the most likely place to find stuff we could use as weapons, I say we head there."

Vivian nods. "It also puts us on high ground, which is probably as good of a place as any to wait. We'll be able to see better and have a bit more time to react if those things make it inside."

Jesus. Did they both take some kind of secret strategy class in school when I was out running around the track and doing drills?

Vivian leans around me and reaches over to tap the map. "Look right there. Once we get into the main manufacturing area, to the immediate left is a room called LAUNDRY. I think we should check there. Maybe for dry clothes or towels."

Of all of us, Vivian is the most together. She is soaked like the rest of us, and she has some goo splattered on her jacket. But her hair is all slicked back and almost kind of cool. Like with some slight tweaks she could be a singer in a goth band.

I wish we could be anywhere but here. Together.

Grabbing the map and the gun, I say, "Okay. Let's move out."

Smentkowski takes over pushing Rachel, and Vivian moves out in front. I figure that this is for the best anyway since she's much better at reading maps than I am. We go down another long gray hall. My flashlight passes over more motivational posters.

Success.

Motivation.

Leadership.

At the end of the hall, Vivian pushes open a wide door labeled EMPLOYEES ONLY.

The building is essentially a large, open production area with rooms lining the perimeter. The ceiling is so high that the flashlight beam can't reach it. Like going up means disappearing into darkness.

I scan the place for threats and am relieved. It seems like we're alone inside.

Then my heart drops into the pit of my stomach.

Vivian had said *manufacturing*, but I hadn't thought to wonder *what* they're making.

My eyes find stacks and stacks of boxes of Metabolize-A bars.

The whole place has the look of an efficient operation. Neat and trim. As if the workers have gone home for the afternoon and will be right back, bright and early in the morning, to resume making those monstrosities.

I have to know.

I have to confirm what is in the boxes. I pick at the tape on the first box I come to. The fucking thing is labeled. METABOLIZE-A BAR 24 CT. I want to believe that this whole thing is a nightmare. That they haven't really made a million of those fucking things. That there might be something else inside these boxes. Brochures. Foam peanuts. Anything but those goddamn bars.

Inside the box, I find twenty-four bars in smooth, shiny silver packaging.

Sort of like evil Rice Krispies treats.

"Shit. Paul. They are actually going to send these things out into the world," I say.

"Correction," Vivian calls. I can't see her, so I move in the direction of her voice. She's made it all the way to the opposite end of the building and is standing near a large silver bay door. Like the kind they pull delivery trucks up to.

She hands me a clipboard. "They started shipping these things out last week."

Tucking the shotgun under my arm, I take the clipboard from her and point my light at the papers. There are pages and pages of shipping manifests. To a bunch of companies that sound like medical research centers. Most of the addresses are outside the US.

"They just went out on Thursday though," I say, feeling a slight sense of relief. "And it's all ground shipping. If we can get out of here, we can warn people."

"The important part being *get out of here*," Smentkowski says. He has wheeled Rachel into the center of the room. "We found the laundry room. Let's check for towels."

"Come on," I say to Vivian.

"We need to take this with us," she tells me, pointing at the paperwork.

I hand it back to her. She folds up the papers and puts them in her backpack.

Smentkowski leads us to the door labeled LAUNDRY. As he wheels Rachel inside, she uses her flashlight to examine one of the bars.

"You need to get rid of that thing," Vivian snaps.

Rachel nods. "I was hoping to figure out what is actually in them. But they're clearly not labeled correctly. I mean, listen to this. Bleached enriched wheat flour, sugar, vegetable oil, eggs, salt, cornstarch. These are the ingredients in a sugar cookie."

Vivian sighs. "Well, I'll go out on a limb here and guess that if you don't mind murdering people, not complying with packaging regulations is probably no big deal." She opens the door to the laundry room. "I saw pallets and pallets of something labeled PRODUCT FLOUR. There's no telling how many of those bars they have already made. Or have the capability to make."

Paul is already inside the room, which mainly consists of several rows of stainless steel washing machines and dryers. "I found some stuff. There are clean scrubs in the cabinets. And I got out some towels," he says, gesturing to a steel bench.

"You know your dad is shipping his mega monster bars all over the world," Vivian says.

"I can't believe my dad would deliberately hurt anyone. Anyway, *I* didn't know what he was doing," Paul says, almost pleading.

"Well, you should have," Vivian tells him. "Allie is dead because—"

I brace myself to bust up another fight.

But Rachel cuts in. "No. No. You can't blame him. Kids . . . can be different from their parents . . . and you can't blame them."

Vivian puts her hand on Rachel's shoulder. "Okay. Okay. Calm down. Let's get you taken care of. So, uh, Four, where'd you say those scrubs were?"

Paul points at the cabinet, and we go over there. Most of the uniforms are the same size, for a shortish, thinnish person. Vivian looks a bit embarrassed, but there is nothing that will fit me or Smentkowski either. We do, however, find a pair of pants that will fit Rachel. Paul grabs some scrubs, and the guys step out and leave the two girls alone to change.

The glass has really messed him up. He has jagged cuts all over his legs and chest. Many are still dripping blood. "Shit, Paul. We need to find a first aid kit."

"Nah. I'm good." He gets the clean scrubs on. For an instant, he looks like he could fit right in with his doctor father. Then he stuffs his arms back into his filthy camp coat.

"So . . . uh . . . you don't think that getting scratched or bitten . . . turns you into one of . . ." Paul's face goes red.

Smentkowski shakes his head. "No. I think you have to eat the bars. That's the only way to change."

Paul's shoulders relax.

The girls come out a second later. Vivian is more or less the same, although she must have dried herself off with the towels. Rachel is back in the chair, wearing clean scrubs and her coat. Her legs are wrapped in several thick towels, and she has another stack of towels in her lap.

She isn't doing too well. Every once in a while, she sort of freezes up, and those freezes are coming faster and faster. She is gonna have her baby, and we are in a race against the clock.

Our only plan is to wait for help. But it's a crappy fucking plan.

Obviously, the elevator isn't working, so we need to carry Rachel up the stairs.

Smentkowski pushes her over to the stairwell, and we, again, both take a side. Fannon carries the chair, and Vivian hustles behind him. When we get to the top, I'm finally winded. I've reached the limits of my endurance.

I can't remember the last time that I was *this* tired.

The stairwell door opens to a railed walkway that overlooks the factory floor. I'm kind of glad it's so dark. I don't want to have to take note of the terrifying scope of things.

To the left, we find a series of lab rooms, each separated by glass panels and doors. To the right, there is a stainless steel wall with a few doors that all have those knobs with keypad locks attached.

Smentkowski points to the secured doors. "I don't think anybody's getting in there."

So we decide to search the left side first. Nothing is locked, and we are able to quickly move from room to room. Unlike Kaiser's space, which had crap all over the place, this lab doesn't have the feel of a place where someone actually works. It seems like a show.

The first room doesn't really have anything of value. Vivian scores a cart that we can use and a couple more pairs of scissors. But it's mainly a room with a few powerless and useless high-tech computers and some office supplies.

The second room is more of the same, with microscopes littered on high-top tables. "Those are the same kind we have at my school," Rachel comments. "I can't imagine any serious professional scientist using them."

In the third room, we hit the mother lode. There is a shit ton of chemicals in here.

Rachel gets up out of the chair.

"You really should stay seated," I tell her.

She snorts at me. Exactly like one of my sisters. "I'm the only one who has any clue what these things do. I need to see what's over here." It's a brave act, but she holds her belly when she speaks.

"Why do you need to see the chemicals?" I ask.

"What if those things get in here?" she says. "There might be something we can use as a weapon. We need to be prepared. Maybe something in here will give us a chance if we have to fight the monsters."

Behind her, Vivian enthusiastically nods.

I have to give it to Rachel. She's tougher than she looks. She comes to stand in front of a shelf that contains a bunch of glass beakers and begins issuing instructions. "Paul, see if there's any safety gear. Gloves. Goggles. Whatever you can find. Steve. Our best hope is to find something that's flammable. Something we could use to burn or distract the creatures. But we'll need a way to light it. There are some Bunsen burners over there. If they actually use them, there should be matches. Vivian, bring the cart and get a bunch of the beakers loaded up. Sheldon, can you help me?"

Rachel moves over to the shelf containing the chemicals. Fannon digs some goggles and gloves out from one of the drawers. He and Smentkowski both suit up while I keep opening cabinets, looking for the matches.

"This doesn't make any sense," Rachel says, more to herself than to any of us. "This is such a bizarre assortment of chemicals. What kind of work would someone possibly be doing here? Look how they're organized. Stuff should be arranged in compatible families. You're not supposed to store acids next to bases. That's day one of AP Chemistry. This is all wrong."

Vivian joins Rachel at the shelf. "It's almost like they're arranged by container size or something. Like, to look nice."

"Rachel, please sit down," Fannon says. "We can get whatever you want."

She snorts at him, but she does sit again.

"Okay. Pick your poison," Smentkowski says.

"Take the benzene and the acetone. Those are the flammables," she says.

I open the next cabinet. There are several boxes of matches. "Found 'em." I drop the matches on the cart with the rest of the supplies.

"Good. Good," she says, still staring at the racks of chemicals.

"These are all things I recognize," Vivian says. "And I got a C in chemistry."

"Exactly," Rachel tells her. "It's a pretty typical setup for a classroom. But geneticists wouldn't be using any of this stuff."

"I bet they do the real work on the other side," Vivian says.

"They might not even do it here," Rachel answers. "I read an article about the CRISPR facility where DuPont edits yogurt and cheese bacteria, and the place is massive. It's millions of square feet and has a computer lab that's larger than this whole building."

Vivian makes a disgusted face. "They edit yogurt? You're saying we've been eating *edited* yogurt?"

Smentkowski thinks for a minute. "Yeah, but there are tons of biotech startups that aren't nearly so big. I think the computer setup in Kaiser's office would work for CRISPR, actually," he says. "Especially these days, when you can buy parallel computing time from server farms or universities if you need it."

Rachel makes one last check of the chemicals. "Okay. I think there is some cyanide down there at the bottom. That's *really* unusual. We should save that for if we get desperate."

I wonder what she would consider desperate, because for me, we're already there.

"What's it used for? Other than to poison people, I mean," Vivian says.

Rachel shrugs. "I don't know. Maybe old-timey . . . photography."

Smentkowski bends down to pick up the large white container. "The seal is broken."

And I know we are all thinking the same thing.

Kaiser.

"Okay," I say. "Let's keep going."

We go into the last room. And this place is really weird. There is a movie camera set up on a tripod and a bunch of iPads lying out on a table. Next to every iPad, there is a Post-it note that reads FANNON TEST 1, FANNON TEST 2, and so forth.

Smentkowski goes around testing the devices. He creates a stack from those with dead batteries. There is only one that works.

"It's got about five percent left," Smentkowski says. "And, of course, no Wi-Fi."

Fannon approaches the table. "What do you think it means? Fannon Test?"

Smentkowski taps the screen in his hands. "I think they were making video tests and using the iPads to review them. I've heard of movie studios doing that. They get a clip ready and then stick a device in some executive's hands so they can say yea or nay."

"Can I see it?" Paul asks.

"I'm not sure that's such a great idea," I tell him. Not only do I really want to find someplace where the walls aren't all made of glass for us to hide, I don't know what we might find on the iPad. And that uncertainty is dangerous.

Rachel clutches her side. "Let him look."

Smentkowski already has the video up anyway.

The face of Paul's father fills the screen. He's posed in front of the wall of chemicals that we've just raided. Rachel was right. The labs are a set.

Dr. Fannon's voice breaks the silence.

Hello, and thanks for watching. I am Dr. Paul Fannon the Third, president and chief medical officer of FannonPharma. For four generations, my family has been tirelessly devoted to providing quality medical care. From advancements in immunizations to cutting-edge cancer research, we've been on the front lines of the fight to keep the world healthy . . .

To me, this is a boring rehash of what we already know. But Vivian and Rachel are staring at the tablet intently.

That's why we've watched the developing obesity epidemic with concern. The physical, economic, and emotional costs of this disease are enormous. But now, I'm thrilled to report we've finally found a cure. We're pioneering a method of gene editing via an ingestible product.

Fannon stops speaking. He pulls an index card from his pocket and stares at it for a moment before he resumes his speech.

The Metabolize-A bar produced fast, safe, effective, and permanent weight loss for sixty percent of participants in the initial clinical trial without the individual making any significant changes to their diet and exercise regimens.

Vivian faces Rachel. "Shit. Is he saying that they knew that forty percent of the campers would be turned into freakish monsters?"

While we have regrettably learned that not everyone re-sponds positively to the process, we believe the astounding results we are achieving represent an incredible opportunity.

"Yeah," Rachel says. "But at least that means there might be more survivors."

I say nothing. I hate to be pessimistic, but if one or two people in each Pod turned into those creatures, everyone else in the bungalow wouldn't last too long.

Join us at Venture to learn more about this exciting new development.

"What's Venture? Some kind of investment conference?" Vivian asks. No one knows.

During the conference, we'll be sharing a bit more on the science behind this medical marvel and sharing the results of the second clinical trial, which is currently underway.

"I guess that's us," I mumble.

The cure for obesity is right around the corner, and you are an essential part of its arrival. We'll see you in Phuket!

"So they need money," Vivian says.

"Research like this can't be easy. Or cheap," Rachel agrees. "Maybe they plan on developing a test to identify those who are resistant."

"Or it's possible that they don't care about killing fat people," Vivian says.

I worry she'll turn her attention to Fannon, who is huddled over in the corner, sickish and green. He reminds me of myself the first time I watched a cow give birth.

"Dad told me they'd found new investors. That they had all the money they needed," Fannon chokes out.

"Some people always need more money," I say, thinking of my

parents' lawsuit. "Monsanto has been suing our tiny family farm for the past two years because a few patented cottonseeds spilled over onto our land. There is no such thing as enough money for those people."

"Monsanto can suck it," Vivian says with a wink.

Smentkowski is still tapping on the tablet. "That file is kind of old."

"Is there anything more recent?" Fannon asks.

"Just this," Smentkowski answers. We all crowd around and lean in to see a lone still image of Dr. Fannon with a bald man in an odd black uniform. Fannon looks like he's aged ten years since the video, and the bald guy has the posture of someone important . . . and menacing.

Vivian stares at the picture. "It looks like a publicity photo or something," she says. "My mom takes those all the time when Pied Piper makes some kind of a big deal."

I recognize the large silver *S* on the pocket of his jacket. "I saw that Silverstone logo at my interview too. And the ranger we met outside the camp was wearing it."

"Silverstone is scary," Smentkowski says.

Vee nods. "I did a report on them for AP Government. They run a bunch of private prisons in Iraq and Afghanistan. They run them the way the Soviets ran the gulag. Those places are supposed to be like the seventh circle of hell."

"Do you know who that is?" Smentkowski asks Fannon.

He shakes his head. "No."

Vivian squints at Rachel. "You think this is a military project?"

Rachel rests her hand on her belly and thinks for a minute. "I guess it's possible. But why would the military care about curing obesity? And if FannonPharma came up with a cure, they wouldn't need a military investment. They'd have a million banks and investors to choose from. They'd basically be able to print their own money."

She's right. There are tons of people who'd pay almost anything to be thin.

People like Allison DuMonde.

Paul returns to the corner, and Smentkowski checks the other tablets again.

Vivian stays next to Rachel. "Allie. Do you think maybe she wouldn't have changed? That maybe she would have been okay?"

Rachel shakes her head. "I think she knew that she was changing. That's why she did it."

Paul hunches over and pukes in a trash can.

"She's right," he says. "We're all going to die. And it's my fault."

God, I'm not sure how many more times I can talk someone off this particular ledge. Plus, we need to concentrate on getting rescued and getting Rachel to a hospital. I open my mouth to speak, but a series of crashes coming from down below drowns out what I intend to say.

It has to be those things.

They are inside.

Vivian is already half out the door that leads to the walkway with the cart full of chemicals. Smentkowski follows, pushing Rachel in the chair.

Paul lingers in the corner.

I grab him and pull him out the door as a horrible scream echoes off the redbrick walls.

VIVIAN ELLENSHAW

The building has no soundproofing or insulation, and the screams of those things are bouncing off the brick walls and the concrete floors and coming from every direction. I push the cart out onto the walkway and swing my flashlight around.

I find the creature.

And it finds me.

The zombie is down there in the manufacturing area, ripping apart boxes and boxes of the very bars that have turned it into the monster. My light catches its attention.

For a second, I honestly think about ending it. I don't want to become one of those things, and I don't want to be eaten either. I could climb over the railing, and it would all be over. But I think about Allie. I have to get out of here and make those fuckers pay for what they've done to her. And Rachel. I can't let her die, too, if I can do something about it.

And there's Steve, who has that super cute little dimple on his right cheek when he smiles. If I take charge, I can keep him from becoming The Courageous Captain. He could stay The Jock with a Heart of Gold and he'd live.

Steve Miller does have a heart of gold.

And I want him to live.

I keep my light on the zombie, almost like a spotlight, watching in horror as it climbs one of the tall storage racks on the other side of the warehouse.

It's coming up here.

The only way we can survive is if we kill it.

Smentkowski and Miller are right behind me.

In the chair, Rachel has the most awful expression on her face. Pain and fear and the understanding that your life might end up being way shorter than you thought it would be.

Miller is getting the gun ready. But we have almost no ammo, and we already know you have to hit those creatures at close range to do any real damage.

"No! You have to get Rachel out of here!" I shout.

"What the fuck are you planning to do?" he yells back.

"I'm gonna torch that thing."

That *thing* is making steady progress scaling the shelves.

"Oh hell no! You—"

"I can't carry Rachel! We won't make it if we don't kill the zombie. Go! I'll catch up."

"Vee! Use the benzene," Rachel says. "It's the . . . most flammable."

"Got it."

Miller and Smentkowski turn to the stairwell. Fannon stays behind.

"Go!" I tell him.

Fannon comes close to the cart. He tosses me a pair of goggles and gloves. "No way. I'm not needed over there, and you know you can't take that thing out by yourself."

I shove the goggles on my face and put on the gloves. There isn't time to argue. Fannon is already opening the amber glass bottle, releasing a sickly sweet smell.

My hand shakes as I take the container and fill a few flasks about halfway.

"What are you going to do?" Fannon asks.

"Um . . . try to make a . . . Molotov cocktail," I stammer, trying to make it seem like I know what I'm doing. And not like my mom made me watch *Night of the Living Dead* a zillion times on late-night TV. "Get the light," I tell Fannon.

I grab the first flask and the matches and run along the walkway toward the side of the building where the creature is about to make the jump from the racks to the second floor. I keep about ten feet between me and *it*.

I strike a match and drop it in the flask. I only barely manage to get my head out of the way as a massive flame explodes upward. A couple of loose strands of hair catch fire, and it takes every ounce of self-control I have not to drop the glass container as the rubber gloves do little to stop the heat.

By the time I launch the thing in the air, the flames have gone out.

And I miss.

My Molotov cocktail attempt is not a success.

"Oh fuck! That is never going to work," Fannon says.

He runs back to the cart and comes back with the entire bottle of benzene.

The zombie jumps from the rack and hangs by the edge of the glass-and-aluminum railing that surrounds the walkway.

"Follow me and get ready," Fannon yells as he passes by.

It takes a minute to understand.

He runs right up in front of the creature and empties the benzene on it.

I have to hurry.

I get the matches ready as I move along.

When I join him, the creature lets go of the railing with one hand and uses the other to swing itself up. It punches Fannon hard in the chest, sending him back ten feet and into the stainless steel wall. He leaves an indentation in the shape of his body as he slides to the floor.

His flashlight skids along the concrete and comes to a stop with the beam pointed in my direction. I light the first match.

And it blows out.

Soon that *thing* will be up on the railing with me.

I keep my hand as steady as possible and strike the second match.

Something on the monster's arm catches my eye. The hand that grips the railing is wearing a watch. A fucking wristwatch. It's black and has a panda on the face.

This is a person.

This used to be a person.

Like Allie.

I hate myself, but I drop the lit match and it lands on the creature's upper arm.

It catches fire instantly and falls to the first floor in a fit of awful screeching.

The monster lands on a stack of Metabolize-A boxes that erupt in flames.

I fight off the urge to watch it burn. To make totally sure it's dead.

Instead, I hustle over to Fannon. His eyes flutter open and closed. The creature really got him. Half of his face is already swelling, and I'd bet anything he has a concussion.

I have to hand it to the guy. He *is* brave.

"Come on," I say. "You have to get up."

He moans and closes his eyes.

I shake him. "We have to get out of here."

He opens his eyes. "Why? Why do I need to get out of here? I just found out that my own father is basically Dr. Frankenstein."

I feel like the worst person in the world. How many people am I going to goad into doing self-destructive shit? "Listen to me. Rachel was right. Our parents don't define us. If you come with me. If you help save Rachel and her baby. Then that will prove it."

He takes my hand and lets me help him off the floor.

"Help me with the cart, okay?"

"What's next?" he says as we approach the stairwell.

"I say we get out of this building and make a run for the van."

"Okay," he says.

But we arrive in the stairwell just as Miller is firing a shot at a zombie clambering up the stairs. The boom bounces off the metal and concrete and feels like it's trapped inside my head, echoing off the insides of my skull.

I can't hear.

The zombie isn't dead, but it's down. Fannon pours the acetone on it, and we light that one on fire too.

Fannon and I move toward the stairs. Miller stops us.

He says something, but I still can't hear.

I shake my head.

He opens his mouth wide and screams. "We can't . . . there's too many . . . Smentkowski and Rachel . . . the roof." Miller gestures with the flashlight toward the stairs.

Fannon nods, and I grab the jug of cyanide and follow him. But I think that this sounds like a pretty suckish plan.

When we get onto the roof, I *know* it is a suckish idea.

Miller slams the door and throws his weight against it.

He almost leans back, like it has taken the last of his strength to deal with the door.

And . . . we're trapped on the roof.

In better times, the roof must have served as an outdoor break room. Smentkowski has cleared off a seat for Rachel on a patio chair near the door. She sits there, bunched up and holding her stomach. She has the remaining flashlights in her lap, pointed upward, the beams cutting into the dark night like panels of stained glass. It occurs to me that, as I move, I'm sinking in the snow. A short ledge surrounds the roof, coming up to about my knee. Then I realize. The ledge is probably at least shoulder-high, but we are standing on several feet of white powder.

A small area has been cleared out around the door.

That's why Miller is so exhausted. He had to tunnel us onto the roof.

A little bit of my hearing has returned, and I'm able to hear Smentkowski when he says, "Come on. Give me a hand."

He wants to fortify the door.

I help him clear the snow off of a wide metal sofa with vinyl cushions. Together, Fannon, Smentkowski, and I drag the sofa over to the roof door. Miller moves out of the way for us to push it in front. The three of us sit down, and our weight, plus the sofa, is enough to keep the door closed.

Miller stands in front of us, hunched over, with his hands on his knees.

The cushions are cold and wet and, if possible, I become even more cold and wet. I can't feel my fingertips or my toes. I'm smooshed in between Fannon and Smentkowski, I've got Allie's camera tucked into the pocket of my sweats, and it digs into my thigh.

Allie.

Allie is dead.

Forever.

As in never. Ever. Coming back.

She sacrificed herself.

Except I wasn't worth saving.

I was a terrible friend.

"How many shells are left?" Smentkowski asks Miller.

Miller pauses before answering. "Two."

Barely enough to take out *one* of those *things*.

A bang.

A sharp pain in my back.

I'm pushed a few inches forward on the sofa.

The monsters are charging the door.

We can hear them hooting in the hall. And down below too.

Heavy footsteps in the snow.

Gripping his flashlight, Miller goes to the edge of the roof and points the beam toward the snow-covered ground. A desperate, animal screech rises into the night.

Another bang at the door.

It's snowing.

Rachel is in labor.

We are almost out of ammo.

The only thing we do have is the cyanide. One of us would have to feed it to the creatures in order to kill them. Which probably requires someone to die for it to do any good.

And the monsters are in the stairwell and all over on the ground down below.

We. Are. Screwed.

We are going to die.

Soon.

ACTION

Update: in the next few hours, one of three things will happen.

     1—~~We'll be rescued.~~ No one is coming.

     2—~~We'll freeze to death.~~ We won't last that long.

     3—We'll be eaten by thin and athletic zombies.

So, that's how we got here. How we ended up on this roof.

     I want to blame Fannon or my mom or evil Coach.

     But I already know.

     I'm the one.

     It's me.

     There's no one to blame but myself.

PAUL FANNON

Vivian is right.

We are all gonna die.

It *is* all my fault.

Miller returns from the edge of the roof. "It seems like we're safe enough up here. Temporarily. If we can hold out long enough for help to . . ."

To? To what?

Vivian stares at Rachel.

We all know that no one is coming.

I wipe the wet ice off my face. Everyone but Miller is sitting on the sofa, and it's sinking. Inch by inch. Our weight pushing it down. The falling snow creeping up around our ankles and then calves and then up to our thighs.

Cold.

So freezing cold.

If this bothers them, Smentkowski and Vivian say nothing.

The thing hits the door again. I stick my feet down into the snow, searching for the floor to brace myself as best I can.

"How many of them are there?" Vivian asks Miller in a cold voice.

He draws in a breath. Waits. Like he'd rather not answer. "I counted twenty before I . . ."

Stopped counting.

There are at least twenty of those monsters out there.

"This is all my fault," I say. I'm surprised by my own voice.

How rough it sounds. How the words feel like sandpaper against my tongue. I'm surprised I'm saying this at all.

I turn to Vivian. "Your friend. Allie. She called it. I *am* The Jerk. I don't know why I'm here instead of her. I don't know why I never asked my father what the hell was happening at this camp. I've been so full of shit. So full of myself. I've never given any thought to how I treat people. It should have been me who went after that thing in the road. It should have been me."

Vivian's shoulders slump. "No. It's my . . . my . . . my fault she's dead," she says through chattering teeth. "We had a fight. She thought I was pissed because some douchelord called Evan asked her to prom. But it was really because she called me out. She told me how ungrateful I was for the life I have. And she was right. Even if my mom got married to Coach, I had it so easy compared to Allie. Compared to so many people."

She sniffles. "She was here because of me. My mom paid for her to come. Allie wouldn't have even been at this camp if it weren't for me. She'd be alive . . . she'd be out there . . ."

Miller takes a half step toward Vivian. Like he wants to comfort her but can't figure out how. He stays back a couple of feet from the sofa.

Smentkowski hangs his head. "Everything is my fault. I . . . I . . . took the camp power systems offline."

"Shit, Smentkowski! What the hell?" Miller says. "Why would you do that?"

"I figured they'd send us home," Smentkowski says in a lifeless voice. "I didn't know that . . . and that girl . . . Zanna . . . she's dead because of me. We're all dead because of me."

"Zanna was dead the moment that Jeep pulled out of the

gate," Vivian says in an equally flat tone. "And I'm not sure we'd be much better off if all the lights were on. The 911 operator said that there are zombies in town."

Rachel groans from her chair a few feet in front of us. "It's *my* fault. God is punishing me. Me and this baby." The flashlights rustle as she clenches her stomach even tighter.

"That's ridiculous, Rachel," Vivian says. "We're not up here because you decided to have sex. We're up here because a bunch of mad scientists don't think you have to treat fat people like people."

"Why did you . . . how did you . . ." Smentkowski tries to put the questions into words.

Rachel pants a couple of times. "I was at the library one afternoon. In April. The weather was perfect. I was supposed to be doing research for youth Bible study. Instead, I found a bunch of books about Henrietta Lacks, and I was there in that section. There was this boy. Tall and handsome, leaning against a cart full of books. You know, the kind who looks like he rides a motorcycle and reads Jack Kerouac and keeps a pack of cigarettes in his jacket pocket. The exact wrong kind of boy. Except that everything about him seemed right, and he was living in this other world, and for a second I thought maybe I could be in that world too. A world where everything I felt on the inside was okay to show on the outside. A world where the real me could live and be free. We went into the bathroom, and I know that it was stupid. I mean, even though my parents pulled me out of school on sex education day in biology, I still know about birth control. And then . . . and then . . ."

We are all guilty. Or we all feel guilty.

She's straight-up heaving and sobbing. I want to go over there, but I don't know how much my weight is needed to keep the zombies from busting through the door.

I flex my freezing fingers and brush the falling snow out of my hair.

Miller approaches her and puts his hand on her shoulder. "It's gonna be okay, Rachel."

She shrugs his hand off. "How is it, Steve? No one's coming to save us. But what if they do? Then I have this baby? You know, I could have gone home and told my parents I was pregnant. I think they actually could have dealt with it. I'm sure my dad could have come up with a sermon about how we're all tested at some point. He could have found some nice guy from church to marry me right after graduation." She huffs a couple of times. "But I didn't because I knew. It would all be over. I would never be able to escape. That's why I came here. To work up the nerve to run away. I wanted to leave camp and never look back. Except I couldn't. I can't be saved. Not tonight. Not ever."

"That's not true," Vivian says. "But . . . do you even want that baby?"

"Vivian . . ." Miller begins. He tries to position one of the towels over Rachel's head to stop so much snow from hitting her.

Rachel chokes on a sob. "Yes. I think so. I think I . . . I love him."

"It's a boy?" Smentkowski asks.

"I think so," Rachel answers.

There's another howl from down below followed by one more sharp bang against the door. "Those things sure are determined," I say. What do they even want? Why are they acting like this?

Smentkowski rubs his hands together. "What's his name going to be?"

"I don't know," Rachel whispers.

Miller sighs. "Look. If you guys want to blame someone, blame me. I knew there was something screwy about this place weeks ago when I was interviewed by a woman who looked like a cyborg. I could have said something. I could have told you all before you agreed to get in the van with me. But all I could think about was getting my tuition money."

"There was nothing you could have done, Steve," Rachel says.

Smentkowski grunts. "Maybe we need to stop blaming us. And also stop thinking about us. We all have families back at home, and we all saw what was going on downstairs. They've made thousands of those bars and shipped them God knows where. We know that around half of the people who eat them get converted into flesh-eating zombies. And the other half tend to get eaten when that happens. I don't know what's going to happen to *us*, but we need to think about *them*. The people we love outside of camp."

Before I can point out how we can't help ourselves, let alone anyone else, Vivian sits up.

"He's right," she says. "We have to at least try to warn everyone. We have to try to go for help. I have to try. For Allie."

I shake my head. "Try? Try what?"

"We have to go for the van," she says.

She says it resolutely. With force. As in, oh yes, *of course* we should go for the van.

Oh. Hell. No.

Miller says it for me. "Go? For the van? You can't be serious."

She stands up. "Trade places with me."

"No. No way," Miller says.

But the things hit the door again, leaving him with no choice but to sit in the spot left open by Vivian.

She takes one of the flashlights and walks around the edge of the roof. "There's a fire escape ladder over here," she calls from a corner on the opposite side of the building. "We just need to release it."

"No," Miller says.

She comes back, swinging the flashlight as she walks, taking a stand in front of us where Miller was a minute before. "What choice do we have?"

"We called the police. They could be on their way."

Vivian puts her hands on her hips. "We called the *Flagstaff* police. Even in good driving conditions, town is more than an hour away. How long do you think Rachel can stay out here? How long can any of us?"

"I'll go," Miller tells her.

"You have to stay here. Rachel needs you. I'll go."

No.

This isn't right.

No.

"I'll go," I tell them.

"You'll never make it on your own," Vivian says.

I don't have time to be insulted. "Neither will you. And if Allie's theory is correct, I'm going to bite it anyway."

Vivian snorts. "If her theory is correct, then you'd never make it back with the van. You don't send a Red Shirt out for help. I'm Action Girl. I should go."

"This whole thing is a really dumb idea," Miller inserts.

"It's not *that* bad," Smentkowski says. "The creatures have obviously breached the electric fences, so it's a straight shot through the woods, back to where we left the van. If we can keep those things interested in us, someone might be able to make a break for it."

"Whoever goes out there isn't coming back," Miller says.

Ever the optimist.

"It's probably two miles or so," Smentkowski says.

"It's at least three," Miller snaps. "In the snow."

"They . . . might . . . make it," Smentkowski stammers.

"Her theory . . . it's not . . . not correct . . . not a movie . . . real life . . . we're real," Rachel says. Her breathing is getting more labored. "We still have our free will."

This settles it. Rachel is having the baby. We have to give it a try.

"I need to find something to use as a weapon," Vivian says.

She leaves us there again, moving around the snowy roof, examining the groups of patio furniture. I can't make out exactly what she's doing. There are a few grunts. Some twisting metal. Vivian returns with what looks like the circular base of an iron patio chair.

"I'm going." As I say these words, I realize that they're true.

That they have to be true.

I don't know if I'm The Jerk. But the only way I won't be him, the only way that I can ever face myself in the mirror again, is if I try to do something. Try to help.

I have to say, the way Vivian looked at me when I charged that creature in the lab. The way people are treating me with more respect. That's what I want. I want to be *that* guy. But if Allie's theory is really correct, do I want to be recast as The Courageous Captain?

Can I go down with the ship?

"I'm going," I say again. With full force.

Vivian waits a second. "If we both go, can you hold the door?"

We're forming a team.

"It doesn't matter," Miller says. "No one is going anywhere."

Rachel moans.

The couch shakes from the force of another pounding.

After it's still for a moment, Vivian says, "We're going."

We.

Miller isn't happy, but what can he do? We push another sofa in front of the door and seat Rachel on it. Smentkowski remains on the first couch. "Whatever you're going to do, you better do it fast. Those things on the other side of the door won't stay quiet forever."

Vivian tosses Smentkowski her backpack. "Keep this safe. It's got all the shipping manifests from downstairs. If we make it out of this alive, we'll be able to tell the police where those bars were sent."

He takes the bag and nods.

Miller, Vivian, and I run over to the corner of the roof. I see the ladder. It's attached to a small metal platform. We'll need to climb off the roof, drop the ladder, climb down, and run like hell. Run like hell past the electric fence and into the tall trees.

"You need a distraction," Smentkowski calls.

"Got it," Miller says.

He doesn't say what he plans to do, and I don't ask. I can't think about too many things or I'll lose my nerve. I climb out onto the platform. The metal creaks and sways and shakes. A feeling of icy cold washes over me, and I don't know if it's the weather or my internal terror.

My father would never do this.

This idea gives me a little bit of warmth.

Miller pumps the last two shells into the shotgun and tries to hand it to me.

I feel incredibly stupid, but I have to tell him. "I don't know how to use it."

"I do." Vivian takes the gun and passes me the chair piece.

It's heavier than it looks.

I end up with my flashlight in one hand and the piece of iron in the other.

Miller stands next to Vivian, who is about to join me on the platform.

"Some people call you the space cowboy," she says.

"Some call me the gangster of love," he answers.

"So we've got time for irrelevant hipster song lyrics now?" Smentkowski calls.

I can hear Vivian's shoes crunch on the rooftop snow.

"Since we're probably going to die. And also for luck," she says. She pushes herself up onto her tiptoes and kisses Miller. Right on the mouth. We're on the roof. Flakes of snow fall onto his blond hair and sparkle in the beam of Vivian's flashlight. It might be romantic. In another place. Another time.

She lets go of him and steps back.

"Don't die," he tells her.

"I won't."

Vivian puts one foot onto the platform and then the other.

"Wait until I give you the signal," Miller says.

She squeezes by me, moving toward the ladder and shining her flashlight all around until it lands on the release hook. For some reason, Vivian whispers. "We both get on the ladder. As soon as Miller gives the signal, I'll flip the hook. We'll go down fast. And then we run."

She climbs onto the ladder as far down as she can go.

I move on as well, taking a position directly above her.

We wait there for a minute.

A few dark, snarling figures swirl around like tornados down below.

I've got my fingers wrapped around the cold, slippery metal. Wrapped so tightly. For an instant I picture what it would be like to let go. To fall into the night. To vanish and disappear into the snow.

I wonder if Vivian is having these thoughts.

Up on the roof, Miller is making one hell of a racket.

Vivian takes sharp breaths.

"We're gonna make it," I tell her.

"We have to make it," she says.

I can't see the monsters down below us anymore.

"Okay. Now!" Miller yells.

It takes a couple of tries, but Vivian is able to pull the ladder hook all the way up.

The instant she does, my stomach does a series of flips like I'm on a roller coaster doing loop-de-loops. We're plummeting down the side of the brick building.

In a blur. A rush. A whoosh.

Down. Down. Down.

The ladder bows and creaks and bends, and when we're down halfway, we're also almost swinging to the side.

I drop my flashlight, but thanks to the side-to-side motion, it doesn't hit Vivian. It lands without a sound on the blanket of snow. I barely manage to keep hold of the metal wheel.

Down. Down. Down.

Vivian lets go right before the ladder crashes to the ground and is thrown a few feet forward. I hang on till the end. Which is stupid, because the force of the crash tosses me up against the brick wall. The iron chair part hits my ribs hard.

I bounce off the wall a couple more times like a pinball.

I know I have to let go.

Let go of the ladder.

I fall back. Flat on my back. Onto the cold sheet of ice.

I'm lying down. Faceup in the snow. The wind knocked out of me.

Here. Existing. Staring up at the dark hole of the sky.

Trying to focus on the snowflakes as they drift down.

Breathe.

I can't.

I need to breathe.

Something's moving around me.

Footsteps in the snow.

Vivian.

"Four!" she screams. "We have to run."

Then.

Bang.

The shotgun.

We have to run.

SHELDON SMENTKOWSKI

The shotgun fires, sending a thunder echoing into the night. Vivian and Paul have barely been gone two minutes and they've already had to use the gun.

Team #SurviveTheZombieApocalypse is down to only one shotgun shell.

Up on the roof, Miller's plan is working.

A little too well.

I mean, if his plan is to make those things *way* more interested in *us* than in Paul and Vivian, then you betcha it's a massive success.

At first, I didn't really get it. Miller grabbed a few of the extra towels off Rachel's lap and took them over to the edge of the roof. In the narrow beam of his flashlight, he started ripping them into strips.

Watching him do it made me think that maybe Brittani is right. That I do need to work out more with the trainer. Miller is tearing through the cotton cloth with ease, like he's shredding paper.

He's still got the lighters from earlier, and he breaks them apart. I can smell the rotten cabbage scent of the lighter fluid even where I am. He sprinkles the liquid over the strips of cloth and lights them, dropping the flaming strips one by one. Miller's not doing much damage, but the monsters down on the ground seem plenty distracted. They hoot and howl and snarl.

Midway through that process, as it's basically taking everything I've got to keep the zombies from crashing through the door, he gets an even better idea.

Rachel kind of pants, "God. Oh. God."

Miller stalks around, making a terrible racket as he tosses chairs and patio tables off the roof, probably hoping that he might actually hit one of the things and take it out. At one point, he has a whole damn sofa lifted over his head, like he's Donkey Kong getting ready to toss the next barrel at Mario.

There are no more shots, and from what I can tell, Vivian and Paul have been able to make a run for it.

Everything appears to be going okay.

Except that we're *supposed* to be keeping the zombies off the roof until Vivian and Paul get back with the van. But now, instead of coming back to the sofa to help me block the door, Miller goes rogue. He scavenges around, finding what looks like a garden hose. He crosses the rectangular space, which is mostly empty now that he's tossed all the furniture over the side. There are only a few patio chairs scattered here and there, a lonely table, and the sofas we are using to block the door. Miller takes long awkward steps, looking kind of like a spaceman as he sinks in the snow between his movements. He ends up on the opposite side of the roof.

Opposite from the door we are *supposed* to be guarding.

I squint at Miller, who is fifty or sixty feet away from me.

As best as I can see, he's fidgeting with the hose.

"What are you doing?" I call.

He doesn't answer for a second, but then he yells back, "There's a metal safety bar surrounding the edge of the roof, and I think we can tie the hose—"

What we should do is use the hose to better secure the door, because those things are punching the hell out of it. But whatever Miller's idea is, he doesn't get to finish explaining it.

Rachel cries out and falls over, forming a ball on the sofa.

I don't know. I don't know what's happening.

From down below, Vivian screams, "We have to run."

I'm beginning to regret not volunteering to be on the expedition that is going into the woods. At the time, it seemed like staying up here was a better idea than going down there with twenty of those things. But now I know.

They can run and we can't.

We have to run.

That's what Vivian screamed. And they can.

They can run.

We are stuck up here.

Miller stays where he is and is still messing with the damn hose.

It's like I can't quite get a grip on things.

Or figure out what to pay attention to.

And then.

I find something to focus on.

A dark blob. Coming closer and closer and closer.

Moving fast.

I barely have time to duck, and the only reason Rachel's head isn't totally knocked off is that she's lying down, writhing on the couch.

It's a sofa.

It flies through the air, coming so close that it actually ruffles my fucking hair. It skids across the roof on its side, at first sliding across the snow. As it sinks and makes contact with the roof, the iron drags against the concrete and creates a horrible, bloodcurdling screech. The couch crashes against the brick ledge on the far side of the roof.

Those things.

They threw the iron couch that Miller had just tossed off the side of the building a couple of minutes earlier. From the ground. Up two tall floors of an industrial building. They tossed a fucking couch.

We. Are. Doomed.

I'm cold.

My heart barely feels like it's beating at all.

Miller is running back toward me and shouting something, and Rachel is crying, and everything and everything.

And too late, too late.

It registers. I get what Miller is saying.

"Smentkowski! They're coming through!"

They are.

At least one of them is.

I've gotten distracted and backed away from the door, and one of the monsters is pushing it open. Hard. With enough force that it hits me in the chest.

My flashlight flies away, another thing that very narrowly misses hitting Rachel in the face, and my lungs deflate like an air mattress with a hole in it.

I can't breathe, and I can't see those hands. Those silver-blue iridescent hands.

But I feel them.

They shove me.

I fly back a few feet, crashing into a patio chair, which flips over and catapults me facedown into the snow on the roof.

Rachel screams. Once. And then again.

I turn my head to the side. My flashlight has landed against the sidewall of the roof, extending a beam of light in my direction, like a beacon. And I think about getting up and going for it. I consider jumping off the roof.

I could jump.

I can't face the possibility of having one of those things on top of me again. Or being ten seconds from having it rip into my jugular. I could jump and the fall would kill me before the zombies could.

Rachel screams again, and I'm reminded why I can't jump.

Her flashlight shakes as she hobbles away from the door. She shines her light over one of those things. One of the zombies is only a few paces away from her. Snow falls and slides down its smooth skin. It paces toward her with slow deliberation.

I have to help.

If I can.

I force myself up off the ground.

Miller whirs by me, picking up the patio chair near my feet as he goes.

"Get Rachel," he says.

Get her and do what? I don't know what the hell he wants me to do, but I guess getting her away from the creature is a good start.

Miller's running toward the stairs, and he hurls the chair through the open doorway with an astonishing amount of force, and again I wish I were the kind of guy who could bench-press patio furniture.

The monsters let out a series of feral screams. Miller's chair sends them far enough back into the stairwell that he's able to get the roof door closed again. So there's only one of those things up here now.

And Miller's leaving me to deal with it.

I don't know what he's doing.

What the fuck is he doing? What the fuck?

I mean, my logical mind does know. He's trying to secure the door so that we don't have twenty zombies up here instead of one.

But still.

He's leaving me to deal with this one.

I have to deal with it.

"Sheldon. Sheldon," Rachel calls out.

I take the last of the patio tables left on the roof. It's small, circular, low to the ground, and almost completely embedded in the snow. Working fast and frantically, I dig it out.

The thing is so close, so close to Rachel.

She's kind of waving her flashlight around. Like a kid with a lightsaber.

I pick up the table, and it's heavy. It's straining every muscle I have to get the solid iron off the ground. My arms burn immediately, but I'm able to lift it.

I take a few steps closer to the creature, close enough that I won't hit Rachel.

And I throw it. I throw a table.

Sort of.

It's more like I kind of lunge in the monster's direction. The table has an immediate downward trajectory, but it's enough to send *the thing* away from Rachel and to the very edge of the roof.

I know what I have to do.

I run forward. Fast. As fast as I can. I pick the table up again, and I lift it as high as I can. Even though I feel like my back might give out at any minute or my arms might fall off. I lift it up. High. Over my head.

With every ounce of strength I have, I throw the heavy hunk of iron at the zombie.

And it's enough.

The thing howls as it's shoved back.

It struggles to find its footing on the ice.

I take one more breath.

Putting my arms out in front of me like a Halloween Frankenstein's monster, I move with as much speed as I can. My fingers land on the monster's cold, smooth, muscular chest, and I push. Its cold, slimy skin slides across my fingertips. I'm holding my breath.

The thing is off-balance enough that I'm able to force it over the side.

I release the air from my lungs in a whoosh as Rachel collapses in my arms.

But I have to see. I take her flashlight and lean over the side of the brick railing, shining the light onto the ground. The thing has fallen onto the snow. It's on its side. Still. Not moving. The other monsters circle it.

One of them is doing something.

They're eating it. Eating the dead zombie.

I grab Rachel's hair and barely have time to pull us both down as a chair cruises overhead, coming to rest next to the sofa.

We have to get off this roof.

Miller runs up. "Nice work," he says in between pants

of breath. "I . . . used the . . . table legs to wedge . . . the door closed . . . but it won't hold forever."

It seems almost mean to keep mentioning how screwed we are.

But he points across the roof. "There's a window on the side of the building. I think it leads to the area we couldn't get into before. The part of the building that you said was secure."

It takes me a minute to realize that *I* am the *you* Miller is referring to.

Since when does anybody pay attention to the shit that comes out of my mouth?

"Yeah. That's . . . that's what . . . I said," I stammer.

He nods. "I think I have the hose pretty well secure. We can use it like a rope."

Great.

Well.

I have to hope I wasn't wrong.

Our lives depend on it.

Rachel moans.

We each take one of her arms and run along the roof, to where Miller has managed to tie the hose in a timber hitch knot that does look pretty secure.

He hands me the end of the hose. "Okay. You go first."

Shit.

He expects me to swing down through the window like I'm Tarzan or something. Like he assumes everyone is up at five pumping iron just because he is.

When I don't take the hose, he shakes it at me. "Whoever goes second has to bring Rachel."

I see his point, and I doubt I have the upper arm strength to support her and keep myself from plummeting to my death.

So.

I am going first.

Grabbing the hose, I pause at the edge of the roof. Miller's made a loop with the end of the hose to make it a bit easier to hang on to. He shines the flashlight along the red bricks, showing me the location of the window. I clutch the hose and do my best to align myself with it. He gives me an iron rod that must be part of a piece of furniture that he's dismantled.

"Use this to break the glass," Miller says. "Once you're inside, try to clear the window as best you can so we can get Rachel through."

"Okay," I say. When what I really want to say is *Please do this without me*.

Those things pound the door again, and I almost drop the metal bar.

"We don't have much time," Miller says.

I loop the hose around my arm several times and climb over the safety bar, taking a minute to stabilize myself on the wet steel. I glance down. We're a long way up.

There's nothing but a dark void below.

Again, I'm filled with all kinds of regret. I could have gone with my dad on that rock climbing trip to Tettegouche. If Dad were here, at least he'd be going over the side of the building with a little bit of training. I didn't go because Brittani suggested it. And now I struggle to remember why that was such a big deal.

"Good luck, Sheldon," Rachel says.

"Thanks."

Okay. Okay.

Here I go.

I make sure I've got enough slack hose and push my feet off the bar.

Too late, I realize that I left Vivian's bag on the roof.

I descend.

Down.

Down into the darkness.

RACHEL BENEDICT

I am Eve.

And this is my curse.

Every Mother's Day, my dad gives a sermon on Genesis 3:16.

I will make your pains in childbearing very severe; with painful labor you will give birth to children.

And yet this . . . this feeling . . . like I'm being torn apart from the inside. It seems like a steep price to pay for fifteen minutes in a library bathroom. I doubt that Dad would take such a view. He would say that we're all tested. We're tested and I failed. Maybe he's right. Look at where I am. Look at what's happening.

My abdomen cramps up again.

I'm on fire.

I put out my hand to brace myself using the icy safety railing that surrounds the roof.

Steve puts his hand on my back.

He really is a good guy.

Too bad he's going to die. Too bad we're all going to die.

Because of me.

Because I sinned. Because I tried to run away from my problems. Because my presence is slowing everyone down and preventing people from saving themselves.

As if sensing these thoughts, Steve says, "We're going to make it, Rachel."

No, Steve. I'm going to get us all killed.

"It's gotta be after midnight," he comments.

I'm sure my parents are locking up the church right about now. They've finished the service, handed out all the candy canes, packed up all the trays of cookies and cakes donated by members of the congregation. The whole front of the church is decorated for Christmas. I wonder if Dad has left the Nativity set outside or if he's brought it in. I wonder if Mary and Joseph are out in the snow like us.

I wonder if my parents have tried to call me or want to know what I'm doing.

Out here, it's so dark. Clouds block the moon and stars. As far as I can see, the landscape is dark and missing everything I look forward to each winter. No houses alight with twinkling lights. No bright shopping malls. No glowing church steeples.

Steve shines the flashlight down the wall, but the beam does a poor job of showing us what's going on. Up where we are, the hose moves around, but we can't see Sheldon. There are some grunts and groans. Breaking glass.

A couple more thuds.

"Smentkowski?" Steve calls.

No answer.

"Smentkowski?"

Oh Lord. He's already dead. He's fallen. Or those things are on the inside of the building. Or he's cut all his limbs off on broken glass. Or he's—

"Hang on, Miller! I'm clearing out the glass."

Sheldon is alive, and he sounds . . .

Okay.

Me and Steve, on the other hand?

The monsters pound again. I flinch as they hit the door with enough force to knock over one of the chairs Steve stacked up to keep them from coming through. It won't be long before they'll be on the roof with us.

In fact, it will be right now.

I scream again. I'm not exactly sure why I'm screaming. I guess it's 50 percent the crippling pain in my abdomen and 50 percent a response to the creaking of bending metal.

Steve whips the flashlight over toward the sound.

The zombies have bent down the top part of the door.

One is busy squeezing through the opening while the pounding continues.

"Smentkowski?" Steve screams.

Sheldon yells something that's drowned out by the sound of my own bloodcurdling scream.

That thing is coming.

The way it moves. Faster than human. More than human.

Steve grabs my hand as he scrambles over the bars of the safety railing. He's not being particularly gentle, but I can't blame him. The zombies are seconds away from ripping us to shreds. He picks me up, hoisting me over his shoulder the way I suspect he deals with bags of animal feed back at the farm, and he lifts me up over the railing.

I barely have time to snatch up the flashlight that Steve has left on the ledge.

Another spasm of pain hits me.

"It's coming!"

I shout this, and it's true. The zombie is making smooth and easy progress across the ice and through the falling snow. It swipes at my ponytail as Steve pushes us off the roof. Its thick fingers brush the ends of my hair as we swing down.

It screeches and howls and snarls as it snatches at the empty air.

We fall straight down for a couple of seconds, and the only thing that stops me from screaming my head off is that honestly, right at this moment, another contraction hits, and plummeting to my death seems like it might be an improvement over my current situation.

Steve does his best to brace us, but the impact with the wall is inevitable. He bears the brunt of it, hitting the brick with an "Oof." The sides of my legs scrape the bricks, but the pain is nothing compared to what's going on inside me.

We're hanging there, and Steve is breathing hard, the strain of everything finally getting to him. Sheldon shouts something, and Steve uses his feet to push against the wall. I realize we're not perfectly aligned with the window and he's trying to maneuver us in the right direction.

Up above, I hear the monsters hoot. I twist around and point the flashlight up, terrified of what I might find.

I hold my breath.

The zombie is up there, pacing around in frustration. But it doesn't appear to have realized that it can untie the hose to kill us or climb down it to get to our level.

I draw in a deep breath.

That's something.

The monsters don't have human-level intelligence.

Which is a break for us.

But the way the thing is staring at me. I get the idea that it might eventually figure it out.

We slam into the wall again.

I do the only thing I can think of.

I pray for a miracle.

Dear Heavenly Father. Please let Sheldon and Steve and Vivian and Paul survive. They're my friends, and they deserve to make it. Please let me survive. Not for myself but for my baby, who deserves a chance at life regardless of what I've done. Please let us survive for all the innocent people who might suffer if we can't get out of here and warn the world about what's happening in this factory. I know I don't deserve one, but I'm asking for a miracle. Please deliver us. Please give us a miracle.

I whisper *Amen* just as a pair of arms reach out an open window and grab on to the hose.

It's Sheldon.

Steve lands in the window frame, bracing us with his legs. We begin this agonizing process of trying to get me through the opening, which, despite Sheldon's best efforts, is lined with shards of jagged broken glass.

It feels like it takes forever, and it's humiliating when Sheldon needs a break midway because he's having trouble supporting enough of my weight. I'm like a grand piano being delivered to a tiny second-floor apartment.

There's the sound of footsteps in the snow below us. Those things must be down there.

Hoping we fall.

The second I'm inside, Sheldon deposits me into another bland office chair and collapses onto a table.

Steve swings in with ease.

But he, too, nearly falls over once he's in the room. He hoists himself up onto a long worktable and lies down, breathing hard.

We're in a large, wide room. On the table where Steve is resting also sits Sheldon's flashlight. With its beam pointed toward the ceiling, it casts a dull glow across the area.

"Sheldon. Your face." He has a horrible gash on one cheek.

"I . . . didn't . . . clear . . . all . . . the . . . glass at first," he says in between gasps of breath.

"We need to find a first aid kit," I say.

He waits a second and then is able to go on more normally. "It's nothing compared to what you're going through."

My pain has let up quite a bit.

Based on the very limited amount of googling I was able to do about what happens when you go into labor, my guess is that these contractions will come and go until they are almost nonstop and I'll finally have this baby.

"Actually, I'm feeling a little better," I tell him.

Steve sits up. "We need to keep track of the time between contractions. That will generally tell us how much time we have. When my sister went into labor, she was mostly okay until the pain started happening every couple of minutes."

I nod but am not sure what he expects me to do. None of us have a watch or a phone, and it's not like I can sit around counting out the seconds. I scoot myself forward, the wheels of the chair crunching on broken glass, and wave my flashlight all over.

Based on what I can see, Sheldon got it right. This part of the building is very secure. The walls that we saw from the other side are thick steel on this side too. I spot a couple of heavy steel doors that probably open via some kind of hydraulic mechanism. They're all closed and locked up tight. And it's a huge relief to be in here, out of the cold and the snow. It's dry and reasonably warm. Up until the monsters took out the transformers a couple of hours ago, this building must have had heat.

It seems safe.

Yet I fight off a shiver.

Steve has recovered somewhat, but he sounds fatigued. "We should look around for supplies."

Sheldon stands up.

"We need to find something to put in front of that window," I say.

"Why?" Sheldon asks.

I stop moving my chair and hesitate, but I feel I have to answer. "I think those things might be getting smarter. That they might be developing problem-solving skills."

The two of them freeze for a second.

"Problem-solving skills?" Steve repeats in a defeated tone.

"Yeah," I say.

But there's no arguing. Which surprises me. I'm not used to having people respect my ideas like this. Unless my ideas concern art projects for the kids in the church nursery. Sheldon and Steve find a heavy filing cabinet against one wall and push it in front of the window. It drags and scrapes against the building's cool tile floor.

When they're done, Steve picks up the flashlight from his table and searches the room, opening supply cabinets and drawers. Sheldon takes over the pushing, wheeling me around with more speed.

Unlike the other side of the building, which was divided into a series of offices and fake laboratories, this space is one giant room. It's a functional workspace. I have to say that I'm momentarily distracted and kind of excited. The tables are full of real, working equipment. I spot a few refrigerated centrifuges, what might be a thermal cycler, and a UVP machine. Stuff I recognize from when Dad let me take a tour of the bioengineering department at U of A.

"What is this place?" Steve asks.

"It's a lab. For bioengineering."

This validates my theory that the Metabolize-A bars work by altering certain genes, but I have the sense that something else is going on. The long wall, the one against the outside of the building, is lined with what look like deep freezers.

They are storing lots of samples.

And manipulating them.

It scares the crap out of me.

I want to say something to Steve and Sheldon, but I'm not sure what the advantage is of terrifying everyone. Instead, I say, "I hope Paul and Vivian get back soon."

"Me too," Steve says.

When my flashlight lands on a few rows of stainless steel computer towers in the corner, Sheldon says, "Now this is more like it."

His enthusiasm quickly wanes though when he remembers that there's no power.

Steve approaches a group of basic blue cubicles with walls that are about five feet high. We can hear him pulling open drawers. "I found some food," he calls. He tosses a couple of granola bars over the wall of the cube. I find myself checking the package with my flashlight, making sure they're regular food and not some zombie-creating monstrosity.

The package has pictures of cute elves on it and reads

Buddy's Gourmet Cookie Company. Flagstaff, AZ. I tear it open, revealing a normal-colored bar with chocolate chips and nuts. It smells okay.

As I bite into the granola, Steve emerges from the cube with a bottle of water, a couple of Band-Aids, and a bottle of Tylenol. I do the best I can with Sheldon's face. Truthfully, he needs a doctor. But then again, so do I.

Steve opens the bottle of water and passes it to me. I hadn't realized how thirsty I was, and I take several long gulps before giving it back to him. The feeling starts to return to my fingers and toes. It's not a nice feeling. The numbness gives way to a cold burn.

Sheldon leaves me at a table to finish my granola bar. The baby shifts in my belly. I don't know if eating and drinking is a good idea.

I don't know much about this baby at all.

"Hey," Sheldon says. "I found some dry clothes."

He's come to a line of employee lockers kind of like the ones back at camp. One of them is full of clean, dry sweats in various sizes.

We're going to be warm and dry.

It *is* a miracle.

We take turns going behind the cubicles to change. The boys go first since they can change much quicker. When they're done, Sheldon gives me the flashlight and I take an extra pair of sweats to the very back cube. It takes most of my energy to get out of my coat and lift the wet scrubs over my head. By the time I pull on the dark blue FannonPharma sweatshirt, I'm out of breath. Getting the pants on takes the last of my energy, and I fall into the nearby office chair in a huff.

The dry sweats smell like floral fabric softener.

And they feel like heaven.

Panting, I bend over and pick up my old, wet clothes off the floor. I'm not exactly sure why I bother except that my mom is kind of a neat freak and there are habits you can't break, even in a crisis. I toss the clothes on the clean desk, and they land on something shiny and metal.

A computer.

"Sheldon, there's a laptop over here."

Steve is still searching through drawers and cabinets.

Footsteps come my way. I point my flashlight into the aisle, and a minute later Sheldon joins me in the cube.

He drags in another chair from the cube next to us. "The charger is still plugged into the wall," he notes. "That's good news. It means that the thing was charging until recently." He presses the power key, and the laptop hums to life.

He frowns. "This security system is good. I can't hack it without internet access. Best I can do is log in using the admin credentials I found downstairs."

Being downstairs feels like another lifetime ago. I don't know how he can remember a username and password that he entered one time, but he does. He makes a few quick clicks and scrolls through a file menu. He taps a bit more on the keyboard.

"This is interesting," he says. He has three different windows open. He points at the screen. "Here are the files that JDALLEN opened. These are the ones that have been recently transferred to a USB device, and these are the last ones printed."

I squint at the screen. "The lists look the same."

"They are. Which is unusual. I think this person was stealing files," he says.

"What files?" I hold my breath as I wait for an answer.

Sheldon makes a few more clicks, and documents pop up on the screen. "They're contracts." His arms fall away from the desk, slack against his body. "For the Department of Defense."

Vivian was right. This is a military project.

My breath releases in a whoosh, and I'm cold again. This time with shock.

And terror and horror.

Words jump out at me.

PROJECT GIDEON.

Grant for research and development of a genetically modified super soldier.

FannonPharma isn't out to help fat people or even to harm them.

They are trying to weaponize them.

"What is this?" Sheldon asks.

My stomach cramps again. Through the pain, I force the words out. "Turning people into monsters isn't an unfortunate accident. It's the point of the project. They're trying to create an undefeatable super soldier. Gideon is from the Bible. In the book of Judges, he led three hundred men to victory in battle against an army with more than a hundred thousand soldiers."

"You have to be shitting me," Sheldon says.

I point at the monitor to a file labeled PROJECT LOG.

"What's that?" I ask.

Sheldon brings it to the front, and we both stare at a series of entries that describe the progress of the project. Most of the entries are written by Kaiser. The first few detail how he made a miscalculation using the CRISPR technology, creating what he called the anomaly, a series of genetic modifications that resulted in something not human, something more than human. Kaiser thought the anomaly was a terrible mistake.

But someone clearly thought the project had potential.

The last entry chills me to the bone.

Silverstone thinks batch 4207-19A is highly promising. Subjects given this cocktail initially appear to lose cognitive function at a similar level to previous test groups. However, early observational data indicates that intelligence and problem-solving abilities recover as the subject adjusts to the modifications. Within twenty-four hours, most subjects are observed as having returned to the preoperational stage of development (see Piaget, figure 4). Intellectual recovery appears to have no impact on the development of preterhuman levels of speed, agility, and strength. Subject 1581 registered an IQ of 105 at eighteen days post-transformation. Its pre-transformation IQ was tested at 108, indicating an almost full recovery of its intellectual capabilities.

The entry is initialed PJF.

It has to be Paul's dad.

"Kaiser was murdered," I whisper. "And this is why."

"Is this saying what I think it's saying?" Sheldon asks.

"If you think it's saying that after twenty-four hours, those things are as intelligent as preschoolers and that they gradually become as smart as adults, then yes, it says what you think it says."

I try to look into Sheldon's eyes, but it's too dark. "Subject 1581 . . ." I trail off.

"Yeah. Yeah," he says in a voice thick with tension. "Where the fuck are they keeping *that* thing?"

Something else is bothering me too. "Do you think that this

means they've made more than fifteen hundred of those things?"

Sheldon taps the keyboard. "Christ. I really hope not." He makes a few more clicks with the mouse. "There's another video file here too."

We lean in toward the laptop. This clip is strikingly different from the other one we watched. It comes from a camera that appears to be hidden in between a couple of objects, like maybe notebooks or stacks of files. The audio is muffled. Dr. Fannon and several military people come in and out of view.

The bald man from the photograph on the other iPad is speaking. "This is the biggest development in warfare since the Manhattan Project. There's no room to fuck around, Doc."

Another man with steely gray hair in a black uniform I don't recognize says, "Command says no loose ends. You're either part of the problem or you're part of the solution. Kaiser is a fucking problem. So is anyone he may have told."

"You have a wife to consider," the bald man says. "And a son."

We catch a glimpse of Dr. Fannon's stricken face before the screen goes black.

"Paul's dad didn't have a choice," I whisper. "They threatened him."

Sheldon nods. "You don't want to mess with Silverstone. They must need Fannon for something. Or he'd be dead too."

On the other side of the room, Steve opens a cabinet with a squeaky door. "Hey. Guys," he calls out. "I think I found something."

"We did too," I whisper.

"Guns," he goes on. "A couple of tranquilizer guns and a shotgun. Man. Look at the size of these darts. These things could put an elephant to sleep."

We hear a series of clicks as Steve removes the guns and gets them loaded.

I tap the computer. "So this admin is some kind of whistle-blower?"

Sheldon shrugs. "A whistleblower. Or a thief. Or someone's dingbat assistant who is operating without any regard to good security practices. If I ran this system, you wouldn't be able to get away with this kind of user behavior."

He picks up the flashlight. "But I guess now we know."

I don't know what to say to that.

"All right. This is good," Steve says from the other side of the room. "We finally caught a break. We can—"

From the dark end of the building where we haven't yet explored comes a series of thuds. A terrible, primal scream. I already know. Subject 1581 is inside with us.

VIVIAN ELLENSHAW

It takes us about twenty minutes to make it to what's left of the electric fencing.

Even after we heard the screams coming from the roof, we kept going. We left our snowshoes back at the factory, so there's a limit to how fast we can travel.

Fannon moves even slower than I do and slips and slides all over the place. I kind of wish Smentkowski had volunteered to come. He is good in the snow. I'm beginning to think that Fannon only came with me because he has a psychotic death wish or something.

What keeps me going is that we're Rachel's last chance. We can save her. Help her.

The way that I didn't help Allie.

And there is Steve.

Ugh. *Focus.*

I have to stop thinking about Miller's kissing and Allie's death and try to focus on what we're doing here. I can't atone for what happened, and there's no time for romance. I'm surviving to ensure that Allie's film gets seen and that Rachel gets to the hospital.

We have to reach the van.

I make myself keep walking through the tall trees that surround the camp.

I'm totally out of breath but trying to be as quiet as I can, taking in small, shallow gulps of air, desperate to be silent.

The way that Smentkowski described it made me think that

once we hit the trees we'd be safe and protected. Back on the roof that made sense to me. We'd be safe once we got out of the open. But it's completely dark in the forest. No doubt those things have chased away whatever wildlife should be out and about. We pass splotches of dark stains in the snow and a few blue gloves tossed here and there but no other people. We are alone out here. Except for those things.

It's quiet and still.

It feels even more dangerous than before.

We huddle near the trunk of a thick ponderosa pine.

Paul dropped the iron wheel right after we came down from the roof. I can't exactly blame him. Still. That leaves us with one gun.

We have one bullet left.

One.

My feet.

They're in my Wellingtons, and they're the only part of my body that isn't soaked through with wet snow.

Don't get me wrong. My toes are freezing. But they're dry.

And that's something.

Never. Never ever. Never been so cold.

Fannon slumps over against the tree. "What do we do now?"

"We . . . we go . . . straight," I say, trying to sound confident. At least as confident as someone with chattering teeth whispering in the complete darkness can sound. But I see his point. It's dark where we are. Like a closet. Or a serial killer's creepy basement. Clouds cover the moon once again, and even if they didn't we could barely see the sky through the thick trees. The beam from the flashlight extends no more than a few feet ahead.

There are no familiar landmarks. No easy way to navigate.

Still. We can't stand here and freeze to death.

"Come on," I tell him.

I'm a few paces from Fannon, who won't get a move on it. I turn my flashlight and point it right at his face, and I can see the warm breath leaving his mouth and his chest moving up and down. He's got the blankest expression on his face. He's just there. Waiting. Like he's stargazing. Or doing yin yoga. Or waiting for the rapture or something.

"Maybe we should go back," he says.

I know why he's saying this. I don't like being out here either. In the dark.

"We can't go back. We said we'd get the van. We have to do it. Fast. For Rachel," I add.

He nods and catches up so that we're walking side by side. Shining the flashlight in front of us, everything looks the same. Like we're passing the same scenery. Wide tree. Skinny tree. Tree with strange knobby features. Over and over on a loop.

We might be lost.

It's oppressively silent. My ears strain to hear something. Anything.

Every once in a while, the moon breaks through the snow clouds and we get a bit better view of the scenery. We're in a thick part of the forest. There are a series of wide dark blobs off in the distance on our right side. It's probably the trailers from the employees-only section of the camp. I bet we're about a mile or so north of our bungalow. A few streams of black smoke rise into the night sky, maybe from campfires that have burned out.

"You ever had any indication that your dad would do something like this?" I whisper to Fannon. It's an insensitive question, but I'm desperate to fill the silent space.

"Aside from the occasional fat-lady joke, no," he answers.

It's quiet again. Then Fannon adds, "I mean, my dad has always wanted to do something big. Groundbreaking. More than running the family company and making antibiotics that are slightly better than the ones we used to make. But he is always really big on ethics. It's hard for me to believe that he would . . . Anyway, he'd never talk to me about his plans."

"Why?" I ask.

"He thinks I'm a loser."

"At least he thinks about you." Those words escape my icy lips before I have much time to think about them. They give away more than I intend.

"Your dad ignores you?" Fannon asks, sounding genuinely interested.

"No," I say. "Ignoring someone is sort of deliberate, you know. It's something you do on purpose." I sigh. "My dad is a big corporate lawyer. Both he and my mom work all the time, but in my dad's case he also started sleeping with his paralegal." I pull my wet coat around me as tight as I can. It's a pointless gesture since the thing isn't doing a lot to keep me warm.

"I get that," Fannon says through chattering teeth.

"You do?"

"I caught Volstead in bed with my dad at our summer house."

"Oh. Ouch." This explains a lot though. Why he kept asking for Volstead. It was much more personal than a stupid kid who wanted to get out of being treated like a normal camper.

"Yeah."

We come to a part of the forest where the tree trunks are narrower and spaced a bit farther apart. At least it's a confirmation that we're not lost and that we're probably getting closer to the road.

"What about your dad and the paralegal?" Fannon asks.

Christine. Ugh. I try to sound casual. "They got married. She's a stay-at-home mom now. My dad has a new family."

"Ouch."

"Yeah," I say. But I smile almost in spite of myself. We're kind of kindred spirits.

Fannon sighs as well. "I guess people are complicated. A lot of layers."

My smile falls away. This reminds me of home. This is how Mom describes Coach. "My mom always says that too. That personalities are like onions and in order to get to know people you have to peel back the layers. To see what's underneath. But what do you get when you peel back the layers of an onion? More onion. It's not like the first layer is onion and the second is chocolate cake. What if people aren't that complicated? What if our parents have already shown us everything that we need to know about them?"

"And what's that?" Fannon asks.

"That they're selfish."

"What if we're selfish too?" he asks.

"I . . . I think we might be."

We're quiet again for a minute.

"I'm sorry about your friend," he says.

Allie. I'm sorry too. "Yeah. Thanks."

He sniffles. "It's thanks to her that I'm still alive. Thanks to you. And Smentkowski. I used to think fat people are . . . well, I pushed you in that chocolate fountain. You know what I thought. But now . . . Allie told me that you're a hero and she's right. If I live, I'm going to be different."

In spite of the cold, I feel my face heat up. I remember the camera in my pocket. I have to finish Allie's last movie. "We have to live."

I have to make sure that the world remembers her. That I remember her.

But we're in almost total darkness. Like a void exists beyond the beam of the flashlight.

It's not much of a shot.

My flashlight catches on the trunk of a ponderosa pine. Its bark has been roughly clawed off, and its lower branches droop down almost to the ground. Pine needles float in a shallow pool of blood. I jerk the light away and pray that I don't throw up again.

"Some night, huh?" Fannon says in a soft voice that sounds like the verbal equivalent of a shrug.

"What would you normally be doing?" I ask. I need something to focus on to avoid thinking about the fact that I'm basically a walking ice sculpture. And I'm curious how you spend the holidays when your family has been on the Who's Who list for four generations.

Fannon's teeth chatter. "Well. Normally my parents would probably be throwing some kind of holiday party. For all their friends. I guess. If you can call people that you sit with on boards or work with on charities your friends . . ." He trails off. "But we have a twelve-piece orchestra on the veranda. My mom hires this chef who makes the most delicious fruitcake."

I force myself to keep walking. "Fruitcake is supposed to be gross."

"This isn't. It tastes like Christmas."

I smile. "So fun, then?"

He doesn't answer right away. "There's the usual old men on their third martini asking for updates on your college applications, but otherwise it's fun. How about you?"

Step. Step. Another step. I sink a bit into the snow each time I move. "We used to have fun. BCE. In the Before Christine Era. This time of year, my dad would usually be coming home from some big trip. We'd pick him up at the airport, and he'd always have special presents. Then we'd make Mom's fancy cocoa. Maybe watch a movie."

"And now?" Fannon asks. He's out of breath. "In the CE?"

I'm tired too, but we have to keep moving. "I get a lecture from Coach on how cocoa has too many calories and too much sugar."

"Nice."

After a minute, Fannon says, "So you and Miller, huh?"

I almost giggle. In spite of myself. In spite of the fact that I'm on the verge of suggesting that we might be lost. I desperately want Steve to be The Jock with a Heart of Gold. I want a shot at a happy ending.

Then I see it.

The dark stains in the snow.

I put my arm up to stop Fannon from walking farther.

He opens his mouth to speak, but I shake my head and point at the spots on the ground.

Blood.

It's deep, black-red blood. Fresh. Wet. Recent.

I don't even dare to look at Four's face. I'll scream if I see that he's as terrified as I am.

Can you force your heart to beat?

From just beyond the end of our light, ice breaks and cracks.

Someone . . . or something . . . draws in a breath.

PAUL FANNON

"Something is out there."

Vivian whispers this. She stops, and I run into her out-stretched arm.

Of course *something* is out there.

We've been getting our asses kicked all night by all the somethings.

The somethings tore what was left of Allison DuMonde limb from limb.

But then.

The rustle of tree branches.

Snow crunching like potato chips.

The somethings have come for us.

Part of me wishes I had died back on the roof.

Or maybe had never been born at all.

I've seen a lot of action movies in my time, and I know what I'm supposed to do. I'm supposed to yell *Get behind me* or some-thing. Of course, I'm also supposed to be in charge, to have the gun and not generally be a jackass whose main skills are knowing how to comb my hair in a pompadour and being able to select the right loafers for any occasion.

So instead I yell, "What do we do?"

It's more of a scream. A shrill scream that, in another time, would embarrass me.

Vivian's got the flashlight tucked under her armpit and the gun up. She is the hero.

I scream again as something massive moves in front of us.

Blocking almost all our light.

There's no way Vivian will be able to take out the hulking thing.

With. One. Fucking. Bullet.

Well. At least I won't have to finish those college application essays.

Another scream leaves my lips.

And then another.

It's like I can't even die with some dignity.

"For God's sake. Stop screaming, boy. Do you want every last one of those animals to come for us?"

A voice.

A human voice.

A man's voice.

"Put that gun down, girl," the man's voice goes on.

Vivian lowers the weapon. "It's you."

"It's you," the man says.

She waves the flashlight beam in the voice's direction, revealing a tall, athletic Black man, probably in his early thirties.

"Is that your blood?" Vivian asks, pointing the light at the snow.

"No," the man answers. "It belongs to one of those . . . uh . . . well . . . I just saw it run toward camp."

I put my hands on my knees and try to catch my breath. "And . . . and . . . who . . . who . . ."

"It's Roger," she says. "He's, like, the head of . . . um . . ."

"I'm the director of camp athletic programs," Roger says.

"How are you still . . ." Vivian begins.

"Alive?" he finishes. "I'm either very lucky or very *unlucky*. I got thrown from the truck after it was hit by . . . by one of those monsters. Broke my arm. By the time I got back into the road, everyone was gone." He hesitates for a second and then forces himself to go on. "Did they make it back?"

"No." Vivian lets the flashlight slip down.

"Zanna?" he asks in a whisper.

"No."

For a second, it's only us and the sound of falling snow.

"What are you doing out here?" Vivian asks.

I notice for the first time that Roger has a shotgun like Vivian's.

"Trying to survive," he says. "Who's left?"

This time, it's Vivian who hesitates. "Us. And three of our friends up on the roof of the manufacturing facility." She jerks her head around, like she suspects that one of those zombies will burst out of the woods at any second. "One of them is pregnant and about to have a baby any second. We have to keep moving."

Roger doesn't budge. "Manufacturing facility? What manufacturing facility? And someone's pregnant?"

Vivian starts walking again. "We have to go. You should know better than anyone that we can't just stand here waiting for those zombies to come and eat us."

Roger steps in front of her, coming more into the light. "What are you talking about?" He's got his left arm in a sling made from a camp T-shirt. "Wait. Wait. You're telling me that out of more than three hundred campers and one hundred employees, there are only five of you left? Those animals killed everyone?"

I clear my throat. "Well. We think . . . we think everyone

either became zombies or got eaten by zombies."

"Come on," Vivian says, waving her arm in frustration.

"Zombies?"

Vivian sighs. "You know those weight-loss bars that they were handing out? They're making them in that big red building on the north side of camp. We think they give people a virus. It changes them into those . . . *things*." She finishes with a shudder.

Roger stays put in front of Vivian. "That's impossible. I've seen those *things*. What they can do. They're . . . inhuman."

"Believe what you want," Vivian tells him. "But we saw someone change . . . my friend . . . she became a zombie. Right in front of us."

"Rachel, the pregnant girl, is some kind of science geek. She can explain it to you later," I add. Vivian is right. We have to get a move on it. Even I can see that standing around here isn't a good idea.

"Are the phones still out?" Roger asks.

"Yeah," Vivian says. "Before we left camp, Steve . . . uh . . . our Facilitator said the phones were out. Then the main power went down."

Roger steps aside to let her pass. "Where are you going?"

She's a few paces ahead of him when she answers. "We left our van outside of the main camp gate. We're hoping that we can find it and make it to town." She stops for a second. "I bet you have a better idea how to get there than we do."

Roger moves past her into the lead. "Oh, I do. I know all the shortcuts." He digs around in his pocket. "And *I* have a compass. Follow me."

Vivian takes up a position behind him, shining the flashlight in his path. "I'm Vee, by the way. And this is Paul."

Roger's movements are smooth and efficient. He even has a broken arm and he moves faster than me. Like Smentkowski. Roger is used to the snow. "I'd say it's a pleasure. But honestly, I'd much rather be at home in my hot tub right about now."

I'm grateful that Vivian doesn't explain who I am or mention my father.

Roger leads us onto a small path to our left. "How many shells you got left?"

"One," Vivian says. "You?"

"Two," he says.

Well. Three bullets are better than one.

We start moving at a pretty fast clip, with Roger checking his compass every once in a while. I'm feeling much better. We have an adult with us, and he seems to know both where he's going and what he's doing.

The snow is still falling. But more lightly than before, and the canopy of trees provides enough cover to keep us dry. Occasionally, Vivian's flashlight bounces upward and I get a glimpse of the white dots dusting the top tree branches like powdered sugar.

It's quiet, and it's almost more like we're on a midnight hike.

Not a desperate fight for survival.

The surge of adrenaline that I got from running into Roger is ending.

The steps are wearing me out.

We keep walking.

Vivian says what I'm thinking. "Is it much farther to the gate?"

She's having an easier time keeping up with Roger, but I have to hustle to catch up to be able to hear his response.

"We're a couple of minutes away," he says.

It's dark on either side of us, and I don't see anything that even vaguely resembles a gate.

"It's best if we stay out of the road until we get to the edge of camp."

I nod to myself. But I wonder. How does he know? I mean, it's not like a zombie attack is the kind of thing you spend your time preparing for.

For all we know, the zombies are scared of the road.

Still, I *have* to believe that this guy knows where he's going.

We keep walking for a few more minutes.

Roger stops us at the edge of the tree line.

Vivian points her flashlight into the open space.

It's the camp's main gate we saw yesterday.

Well. Sort of.

The huge metal gate has been torn apart and tossed with an almost casual air into the middle of the road, leaving a gaping hole of darkness.

"Wait!" Roger whispers.

But he doesn't know Vivian.

She never waits.

Vivian marches into the road with deliberation.

Like a cop walking a beat.

She's got the only flashlight—which leaves little choice except for Roger and me to follow her—and is shining it all over the place.

Murmuring to herself.

"Those things . . . they ripped this gate apart. The metal . . . the masonry . . ."

I can see what she means. The flashlight beam travels over pieces of discarded iron, pulverized river rock pillars, planks of wood, and . . . oh God.

An arm.

Shit.

There's an entire goddamn arm lying right in the middle of the road.

Vivian quickly moves the light away. "I think it's the guard."

The guard from yesterday.

Yesterday.

Or if it's after midnight then maybe it was the day before yesterday.

I can barely remember.

And yet she has to be right.

The arm is still partially tucked into one of the official blue camp jackets.

This is the arm that waved us into camp.

Oh God . . . I'm going to . . .

The only thing that keeps me from vomiting whatever might be left in my stomach or from screaming like a little girl again is this pronouncement from Roger.

"Being out in the open like this isn't a good idea," he says.

Vivian doesn't listen.

She's formed her own *Law & Order: Zombie Victims Unit* and is hell-bent on finding out exactly what happened to the guard.

We catch up to her when she's a couple of feet from the beat-up shack. She's got a small silver camera out and is moving it slowly over the devastated scene in front of us. I don't know how she managed to get that camera into camp or why she thinks filming is a great use of time when we really should be getting our asses to the van as fast as humanly possible.

She freezes as she points the camera at the guard shack.

"Don't go in there," Roger says.

In there is pretty much an impossibility since two of the shack's walls have been torn apart.

Anyway, Vivian finally does stop walking.

I'm not sure what gets to her.

The blood spilling onto the snow.

Or the fact that we find another finger.

It's pointing up at us. Sticking out of the snow.

It's pointing at me. The bloody finger of blame.

"What a horrible way to go," Vivian says softly with a sniffle.

I'm sure she's thinking about Allie. I fall onto my knees. Onto the wet, hard ice.

There's nothing in my stomach to throw up, so I dry-heave.

And it's loud.

Too loud.

This combination of coughing and retching that echoes all over.

And it's petty, but I'm thinking about the way that the stomach acid tastes in my mouth. Like corroded metal. And wondering if or how I'll ever get back to normal.

"Shh! Four! Shut up," Vivian says.

Roger takes a few steps in my direction. "Let's get through the gate and into the tree cover on the other side," he adds in a tense whisper.

I cough again, and Vivian has her shotgun up, and I know.

I know.

They're coming.

There's another one of those screams.

A sharp, horrible sound that could pierce your heart.

"Run!" Roger shouts.

He points toward the gate and into the darkness. Vivian turns that way for a second but then runs a few paces in my direction, sliding to a stop right in front of me.

The two of them tug on the ribbing of my sweatshirt, trying to pull me up off the snow. "Come on! Come on! We have to run," Vivian says.

I shrug out of Roger's grip, landing on all fours on the snow. I don't want to run. This is my fate, and I accept it. "You go. I'll hold them here." It sounds ridiculous. I'm obviously no match for one of those zombies. I'm not holding them anywhere.

"Go. Go without me." I retch again.

"Get the hell up off the ground, son," Roger whispers through clenched teeth.

But I deserve this.

I deserve to die.

One of those things is ahead of us in the road. I can't see it, but I know it's out there.

I look up at Vivian. "You know who my father is. What he did."

Another screech.

"Go," I say.

Vivian flings herself down in the snow next to me. "You have to listen to me. I was wrong. What Rachel said. She was right. We're not our parents. You're not responsible for what your father did here." She almost punches me in the heart. "You said you want to be different. You are the choices that you make. You have to get up. For Rachel. Or for me. I can't . . . I can't lose anyone else. You have to get up. Now."

Roger is fiddling around his gun, probably trying to figure out how to get a shot off even though he has a broken arm.

Maybe that's what does it.

They need me.

My friends need me.

Vivian puts out her hand.

And I reach out and take it.

The instant we're both on our feet, I'm knocked right back down again.

One of those things runs by us so fast that it actually creates a breeze.

Roger is down too. Right next to me. Kind of moaning.

He can't possibly still have the rifle.

The only sound is my own huffing and the scratching of the creature's feet on the ice, just out of sight, just beyond reach of Vivian's flashlight. She swings the light around, landing on the shiny, disco-ball skin of the monster. It almost sparkles blue and green as it crouches over Roger.

I scream again.

That thing.

It's like two feet from my fucking face and frenzied with a horrible hunger.

As I brace myself and get ready to be eaten, Vivian tucks the light under her armpit and gets a shot off.

Her last bullet.

Except it works.

Sort of.

It works in the sense that Roger is able to get out from under that thing, and I can see his silhouette scramble toward the other side of the path. I can no longer hear the monster's shuffling right in my ear.

Vivian has the flashlight again, and the beam of light darts all over as she searches for what became of the thing.

The light freezes as she finds it.

It's a few paces in front of her, snarling as the light hits its face.

The monster.

It swats at the red blood gushing from a large wound in its shoulder.

But the thing appears otherwise unfazed.

And it's on the move.

Vivian has the shotgun in one hand and the flashlight in the other.

She digs her feet into the snow.

I scream one last time as the zombie charges in her direction.

SHELDON SMENTKOWSKI

We have found the anomaly. Subject 1581.

Rachel, Miller, and I stare at the zombie through the glass.

The thing seems every bit as surprised to see us as we are to see it.

We're on the other side of the long room, away from the window we came through. We each have a flashlight now and are shining them into the monster's . . . well . . . cage. It's basically like a glass box surrounded by carts and workstations and small desks. Like people were constantly milling around over here.

Watching the creature.

Well, they figured out how to contain those things.

Score one for the good guys.

If you can call anyone working for FannonPharma a good guy.

It's an odd environment. Like someone built a zoo for people. On one side, there's a narrow slot with a handle. Probably how they feed the creature. Inside, there's a low stainless steel toilet, a cot with a small pillow, and . . . a stack of books.

That kind of punches me in the gut.

The thing is reading in its spare time.

It appears to like fantasy novels.

"That's one of my favorite books," Rachel says, pointing at a book with a purple cover.

Miller runs his fingers over the clear surface. "Shit. You guys. I think this is transparent steel. I saw some when my dad took me to an animal expo last year. It's bulletproof. Virtually indestructible. They were promoting it to use in containing large animals."

"What do you have on a farm that would need a cage like this?" I ask.

"Bulls, maybe. But the company was advertising it for zoos."

"Right," I say.

This *is* a zoo for people.

Or things that used to be people.

Rachel is clutching her belly again, but this whole thing has her distracted. She's walking around the cage. I follow behind her.

Miller is staring at the monster.

I can sort of see what the file on the computer was talking about. There's something way more human about Subject 1581. It does certain things. It tilts its head. Holds its hands the way a person would.

But when it walks.

It still moves like the other zombies. Quick. Smooth.

Unnatural.

It is also staring at us.

With eyes that never blink.

Rachel spots a stack of file folders, and because, of course, this is the perfect time to do more research, she picks them up and begins reading.

For a while, the monster is pretty interested in Miller. Which makes sense. If the zombie is smart, like the file says, it makes sense to pay attention to the guy with all the guns.

But as we stand around a little while longer, the creature shifts its focus to Rachel.

Maybe the two of them can start a book club.

With her flashlight tucked under her arm, Rachel has a file folder in one hand and presses the other up against the glass.

"His name is Brian. Brian Quimby," she says quietly.

She flips through more papers and then holds up a missing-person flyer. "Whoa. I remember this kid! He's from Flagstaff too. After he went missing, my youth group hung a bunch of these posters up all over town. I remember seeing his mother. She was . . ." Rachel hesitates and finishes with a breathless "devastated." She clears her throat. "The file says that he was at camp a few months ago as part of some kind of scholarship. Or grant." She flips a couple more sheets of paper. "His parents believe he ran away."

"I guess that explains what his family thinks happened," I say. Truthfully, this is one of the things that has been bothering me since we found the notes on Subject 1581. If FannonPharma made over fifteen hundred people disappear, where does the world think they are?

But also.

"They might be able to make a few people vanish here and there," I say slowly. "But you can't just kill off an entire camp full of kids and expect nobody to notice."

"The blizzard," Miller says.

Rachel stops reading. "You think they predicted the storm?"

Miller continues to stare at the zombie. "You can't really predict the weather. But this is Silverstone we're talking about. If you believe the internet, they ran a death squad for the CIA. They shot fifty civilians in broad daylight in Baghdad. This is a remote area. Hard to access. So they could pretty much do what they want. My guess would be that they had some kind of a plan, but the blizzard is saving them the trouble of coming up with a cover story."

A jolt runs through me as I realize that he might be right. I'd set up alerts on my laptop and phone to monitor the weather and gotten a ton of notifications about snow. Which I'd disregarded. Because I'm from Minnesota, where I regularly have to dig my car out of the ice with a shovel.

But what he's saying makes sense. "That's why they're suppressing all the comm. They don't want anyone to be able to send out messages that would show what's really happening."

Rachel closes one of the file folders. "But how does that help them? What does it accomplish?"

Miller pauses for a second. "When we came in, there were a bunch of rangers trying to wrangle one of those things down by the lake. They had these Silverstone logos on their jackets. I didn't understand it at the time . . . but now . . . I think they were ordered to wait there. To wait for kids to change into those monsters and then round them all up."

"They're not monsters," Rachel says. "They're people."

Miller's head jerks in her direction. The two of them watch each other through the glass box of the creature's cage. "They *were* people, Rachel. Now they're . . ."

"Something new," she finishes.

I shiver.

But I try to focus on what's happening right in front of us. I almost drop my flashlight. "They have more money than God. It would be no problem for them to fund an operation like this. If Silverstone has a team out there, where are they?"

"Maybe hanging back until things settle down?" Rachel suggests.

"Or dead," Miller adds in a dull voice. "I mean, you saw what those things did to Zanna's caravan. Maybe these monsters are more dangerous than even Silverstone can handle."

I glance at Rachel through the glass box. "You need to sit down again."

Her mouth is pressed in a tight line, and it's pretty obvious that she's having another round of contractions. She stands near the far corner of the cage. "I'm fine," she says through clenched teeth.

"Smentkowski is right," Miller says. "You need to stay still. And calm."

Rachel glares at him. "I am calm." She leaves the side of the cage, walks over to one of the low desks, and rifles through it. Opening the drawers. Like she's looking for something.

Miller leaves the side of the cage too. The zombie turns away from me, pacing around the cage and mirroring the jock's movements.

"It's only been about fifteen minutes since your last round of contractions. I really hope Vivian and Paul show up with the van soon." Miller's out of sight now and on the darker side of the room. His flashlight beam bounces all over the ceiling.

Wheels scrape the concrete floor, and I realize he's gone back for one of the office chairs. I shine my flashlight into the cage again. The zombie has a patch of reddish scales on its back. Kind of like freckles. Kind of like.

A person.

For a second, I also realize how quiet it is in here. Either the FannonPharma people did a great job with the soundproofing in this area—which is possible, given all the reinforced steel—or those monsters are no longer rolling around the first floor of the building, smashing the manufacturing equipment all to hell.

Maybe it's wishful thinking, but I really hope it's the latter scenario.

I've gotten wrapped up in these thoughts and have lost sight of Rachel.

She comes back to the cage with a sense of purpose.

She has something silver in her hand, and it glints in the light of my flashlight.

Too late, I realize what she's doing.

Miller's a few feet behind her.

Pushing the chair along.

The two tranquilizer guns rest in the seat.

"Rachel," I choke out. "No. You can't . . ."

A series of thick locks are attached to the corner of the cage.

Like the kind they use in high-security prisons.

It's the door.

And Rachel has the key.

She inserts the key into the first lock.

And turns it.

Rachel Benedict is going to open the fucking door.

And let that thing loose.

RACHEL BENEDICT

Brian Quimby lives less than half a mile from me.

I hung pictures of his face on the bulletin board at the White Dove coffee shop.

My dad held a candlelight vigil at the church. His mother showed up with three boxes of tissues. She couldn't stop crying.

The team at FannonPharma did a whole workup on him before the experiment. In many ways, he's the perfect subject. Smart but not confrontational. Nice but not known to be a pushover. Somehow, they got ahold of his student files. He won two character awards at his high school. One for integrity for turning in a cheating student and another for compassion for helping a kid being targeted by bullies.

I guess you could call him fat, but the notes indicate that he's in good shape. Or was in good shape. I mean, if you want to be super technical about it, maybe now he's in better shape. Sort of. According to the file, Zombie Brian can run at cheetah speed if he gets out in the open and can jog for close to two hours without needing a break.

But before . . . he used to hike and play baseball and volunteer at an old folks' home.

It's also clear from Brian's file why this program requires fat people. Whatever they're using to trigger the genetic mutations eats through fatty tissue at an alarming rate. There are long tables recording Brian's body weight in the days following the transformation. Sometimes he loses as much as ten pounds in an hour.

It stabilizes after time.

But a thin person probably wouldn't survive.

His family has a trailer behind Black Bart's, the steakhouse where my dad likes to eat on his birthday. They get students from NAU to come sing Disney tunes while you eat.

They always overcook my steak.

Brian's file also records several escape attempts.

FannonPharma had to keep building better and better cages to keep him in.

On the opposite side of the transparent cell, Sheldon pounds his fists on the glass.

He knows what I'm doing.

Matthew 10:28.

And do not fear those who kill the body but cannot kill the soul. Rather fear Him who can destroy both soul and body in hell.

My dad uses that verse in his sermons a lot. Usually when he wants to talk about how some book or movie is going to rot away your brain.

But right then, I understand what it really means.

The first lock clicks open.

We are being tested.

Sure, these zombies can kill us. Kill our bodies. But if we go along with what FannonPharma is trying to do here, we'll jeopardize our souls.

We have to let Brian Quimby go.

I open the second lock.

Steve is off somewhere in the dark corner of the room.

His flashlight bounces all around, kind of like a searchlight.

The baby gives my belly a swift kick, but it's more like an encouraging push.

We have to do this.

If we don't do this, we're no better than they are.

"Rachel. No!" Sheldon says.

If we don't do this, we're not human.

We all want to go home.

Steve is back and is a few feet from me, pushing one of the office chairs. He shouts something, but I don't listen. I can't listen. I twist the key in the final lock. Holding my breath, I tug the glass door open a couple of inches.

Brian Quimby screams.

The sound echoes off the walls of the cage and into our steel room.

VIVIAN ELLENSHAW

This is it.

The end.

I'm expecting my whole life to flash before my eyes.

The way it always happens in the movies Allie loves to watch.

Loved to watch.

Instead.

What happens is a single memory hits me.

It's more of an image, actually.

Of Allie's face.

We were twelve and in a yellow raft on Gauley River, and I'm pretty sure the expedition we were on wasn't for beginners. But when your parents have unlimited money and you say you want to go white water river rafting, they sign you up for the best. And best means most expensive—not the best for you personally.

So there we were, and Allie was pointing and we were laughing and annoying the absolute hell out of the guide, who kept telling me over and over that I wasn't holding my oar correctly.

I never listen.

When we hit a big break, the water knocked my oar out of my grip. Right smack into the face of the guide sitting behind me.

There was complete mayhem in the raft. The guy was bleeding, and some people were rowing and some weren't, and there was yelling, and we were sort of spinning around and around.

The raft capsized.

I went down.

Down below the surface of the greenish, murky water.

I was cold then too.

Just like now.

I thought I might vanish. The water pushing me farther and farther and farther down until I disappeared into the mud.

Somehow, I found Allie's hand.

She pulled me up.

I came above the surface of the white rapids. Almost like I was born again.

The first thing I saw as I emerged was her face.

She had several strands of her long hair running down her cheeks.

But that look. Her eyes were so wide and round and full of shock and terror.

Like the thing that you love the most might be gone.

And the thing she loved the most was me.

I saw her face. *That face.* That's what I saw as the monster turned to charge me.

How could I have wasted the last six months being so pissed? How could I have let Allie die? How can I get her back?

I'm in the narrow road only a few feet away from the nightmare of the guard shack and the gate that's been torn open. I'm actually relieved that it's so dark in the clearing. My heart already feels like it's about to explode. Without the sight of blood and mangled body parts. I dig my heels into the snow, trying to find firm ground.

I could let that thing get me and end it.

But if we don't manage to find the van, things will only get worse.

I make a decision. If I'm going out, I'm going out swinging.

Bracing myself, I grip the empty gun and get ready. Without bullets, it's not going to be much of a weapon against the monster. But it's all I've got.

The zombie is inches from my face. So close that I can hear it breathe. So close that I can smell its warm, fishy breath.

Using the gun like a baseball bat, I'm about to take my first swing at the creature when Fannon scrambles up off the snow. He charges the monster, grabbing it by the waist and sending it sprawling and sliding along the slick ground.

The zombie is wounded, and the two of us together might have a chance.

And Fannon. Whoever he is, whatever he is, he does have courage.

If Allie were here, maybe she'd recast him as The Courageous Captain.

Fannon dives out of the beam of my flashlight. Tackling the thing. Like he's going to beat the monster in a fistfight. Like a bar brawl.

We might be able to beat the thing.

We could win.

The zombie snarls and screeches.

Fannon must be punching the monster or something, but I don't have time to aim the light and really figure out what's happening. I find I've gotten used to the squishy sound that the zombie's firm yet fluid body makes when you hit it.

This scares the hell out of me.

Fannon screams.

I run toward him, nearly tripping over pieces of splintered

wood and a broken-off tree branch and almost falling into the bloodstained snow. Fannon and I have to take that monster down and get the hell out of this clearing and back into the relative safety of the trees.

There's a sickening rip of flesh.

The flashlight is tucked under my arm, and the light bounces up and down as I travel away from the shack and toward Fannon. I catch a glimpse of him on top of the zombie. There's a flurry of activity that's hard to process. The creature shrieks again.

I skid to a stop in front of Fannon. The flashlight falls to the ground when I take my first whack at the monster with the barrel of the shotgun. I get a few hits in before it manages to buck Fannon off its chest.

He crawls through the beam of light created by the flashlight lying in the snow. He's moaning and trailing dark blood. More blood dripping onto the snow.

I fight off the urge to scream.

Focus. Focus. Focus.

The monster is still down. Whatever Fannon did was enough to temporarily immobilize it. I take swing after swing, doing my best to aim for the shoulder where I know it's wounded, but I have limited success. The monster manages to dodge several of my attacks.

Fannon coughs and moans again.

The zombie scurries up, punching me in the chest as it rises.

I fall onto my back and glance up, staring up into the abyss of the dark, cloudy night. I can barely make out the pointed tops of a few pine trees at the edge of my vision.

I struggle to take even a small breath.

And it doesn't matter anyway.

The *thing* is coming.

And I can't breathe.

As I choke out a small breath, I hear footsteps moving fast behind me.

I know it's not Fannon.

It's probably another one of those things.

A dark blur hovers over me, and I'm seconds away from being torn apart.

Maybe it won't take long.

I fumble around in my pocket and get out the camera. One of its big selling points was that it has a special night vision mode. Allie was always talking about the money shot, and an inhuman monster bobbing around in front of my face *has* to be it.

Turning on the camera, I point the lens up toward the zombie.

Then.

Bang.

And.

Bang.

Two shots.

It must be Roger.

The relief fills me with warm adrenaline. Like a cup of hot cocoa.

Above me, the monster chokes and gurgles and wheezes.

Fannon is shouting something, and I realize.

I have to move.

Now.

The zombie is coming down.

It's going to collapse right on top of me.

Tucking the camera back into my pocket, I roll over a couple of times and push myself up onto all fours. Dirty ice sticks to my nose and forehead. The instant I move, the creature comes to a crash where I was lying only seconds before.

I crawl over to my flashlight and wave it first at the thing. I quickly move the light away. The monster is missing half its head, and blood is running everywhere, forming a series of rivers that flow into the night. New splotches of gray flesh dot the snow here and there.

The zombie twitches a couple of times.

And then is still.

I shine the flashlight all over the place, looking for Fannon. He's a few feet away from me, collapsed on the ground, clutching his arm and grunting in agony.

Oh holy hell.

What if that thing ripped his arm off?

I make myself crawl over there and not into the bushes to hide or throw up.

Okay, Fannon still has his arm, but that's not saying much. Blood has already soaked through his jacket sleeve and is dripping onto the snow.

"Shit. Shit. Four! Did that thing bite you?"

Don't die.

"I don't know . . ." he pants. "I mean, I guess . . . It was kind of gnashing its teeth at me . . ."

Don't die.

Okay. Do I remember any part of that one first aid class that I took that summer I wanted to form my own babysitter's club?

Um.

Well.

Let's see.

There was this.

Wash your hands thoroughly to avoid contamination.

Nope. Not helping.

Thank God that Roger emerges from the trees that surround the road. "You kids are gonna be the death of me."

As he's used his last bullets shooting the monster attacking us instead of running off to save himself, he's probably right. He tosses the now empty gun on the ground alongside me.

Roger kneels next to me and grunts as he has to straighten his injured arm to shrug out of his jacket. He removes the long-sleeve camp sweatshirt and puts his jacket back on. "Hold that light steady, girl," he says. It's actually more of an annoyed growl.

I help Fannon take his jacket off too, leaving my friend in the freezing cold in nothing but the medical scrubs from the FannonPharma plant.

"It's not too bad," Roger says.

Pointing my flashlight at Fannon's arm, I grimace. To me, it looks bad. Like we might need to stop and figure out how to amputate it.

"That thing tried to eat your arm off, eh, son? Well, we can stop the bleeding for now. And it's cold, so that helps matters a bit," Roger says as he presses his sweatshirt onto Fannon's bloody arm.

Fannon starts to scream, but Roger shushes him. "There's more of those things out there."

Roger jerks his chin at me. "Keep the pressure on the wound and keep him quiet."

I do what Roger says and grab Fannon's hand. "Four. Listen. It's going to be okay. Squeeze my hand if it hurts." This is always what my dad would do when I had to go to the doctor, and the technique always seemed to work.

Fannon gives my fingers a light squeeze.

Roger picks up a handful of snow and rubs it with his palms until the ice is kind of watery. "Okay," he says, and takes the sweatshirt from me. Fannon's blood covers the Featherlite crest.

I watch as Roger pours the water from his palm onto Fannon's bloody arm. I don't know why I watch. I mean, it's gross as hell and I've already seen enough disgusting stuff tonight to last me a lifetime.

But I guess I have to know.

How bad it is.

Some of the blood washes away, revealing a series of deep, jagged gouges. Like someone pressed their fingers into Fannon's arm and kept pressing and pressing.

Someone with superhuman strength.

It does look bad.

But also like he'll live.

But also. Now we have another person in desperate need of a doctor.

We *have* to get to the van.

While Roger tears the ribbing off the camp sweatshirt and ties it very, very tightly around the wound, Fannon squeezes my hand hard. Roger uses the rest of the sweatshirt to make a basic sling. We help Fannon to his feet and slide his arm into the sling.

Fannon almost immediately falls down, but Roger catches him.

"Listen to me. Both of you," Roger says through clenched

teeth. He jabs his finger at Fannon. "*You* need to pull yourself to-gether. The longer we're out here, the more we increase our odds of getting our asses kicked by those . . . zombies . . . or whatever the hell you want to call them. We've got to move quick." He turns to me. "*You.* Young lady, you need to listen. If I say stop, you stop. If I say run, you—"

"Run. I got it," I say.

Roger cocks his head. Almost like he's thinking about leaving us here. "If you take off again, you're on your own. Understand?"

"Yes."

He wraps his arm around Fannon, and the two of them scurry fast toward the open gate. I hustle to follow along. The instant we're on the other side, Roger guides us off of the wide trail and back into the cover of the thick forest. It's somehow colder under the tree canopy, and I struggle to keep up with the break-neck pace. After a few minutes, I'm out of breath.

But it's working. We haven't attracted any more of those things.

And.

The van.

The van!

The van! The van! The van!

The beam of my flashlight lands on a bit of the chrome bumper sticking out of the snow. I can't help it. I'm almost grinning.

We. Found. The. Fucking. Van.

In a few minutes, we might be warm and on the road. We can find Miller. Get Rachel and Fannon to the hospital. Tell the world what is happening here. Tell them about Allie. This will become a nightmare that I can wake up from.

Roger slows down as we get closer to the van. "We need to be cautious."

I don't totally agree with him. Those zombies might be tough, but they're also stupid. I saw one jump out a glass window rather than open a door. And they kept charging at us even when we had guns. But. They clearly figured out how to get over the camp's fencing and through the gate. Maybe they're getting smarter. Or stronger. No, I can't let myself think about stuff like that. Anyway, I seriously doubt that they have some secret plan to sneak up on us as we try to get in the van.

Our brains are the one advantage we have.

But I said we'd follow Roger's orders, so we stop.

He transfers Fannon to me and leaves us behind a large, knobby tree as he takes off to inspect the van.

"You okay?" I ask him.

Fannon coughs. "I'll survive."

He doesn't sound so sure.

After a couple of minutes, Roger calls out, "It looks okay."

As we approach, Roger says, "We need to dig out the tires, otherwise it'll be a real short trip."

I lean Fannon up against the van. "You should rest."

"I'll help," he says. He falls in front of the passenger-side front tire and insists on scooping snow away with his uninjured arm.

Since Fannon and Roger seem to have the front under control, I head to the back. The passenger-side rear tire is right up against a tree trunk, so there's not much I can do there. My hand glides along the rear bumper as I move to the driver's side. Sticking the flashlight into the snow, I pull the sleeves of my wet jacket over my fingers and pick up mounds of ice, tossing them a couple of feet from the tire.

On the opposite side of the van, something rustles.

Maybe a tree branch. Or some leaves.

I freeze.

I can see Roger's form up at the front of the van. "Did you hear that?" I ask.

"What?" He stops working.

"There's something out there."

"You keep saying that," Fannon grouses.

"Those things keep coming for us," I say with a shiver.

"Okay," Roger says. He's already opening the driver's side door. The dome light pops on. That's a good sign. The van's battery is working, at least. "That'll have to be good enough. Let's get inside. You said the keys are still in this thing?"

I get up and go to help Fannon on the passenger side. "Miller left them in the ignition."

I help Fannon up off the ground, and we hobble over to the sliding door. It's seems like another lifetime ago that we were all in the back seat of the van and our biggest problem was that we had to walk to camp and carry our own bags.

Fannon puts his hand on the side of the van to brace himself.

I slide the door open.

Twelve inches from my face.

In the seat that Fannon used on the drive to camp.

A monster sits there.

Like it's waiting for a ride.

I scream.

STEVE MILLER

Time keeps on *slipping into the future.*

I hate to admit it, but yeah, my parents really did name me after that old singer Steve Miller. Most people my age don't even know who he is, and those who do all smoke a lot of weed. "Fly like an Eagle" was my dad's favorite song when he met my mom. But seriously, what the hell does it even mean?

And how much does it suck that I'm not even gonna live long enough to figure it out?

Oh well.

"Rock'n Me" was always more my vibe anyway.

Of course Rachel is gonna let that thing out of its cage.

I should have seen that coming.

City people are always sentimental about animals. They've seen a lot of cartoons with talking rats or cows that fall in love. But rats bite people all the time. Cows often try to kick farmers in the face. Believe me, a chicken would eat you if it could.

City people pay no attention to the reality of dealing with animals.

And, like it or not, that *thing* in the cage is an animal.

Plus, Rachel's whole life is kind of like a cage that she wants to be released from.

So here we are. She's gonna let the thing out of the cage.

And I have to let her, because my two choices are to either allow her to open the damn door or knock over a pregnant girl in labor so I can keep it shut.

I have four sisters.

Rachel pulls the glass door open a few inches.

She's got this look on her face. Her eyes are wide. Her mouth is kind of hanging open. It's almost an expression of awe. Like a kid opening up an unexpected present on Christmas morning. Like someone unraveling the mysteries of the universe.

Someone wonderstruck.

The monster screams its head off.

Smentkowski pounds on the glass and mumbles something that I can't make out.

Everything is going in slow motion.

Like every moment for all of eternity will be filled with the smooth, swinging motion of that transparent steel door. Silently creeping open.

That monster will always be screaming, sucking all the oxygen from my lungs.

I take in a deep breath.

Things start moving fast again.

And again, I have a split second to make a decision.

Get Rachel away from that cage.

Or grab the tranquilizer gun off the chair, hope I can get a shot off, and hope the darts are effective in bringing that monster down. Which is a big if. The flashlight isn't enough light for the whole room, and there are huge pockets of darkness where the zombie can hide.

Anyway, I have four sisters.

So I have to help Rachel.

I swipe the guns off the chair and tuck them under my arm. Moving as fast as I can, I push the chair right behind Rachel, forcing her to sit in it. Smentkowski is coming in our direction, the beam of his flashlight swinging all around. This seems pretty stupid to me. He's safer where he is. The monster can't attack on all sides at once.

He probably wants to help Rachel too.

Drawing in a deep breath and trying to stay as calm as I can, I wheel Rachel behind one of the short walls of the cubicles and give her a swift push over toward the corner.

I've got this feeling. Like the time Dad accidentally almost ran me over with the tractor. It was right before first light and he couldn't see me out there, trying to get Meagan's goat out of the fields. That feeling. The kind of feeling where something is bearing down on you. It stays with you.

The feeling of imminent doom.

I shout, "Get ready," at Smentkowski, who is only now joining me behind the low cubicle wall. Tossing him the second tranq gun, I lumber up onto the empty white desk, placing the barrel of the gun on the metal bar that lines the top of the cubicle wall.

I brace myself.

I'm ready.

Except.

Nothing happens.

The monster remains in the glass cage. Kind of poking at the door. Like it's shocked that the thing is really open. The monster isn't screaming anymore. It's standing there.

Confused.

Smentkowski is doing his best to handle the gun, and I'm up on my knees on the desk, yelling my head off. For a second it seems a little ridiculous. We're breathing heavy, and I'm shouting and clutching the gun.

Rachel is up out of the chair. "Steve. Relax. Brian isn't going to hurt us."

Brian.

She is calling that thing by its name.

Rachel moves to go around me and out of the row of cubicles. I try to block her, but she does this thing where she clutches her belly and makes a kind of pained expression.

I let her pass.

She walks toward the cage. Very slowly. The way I might approach a skittish dog. With her hands slightly up in the air. Cautious. Step by step. The back of her hair swings. Side to side.

"Hi, Brian," she says. "You can come out now."

Rachel puts her hand on the handle of the clear door.

The creature—Brian—jerks at the sound of her voice and then pushes the door open the rest of the way.

Fast. In a blur.

Rachel has to jump back to avoid getting hit by the door. She's a few paces from the monster. In front of me. Blocking my shot.

The thing kind of snarls at her.

I've got my finger on the trigger of the gun.

"Get back, Rachel," I say through clenched teeth.

She ignores me and takes a soft step toward the zombie. "Brian. Listen to me. We're from the camp. We're campers. Like you were. Or . . . um . . . are. And . . . there's a blizzard. The FannonPharma people mostly deserted camp. Dr. Kaiser—"

The creature snarls again at the mention of Kaiser's name.

Rachel continues talking to the zombie in a calm voice. "And some others . . . well . . . probably everyone else except us and a couple of our friends are dead."

The zombie stands in the doorway of the clear cage.

With its head cocked to one side.

Listening.

"You have to get out of here," she tells the zombie.

"Rachel. What are you saying?" I ask her. We can't even get *ourselves* out of here, but she's worried about what will happen to the creature? I picture Vivian. I'm hoping she's out there with that determined look on her face. That she and Paul found the van.

That they're on the way.

Brian sniffs the air. And before I can even register what's happening, he's almost on top of me. Bluish, scaly flesh fills my line of sight. The zombie swats at the tranquilizer gun, knocking it out of my hand with ease and sending it bouncing along the thin blue carpet. It lands a few feet from my reach.

I would scream except that the fall has totally knocked the wind out of me.

"Smentkowski! A little . . . help . . . here," I pant.

"No. Sheldon. No," Rachel says.

Out of the corner of my eye, I wait for Smentkowski to do something. Instead, he hesitates, an expression of uncertainty on his face.

Rachel waddles as fast as she can over to me. As she gets closer, the creature stands up and moves over to make way for her. "Steve, I think he's just hungry."

As I scramble to my feet, she digs around in the backpack that I'd forgotten I put on. She pulls out a couple of the peanut butter bars we took from the supply cabinets. "According to the chart, someone was supposed to come this morning with a food delivery," she says. "But they probably didn't because . . ."

"Because FannonPharma was extra busy making way more Brians," I finish.

She holds the bars out for Zombie Brian to take.

He actually zips back a few feet. Like the bars terrify him.

"It's okay," Rachel says. "They're regular energy bars. We've been eating them." She opens one and takes a small bite. "See. They're fine."

I see what she's getting at. Zombie Brian clearly knows how he ended up in this position.

Zombie Brian reaches out to take the bar from Rachel. Again, there's something wrong with his movements. They're too jerky. Too fast. But there's something else too. It's like Brian remembers being human but can't get a handle on the controls of his new super soldier body. He snatches the bars from Rachel and eats the first one in a single bite.

"If the charts are correct, the transformation makes you hungry all the time. The . . . um . . . zombies are attacking us because they're hungry and they don't know how to find food," Rachel murmurs, talking more to herself than to me.

As all of this is going on, I'm desperately trying to catch my breath. I put my hands on my knees and lean forward. Smentkowski is over on the side of the room, watching things transpire, holding the gun kind of slack against his shoulder.

"Thanks for nothing," I say when I can breathe again. I can't keep the bitterness out of my voice. He stood there and let that monster attack me.

"You seemed okay," he answers, eyeing Rachel.

That's just great. He was willing to risk my life to avoid upsetting the pregnant girl. "You're lucky Vivian didn't take that position when you had one of those things on top of *you*."

Smentkowski's face turns red. "Okay. Sorry. Point taken."

I have to get control of this situation. To get back in front again.

"Rachel," I say in my firmest voice. "I know it sucks, but Brian is—"

"A person, Steve," she interrupts. "He's a human being. With a mother who misses him."

I take in a deep breath to stay calm. "He's a human being who has been the subject of a series of terrible medical experiments. That's unfair. Tragic, even. But we don't know what the consequences of releasing him will be. For the world. Or for him. You might not want to admit it, but we're all safer if he remains where he is."

"I'm not sure that's true," Smentkowski says. His forehead is squished up. He's deep in thought.

"Of course it's true, Smentkowski," I snap. "For all we know, Silverstone is waiting to scoop Zombie Brian up the second he gets out of the lab. And even if they don't, *someone* is gonna come looking for him. We need to focus here, people." To my left, Rachel sinks into the office chair with a pained expression on her face. She's on the verge of another round of contractions. "We need to put a plan together to get out of here once Paul and Vivian get back with the van." I say the last part with as much force as I can muster. Like I won't allow any discussion of the possibility that something might have happened to the two of them.

Brian watches me with what I would describe as a glare.

If zombies can glare.

I draw myself up as tall as I can and glance around at the

steel walls of the long room. "We have to figure out how to get out of here and down safely to the ground floor."

Rachel moans, and the creature twists around to face her. His head pulses from side to side. He's nervous.

"She's pregnant." Now I'm talking to it. To him. Explaining myself to Zombie Brian. "About to have the baby any second."

There's a pause. Zombie Brian holds himself very still.

"No one is going to come looking for Brian," Smentkowski says with a grim finality.

"What are you talking about?"

He puts the gun down on the desk nearest to him. "We're going to destroy this building."

Rachel's mouth falls open.

I remember what Zanna told me.

Watch out for Ellenshaw and Smentkowski.

They're Pod destabilizers.

Brian whirls around to face Smentkowski.

"I have a plan," Smentkowski says.

He points to Brian. "And *he's* going to help us."

SHELDON SMENTKOWSKI

It's the only way, really.

I lost the shipping manifests and the laptop up on the roof. Our best hope of stopping Silverstone from making more Metabolize-A and more monsters is to destroy their operation. No, this won't do anything about the bars they've already made, but it will certainly make it harder for them to produce more, and wrecking most of their computers and equipment will hurt too.

Plus, those zombies are still trolling around all over the factory. The more of them we can take out, the more we'll increase our odds of survival.

I know how we'll do it.

"You want to destroy this building?" Miller asks. "Even if that was a good idea, how would we begin to do it?" He keeps his tranq gun tucked under his arm. "And how does that help us? We're supposed to be waiting for the van."

I left my gun resting in one of the cubicles. "There's so much soundproofing in this part of the building that we'll never be able to hear the van. And what happens if it shows up?"

"When it shows up," Miller says with an edge to his voice.

"Yeah, well, *when* it shows up . . . well, in case you've forgotten, there's like twenty of those things out there by the building. Twenty of those things that'll be chasing the van. *Three* of those monsters ran down that blonde girl and—"

"I remember," he says even more sharply.

The zombie is staring at me with its deep black eyes. It's unnerving.

Zombie Brian. That's what Miller calls him.

I clear my throat. "Anyway, we need to take down as many of those creatures as we can." I glance at the monster. "No offense, bro."

Putting my hands up defensively, I go on. "Steve, look. Rachel's contractions are coming faster. We can't wait around here forever. We might have to go for the van ourselves. If we do, it'll help a lot to have one of those—"

"Brian," Rachel interrupts with a snort.

Zombie Brian's head whips around toward Rachel at the sound of his name.

Rachel frowns. "So what exactly do you want Brian to do?"

I find myself stepping back. "We . . . uh . . . need . . . him . . . to keep the monsters busy while we set things up. And then . . . um . . . protect us until we can get to the van."

Rachel shakes her head. "You saw what the zombie did to Allison. He can't handle too many of those . . . former people on his own. He'll be killed."

Zombie Brian makes what, in his human days, might have been an impatient noise. But now it's more like an animal's indignant grunt.

I step back farther. Miller's right. Rachel's lost it. Become too attached to the creature. Or what the creature represents. But we have to make this work.

Drawing in a deep breath, I force myself to go on. "Allison was still almost fully human, and she didn't know what we know." I glance at Zombie Brian. "You said it yourself. Those things down there are basically like toddlers. He's as strong as those things, as fast as they are, but he has his full intelligence. It's like sending a

294

teacher to deal with a class of preschoolers. He just has to babysit them for a few minutes. Long enough for us to get set up."

Miller frowns. "And what, exactly, will we be setting up?"

I hesitate. We'll basically be recreating my dad's worst industrial disaster. Maybe they won't realize how dangerous my plan is. "An explosion." I pause again. "Combustible dust."

Rachel and Steve watch me with matching skeptical expressions, and I go on. "Remember how I said my dad investigates industrial accidents? A few weeks ago, he started dealing with this explosion at a dog food plant. Basically, the place was covered with the grain they use to make dog biscuits, and then some welders came in and the whole place went up in flames."

Rachel frowns. "I read about that in the *Wall Street Journal*. Four people were killed."

"Great," Miller grouses.

I ignore them. "Vivian said there were a bunch of boxes labeled PRODUCT FLOUR. Whatever they're making those creepy bars out of—"

At the mention of Metabolize-A, Zombie Brian jerks his upper body and growls.

Miller raises his gun.

"Relax, Steve," Rachel says.

"—has to be every bit as flammable as ordinary grain. We'll disperse it and head for the exit. When we're almost out, we'll light it up."

Rachel is about to object again.

"The only way these people will let Zombie Brian go is if they think he's dead. We destroy the factory and get to town. He can ride off into the sunset," I say.

She shakes her head. "He's not our property, Sheldon."

I roll my eyes. "Then we ask him if he'll do it. If either of you have a better idea, now is the time. Paul and Vivian have been gone over an hour. If they're coming back, they should be here soon."

"Well, if I know anything about animals it's that, on the whole, they like to avoid big fires," Steve says, lost in his own thoughts for a minute.

Rachel clutches her belly and winces. "They're not animals, Steve."

"We have to get Rachel to a hospital," I say. If we can agree on that one thing, maybe we won't keep arguing.

"They're coming back," Miller says.

"Then let's get ready," I say.

We pause and stare at Zombie Brian. Apparently, it's on me to pitch this idea to him . . . or to it . . . or whatever. "Look," I say. "You gotta know that those Silverstone people . . ."

The zombie dramatically flinches, almost knocking into Rachel. He clearly knows all about Silverstone.

"Yeah. Well, those guys. They're gonna hunt you down. If you help us, you get away. We survive and go home and tell the world that we saw you bite it. Then you can . . . ah . . ." I trail off. Truthfully, I have no idea what on earth a sci-fi super monster could do, or wants to do, or would do.

Rachel draws in a deep breath. "Your mom came to our church. I saw her, and she was so . . . devastated . . . she needs . . . I promise. I'll find a way to tell her what happened. So she can stop . . . wondering."

Next to Rachel, Zombie Brian's head jerks around, his gaze

moving from person to person. Then he slowly and deliberately gives us a nod.

Shit.

Yeah.

He'll do it.

Okay.

"You're one of us now," Rachel tells Brian.

Okay. All we have to do is implement this insane plan.

Miller sighs. "All right. I'll get everything packed up."

He collects all the guns and ammo and makes a show of getting everything organized. Like the plan will go better if he has certain bullets in certain pockets. Miller insists on packing the laptop even though we keep losing all the shit we try to collect.

"We'll need something flammable," Rachel says.

Zombie Brian takes off toward the corner of the room and almost crashes into the wall. He really doesn't have a very good handle on how fast he can run. Or good control of his strength. He rips a drawer out of a desk, and it hits the wall behind him. Rachel takes one of the flashlights and heads in that direction.

"Ah. Whoever sits here is a smoker." She returns with two lighters and a pack of Marlboros. "We can probably use these sort of like fuses. You know, toss a few cigarettes around to ensure the spread of the flames."

I do not know, but I nod along anyway.

"It's not enough, though. That alone won't make a large flame." She keeps looking around the room and finds a desk with a small refrigerator underneath. "Oh, perfect. Did you know non-dairy creamer is seriously flammable? We once did an experiment in . . ." She trails off, mostly talking to herself.

Miller hands me a flashlight and my tranq gun and pushes the office chair up to Rachel.

The creature snarls.

What if this isn't a good idea?

What if I get us all killed?

I shake that off and follow behind Miller as he pushes Rachel in the office chair. Zombie Brian zooms around us, disappearing into the darkness beyond the flashlight. He's resting near the door when we arrive. Like he's been there forever. Waiting on us.

It hits me.

The monsters can see in the dark.

Fuck.

We all stand around pointing our flashlights at the hulking stainless steel door.

"Now what?" Miller asks.

Oh. Yeah.

I'm in charge now.

I shiver. "Okay. Well. Zombie Brian should go first. Clear the path. When we get down there, well, one of us needs to disperse the flour. The rest of us should wait by the door. The instant there's enough powder in the air, we light it and get the hell out."

"Someone has to help Rachel," Miller comments.

We both glance down at the pregnant girl with a pack of cigarettes and a large container of hazelnut coffee creamer in her lap.

And here's a problem. Miller would probably be better and faster at dispersing the flour. Miller would also be better at protecting Rachel. I'm tubby. He's fit and better with guns.

I'm a nerd who got sent to fat camp during winter break.

He's a jock who works at said fat camp.

Miller thinks for a second. "Okay. You dump the flour. I'll cover you."

On the plus side, Miller is back in charge.

But.

Me dumping the flour sounds like a shitty idea.

"Right," I say. That sounded confident, right?

"I hope *Brian* is as good as you think he is. Or we'll all be dead," he says.

"What about the door?" Rachel asks.

She's staring at the thick lock on the thick door.

Zombie Brian reaches out and tears the door open. It bounces off the wall a couple of times and then comes to rest in an open position. The door handle has been squished into a small sphere and hangs by a single screw.

Something tells me Brian is pretty good.

"Now we know why that cage door had five locks," Miller says.

You betcha. Now we know.

We move out into the open space of the second floor. Out here, the smell of burnt acetone and zombie flesh lingers from earlier. A bit of smoke has risen toward the high ceiling. It smells gross, but I remind myself that this probably helps our little science experiment.

I follow behind Zombie Brian, struggling to keep up. He moves like lightning.

My flashlight shines across his back. The grayish-blue scales shimmer and create a strangely fascinating pattern as he runs.

We can already hear more of those things down below.

Behind me, Miller pushes Rachel. "Tell your pal not to get too far ahead," he says.

"I don't control him," Rachel says with an edge to her voice.

"Well, someone needs to," Miller shoots back. "The whole point is that he's supposed to clear a path for us. He can't do that if he isn't *with* us."

We walk as fast as we can. The wheels of the chair make a ton of noise as they scrape across the tile floor, and for a second, it gets quiet. The creatures are listening.

For us.

I walk faster.

When we arrive at the staircase, something crunches under my feet.

Glass.

Using the flashlight, I trace a trail of jagged shards on the floor that leads to the fake lab we explored a few hours ago. The place looks like it's been through a war. All the windows and partitions have been smashed, the lab equipment lies in ruins on the floor, and the shelves where we found the chemicals are empty.

And.

Two of the monsters are in there.

A pair of them. Standing together in the far corner of the lab. The flashlight nearly falls from my sweaty palm.

Miller sees them too. "Run!"

One of the zombies screams while the other watches us, cold and frozen.

Zombie Brian races forward, positioning his body in front of Rachel. Whatever else happens, I get the idea that Brian will make sure that Rachel survives.

Miller picks up the chair Rachel is sitting in and hurries past me, carrying her, huffing and puffing as he goes. He's made his way down the first couple of steps before I realize.

I have to run.

Now.

Run. Now.

One of the zombies takes off in a blur. Coming fast in my direction.

Zombie Brian roars.

And it *is* a roar. It's intense. Loud. Like a lion. He might represent the next evolution of humanity, but there's something about him that harkens back to caveman times. Something raw. Something primal.

I remember what Rachel said. Zombie Brian is something new.

The thing in the lab slows its pace and even shrinks back. It lets out a scream, but not the same as before. My plan seems to be working. Zombie Brian is getting control of this.

Miller is at the base of the stairs. "Smentkowski! Get a move on it!"

He's right.

I zoom by Zombie Brian and meet Miller and Rachel on the first floor. He's out of breath, which makes sense considering he carried a pregnant girl in a chair down a flight of steps. Our flashlights reveal several of those things over by the machinery. Frozen.

Watching Zombie Brian.

This is a really stupid idea. I count at least five of those creatures, which means there are probably even more out there.

Miller's scanning for the best way out.

"There's a door back there," Rachel says, pointing to a glow-in-the-dark EXIT sign.

That's true. But it's an emergency exit down a long, narrow hall. If we get trapped back there with one of those creatures, we'll be dead for sure.

"We go out the front," Miller says in a tone that doesn't invite arguing. "Smentkowski, you're up."

Yeah. About that.

I'm about to suggest that Miller go dump the flour. The pallets of flour boxes are off to the left, very near where one of the zombies was jumping on a fulfillment machine conveyor belt just minutes before. If anyone can do this, it's Miller, not me.

He's the athlete.

It's like Miller senses these thoughts. "Smentkowski, you can do this. For God's sake, an hour ago, you tossed a zombie off the roof. You swung from a hose into a glass window. Anything gets near you, it's gonna get shot in the ass with a tranquilizer dart so big that the thing will be asleep until next Christmas. You're a badass. Let's go. Meet us at the front door."

Without waiting for me to respond, he pushes Rachel's chair toward the wall behind us. A couple of seconds later, the beam of his flashlight bounces around the warehouse like a searchlight.

He's looking for those things.

He finds one, and a second later the first shot of the tranq gun echoes through the warehouse.

I have to move.

Tucking my own flashlight under my arm, I run toward the boxes.

Miller must have hit one of the creatures, because there's a series of pained shrieks.

This also breaks the silent standoff between the monsters and Zombie Brian.

Fast, heavy footsteps echo off the stairs.

Zombie Brian is coming.

There is the pitter-patter of light footsteps too. Rachel is running around. Something is happening. Going wrong.

Another shot.

I make myself keep going toward the flour. I find it, and with a mounting sense of desperation, I rip the plastic wrap off the stack of boxes. I catch a break and find a box cutter on the top of the stack. I'm able to get the first box open pretty quickly and drag a fifty-pound industrial bag out. It's labeled METABOLIZE-A PROPRIETARY FLOUR BLEND and lands with a whack on the factory floor.

Another shot.

My ears are kind of ringing now. Maybe from the noise.

Maybe from absolute fucking terror.

There's more shrieking and screaming, and about twenty feet in the distance, something lands hard on the floor.

I'm flooded with a momentary sense of relief. Miller has managed to take one of those monsters down.

The feeling is short-lived though.

There's another series of shrieks, the creak of metal, and a horrible scraping, a thousand times worse than nails on a chalkboard. I have to jump to avoid a forklift skidding along the concrete.

One of the monsters has tossed a fucking forklift.

Even worse, when I cut open the bag of flour and dump it, a disgusting, glittery, greenish powder empties out. Some of it rises into the air, but most of it settles neatly on the factory floor, and I watch the airborne particles fall and start to land.

My blood is cold as ice. My heart is frozen.

This isn't going to work.

The factory is squeaky clean and, working by myself, I won't be able to spread enough flour for us to create a fire. I remember my dad saying that the conditions at the pet food factory were the results of years' worth of negligence. I thought he was full of shit.

Now I'm not so sure.

Another shot.

And then another.

Rachel screams.

My stupid fucking plan is going to get us all killed.

But in for a dime, in for a dollar. I open the second bag.

I let out a silly horror-movie scream when Zombie Brian slides up right next to me and yanks the open bag from my grip.

Another shot.

Zombie Brian is being trailed by a group of the creatures. He tosses the bag of flour at one of them and then knocks me back, sending me flying against the wall. I see double for a second after my head hits the bricks, and a blurry Zombie Brian tears the first pallet apart quickly and with ease, continuing to throw the sacks to the other monsters. They pass them back and forth between each other. Hooting and hollering as they run around.

He's created a game.

A game for monsters.

Zombie Brian hits the second pallet. This time a few of the other creatures join him.

Shit. He's getting the other zombies to disperse the flour.

And it's working. They're tossing the bags all over the place and kicking up dust as they zoom around the room. The air is full of that creepy green dust. Plus, they appear to have forgotten all about me and Rachel and Miller.

Suddenly the danger of what FannonPharma is doing here is so clear. Miller thinks we should have left the monster in his cage. He might be right.

Zombie Brian is stronger than us. And faster.

And now. He is also smarter.

His plan is better.

An army of Zombie Brians would be unstoppable.

"Smentkowski!" Miller screams.

It's time.

Time to light this place up.

Pushing up against the wall, I take off hard toward the front door.

I'm running as fast as I can, and as I go the fire is already starting.

Rachel Benedict is some kind of an evil fucking genius. She's made a trail out of the creamer and placed lit cigarettes along the way. Flames burst out as I pass, and the only thing that keeps my sweatpants from catching fire is probably that they are still wet.

It's a strange feeling though. The way that my skin is both hot and cold.

Also.

I might not make it out.

A second later, Zombie Brian arrives right behind me. He puts his cold hands under each one of my arms and scoops me up, the way a parent might handle a small child. He breezes past Miller and Rachel.

Rachel has a piece of a flaming camp T-shirt, and Miller has the coffee creamer container. They both toss them as far as they can into the factory, which is smoky with the ominous green Metabolize-A dust.

Hot flames explode in every direction.

Zombie Brian pulverizes the front door, and the fire pushes us out into the snowy night.

PAUL FANNON

There's something surreal about the feeling of *being* dinner.

Humanity is supposed to be at the top of the food chain.

But maybe not anymore.

My arm throbs, and the bandages Roger wrapped it in are soaked with cold blood.

Vivian Ellenshaw is Action Girl.

She's at the side of the van taking whacks at the monster with the end of the flashlight. The beam of light bounces all over the snow, crossing my face twice.

The zombie screams and screeches and takes a couple of swipes at Vivian that she somehow manages to dodge. She's going to get killed trying to get that monster out of the van, and I'm going to sit here and let it happen.

Except that's not me anymore. I lit a zombie on fire and almost got my arm eaten off when I tried to charge one of those things. I'm not going to be The Jerk.

I'm going to choose to be something different. Something else.

I grunt in pain as I will myself to my feet. I'm moving as fast as I can toward Vivian when a few things happen at the same time.

Roger attempts to start the van. It takes him a few tries, but the engine turns on, making noises like an angry espresso machine.

Then.

A deep, low roar and flames that erupt over the tops of the tall trees.

In the direction of the factory.

Some major shit is going on over there.

What if it's taking us so long that everyone is dead?

There's another boom.

How could anyone survive that?

Roger is screaming, and Vivian is yelling something, and the creature is hooting, and smoke rises above the forest, and only one thing is clear.

What we're doing isn't working.

From the front seat, Roger jabs at the zombie with the barrel of the empty shotgun. In the back, Vivian pounds it with the flashlight. Occasionally, Roger inadvertently hits a button in the van's control panel. The headlights go on and off, the windshield wipers activate, and the horn sounds. This is enough to keep the monster distracted, but it's pinned down. Trapped.

We need the creature out of the van.

The thing lands a pretty good punch, like *pow*, right in Vivian's face. She stumbles back, landing in the pile of snow I created with my digging. She moans, but I think she's okay. She just took a big knock.

This is the opening I need.

But I have to get a move on it before I lose my nerve.

I make a dash at the zombie where it sits, dazed and confused.

Let's hope it doesn't try to eat my other arm.

I'm in the back seat of the van, inches from the monster and its hot, fishy breath. Roger is turned all the way around in his seat, continuing his frantic attempt to pummel the creature with the shotgun.

Grabbing the monster by the waist, I try to tug it out of the van. It's like trying to move that horrible Neptune marble statue my mom insisted on buying at an art fair and sticking right by the front gate. When she was out one day, Dad and I moved it into the bushes. It took forever and almost killed me. This is basically like that.

The zombie digs its strong, pointed, spiny fingers into my back.

Roger must have some concept of what I'm trying to do. He squeezes through the small gap between the front seats and pushes the monster from behind. He continues to shove the barrel of the gun into the zombie's back, leaving the thing trying to fight us both in the cramped back seat.

Together, we're able to shove the creature out of the van and into the snow.

While Roger and I keep beating the zombie, Vivian gets up and runs to the driver's side of the van. She gets behind the wheel of the van and takes off. At first, I think she plans to leave us here. But after about ten feet the brake lights cast a red glow over us.

She's backing up the van.

Fast.

Roger and I have to jump out of the way to avoid getting rammed by the van.

The van hits the creature hard, and it's thrown backward about ten feet, into the trunk of a massive tree. It's not dead, but the collision causes enough of a delay for me and Roger to climb into the back of the van.

He goes first and then me. Vivian hits the gas the second we're inside.

And I seriously wish Roger was driving, because Vivian can't drive in the snow for shit. She isn't able to get the right pressure on the gas, so we're not going nearly as fast as we could be and it also feels like we're one jerk of the steering wheel away from skidding to a crash.

It's gonna be ridiculous if I survive a horde of superhuman, screaming, flesh-eating monsters only to be killed in a car wreck.

I'm doing my best to slide the van door to a close when the monster's hand wraps around the edge of the door, compressing the metal with its grip.

The zombie has caught up with us and runs alongside the van. We're probably going around twenty miles an hour, which means the monster is fast.

Incredibly fast.

And it's climbing into the van.

I scream yet again, and Roger pushes me aside, climbing over me toward the open door. He gives the creature a hard, swift kick.

Or he tries to, anyway.

The thing anticipates Roger's move, and it grabs his leg instead.

Now it's Roger's turn to scream.

I don't know what to do. We're dragging the zombie along with the van, and one of two things is going to happen. Either the creature is going to succeed in getting back into the van or it's going to pull Roger out with it.

I scream again.

The windshield wipers slide back and forth. It's snowing, and they're barely effective at keeping the front window clear. I don't even know how Vivian can see what she's doing.

Vivian glances back at me. "Hold him!" she yells.

I don't know what she has in mind, but I've learned not to argue with her. I grab Roger's shoulders and hold him as tight as I can.

Breathe. I have to remember to breathe.

Vivian steers the van inches away from a tree. There's a loud whack, and then Roger and I are almost thrown out of our seats by what feels like the van running over a massive speed bump. The monster was pushed away from the van. And.

We ran over it.

We ran over that thing. We hit it with the van.

Again.

I do my best to look out the back window. The moon is still behind the clouds, but I can't see anything. The zombie appears to be down.

It doesn't seem to be following us.

I help Roger into the seat next to me.

Both of us are breathing hard. Huffing and puffing. Sitting there. Staring at each other but saying nothing.

Vivian continues to drive. She's getting a little better at the controls. She steers us onto the main road. We're not sliding around as much, and we're going a bit faster than before.

Because.

Well.

That massive fire is providing a little bit of extra light and making it easier to see.

"Roger," Vivian calls back. "Any suggestions on how to use the service roads to bypass camp and go straight to Fannon-Pharma?"

He leans forward. "Yeah. Plenty. Beginning with how about we not do that? In case you haven't noticed, there's a massive fire in that direction. Things are clear over here. We need to get to town."

Vivian ignores this. "Four! See what you can do about the door. We're gonna freeze if you leave that thing wide open."

Her conversation with Roger goes on as I try to slide the door closed. But the monster crushed the middle part of the door, and it won't stay shut. I end up sitting on the edge of my seat and holding it closed. Vivian cranks up the van's heater, and a couple of seconds later it's much warmer inside.

"If your friends were in that building, they're probably dead," Roger is saying.

"They're alive," she says with absolute certainty.

I think she means Steve Miller is still alive.

"And we told you we were going for the van and going back for our friends. You chose to come with us."

Roger snorts. "I chose to save your ass back there. I could have left you to deal with those things by yourself and taken the van."

Up ahead of us, the road branches off in two directions. Roger rubs his broken arm. For the first time, I notice that he, too, is bleeding.

Vivian stops the van at the fork. "Then do it now, Roger. Push us out of the van and go on your merry way." She waits for him to do something, but Roger remains in the back seat, scowling at her.

"We have to save our friends, Roger," she says in a quiet voice.

"Fine. Go left," Roger says through clenched teeth. "That

should take us north and toward that burning mess. What happens next is on you."

I guess now that Vivian has the van, she's back in charge.

Which is just as well.

He gives Vivian a series of directions, guiding her through the back roads that surround the camp. When we get closer to the flaming building, we're able to drive right across the electric fence that we climbed over a few hours before.

Roger presses his face up to his fogged-up window to get a better look at the fiery red brick structure. "What the hell is going on over there?"

Black smoke rises into the even blacker night.

Vivian makes the turn into what must be, in better times, the driveway leading up to the manufacturing plant but immediately hits the brakes. We skid a few feet forward, but she's able to stop the van before things get too out of control.

I spot three familiar figures. Miller and Smentkowski have their arms around Rachel to support her weight. They're filthy and haggard, but otherwise they seem okay.

Except.

Right behind them.

Towering over them.

Is one of those things.

They're about to be torn apart by one of the monsters.

Vivian screams.

I let go of the van door, and it whips open.

I grab the shotgun and push myself into the night.

RACHEL BENEDICT

Outside, the night itself is on fire.

On the bright side, at least it's warmer. The FannonPharma building is a massive campfire, and its flames create a glow that's weirdly cheerful. Sheldon's plan seems to have worked. The building has been destroyed. Mad scientists won't be making any more of those Metabolize-A bars. Not in there anyway. And we seem to have taken quite a few of those monsters out with the fire. Should I still keep calling the victims of FannonPharma's terrible experiments monsters? Should I still be happy if we're able to kill them? The only reason that they're doing what they are doing is that they've been genetically engineered to be . . .

Hungry.

These thoughts send cold shivers through my body.

Behind me, Brian is breathing loudly. He has almost dragged us away from the factory, dodging the shards of glass shooting out from the exploding second-story windows. In a blur, we traveled up the road and to what must have been the main gate. It's more or less destroyed. The iron looks like it's been trampled by a herd of buffalo.

We land in the snow a few feet from the beat-up van that skids to a stop in front of us.

The. Van. A nice, warm, comfortable van waiting to take us to the hospital.

The van's side door is thrown open, and Paul runs in our direction.

A second later, Vivian is right behind him.

They're covered in blood.

That's what hits me as they rush forward.

Vivian, Paul, and some strange man.

Half of Vivian's face is all swollen up. Paul holds his own arm like it might fall off if he lets go. The pair of them have blood on their coats, on their faces and hands, and even running through the strands of their hair.

They've managed to find an adult, an athletic Black man in a staff uniform. One of his sleeves is dark with blood. I vaguely remember seeing the man while Sheldon and I waited in the Lodge for the rest of our Pod to arrive. How long ago was that? How long has Allison been dead?

Even though they've been to hell and back, the three of them roll out of the van like a pack of army rangers. Paul has a gun. They wear identical expressions of terror and horror on their faces.

They're moving fast.

Toward Brian.

"Get in the van!" Vivian shouts.

They think Brian is a threat.

I try to step in her path, but a fresh wave of contractions hits me. They're like an earthquake inside my body, and they're coming faster now. I'm going to have the baby soon. Really soon. It takes everything I've got not to fall down into the snow.

"Wait. Wait," I say as Vivian breezes right past me.

Sheldon is too worried about me to care much about Brian.

Brian's muscles tense slightly. I'm the only one who notices. He's getting ready. Looking at the gun with his midnight black eyes. He snorts a couple of times. The sound is full of menace. I can't move. But I also can't let this situation get out of hand.

Brian could kill Vivian and Paul without even meaning to.

My abdomen pulses and throbs. Everyone is rushing all over the place.

Luckily, Steve intervenes. He blocks Vivian. "Stop. It's okay, you guys. It's okay." He glances at Brian. "He's . . . uh . . . with us."

Paul slides across the snow, coming to a halt in front of me.

Vivian tries to go around Steve. "*He? He's* with you? What the hell are you talking—"

Sheldon has come to stand next to me. I hate to admit that I need help, but I find myself leaning up against him for support.

Steve puts his hands on Vivian's shoulders to keep her from going any farther. He leans around her. "Is that you, Roger?" he asks. "You're . . ."

"Alive?" the man who must be Roger says. "Yeah, that seems to keep surprising people."

I dig my fingernails into my palms to avoid crying out.

We pause there for a minute or so in a snowy standoff. It only ends when something rustles in the forest and reminds us that we're not safe.

And the pain. I groan.

"We have to get Rachel to town," Steve says.

Roger nods and makes his way to the driver's seat. We have an adult in charge. For some reason this creates a warm surge of reassurance.

Vivian mutters something as Steve guides her to the back seat of the van. Paul and Sheldon hover behind me. I take a few steps toward Brian. He's staring at me, and it hits me that his gaze from now on will always be alien and cold. His life in the normal world is over. The old Brian will be on that MISSING poster forever. He will always be gone. Lost and missing.

"I'm sorry," I whisper. "I'm so, so sorry. I wish . . ."

I wish this had never happened to you. I wish you could go back to your old life.

Brian holds himself very still and gives me a small nod.

Then he turns and takes off in a run. In an instant he's gone. Disappeared into the trees.

Sheldon helps me into the middle row, leaving Paul to take the front seat.

The moment we're all in, Roger hits the gas. It takes Sheldon and Steve a few minutes to get the van's rear door closed. They end up tying it shut with a piece of torn T-shirt. There's a small gap that lets cold air in and rattles.

But still.

Roger has the heater cranked all the way up. He seems to know where he's going on a series of back roads, and he knows how to drive in the snow. Paul tries turning on the radio, but we don't get any reception. After a few minutes of static, he turns it off again.

Behind me in the very back seat, Steve introduces everyone to Roger, who we learn is the camp athletic director. Then he explains what happened in the factory. How we escaped from the roof. How we found out that the Metabolize-A bars were a big military conspiracy designed to turn fat people into the ultimate warriors. How Brian helped us destroy the factory. I'm relieved that I don't have to do anything but concentrate on my breathing.

Breathe in.

Breathe out.

Slowly.

Knowing that Brian can never ever go back to his home makes me miss my own. I should have tried to talk to my parents sooner. For the first time in a really long time, I wish I could talk to my mom. She'd hug me and tell me everything will be okay and make my favorite gingersnap cookies. Dad would let us roast marshmallows in the fireplace.

When Steve is done, Vivian asks a question.

"I don't get it," she says. "If these things can control their behavior, why are they running around trying to murder everyone in sight?"

"Um, well," Steve begins.

I sigh. "Going through the process of the mutation, of changing, it's like being born. It takes time to become mature. Brian had been at FannonPharma for months. He'd regained all his intellectual capabilities and learned to control his body. The . . . um . . . others. They're like toddlers. There's nothing that can control them, and they're hungry."

"Great," Paul mutters.

It's quiet again for a while. Roger succeeds in getting us onto the main road. We're on a stretch of the state highway that I vaguely recognize from when Dad takes us out to cut down our own Christmas tree. It's no longer snowing, and we're making progress. We pass a sign advertising a breakfast buffet in Flagstaff.

We're headed toward civilization.

Vivian leans in between me and Sheldon, resting a small video camera on the seat right between our heads.

"What are you doing?" Steve asks.

"Trying to finish Allie's movie," she answers with a sniffle. "She'd want this shot. The return to the ordinary world."

"You got video footage of those things?" Sheldon asks.

"Yes," Vivian says in a tight voice.

It's quiet again. Vivian Ellenshaw wants to avenge her best friend's murder.

Roger tries to lighten the mood. "When we get to town, what's the first thing you're gonna do? You know, after we call the police and your parents and all that? When I get home, I'm gonna sleep for a week."

"I'm going to get this baby out of me," I say as my insides ache.

Light laughter breaks out in the van.

After a pause, Vivian answers. "I'm going to finish Allie's movie. But after that? I think I'll get a stack of the dumbest magazines I can find. You know, the ones that have articles like 'Use Your Horoscope to Pick the Perfect Pedicure' or 'One Hundred Ways to Organize Your Desk Drawers' or something. I'll get the world's biggest cup of cocoa with so many marshmallows that I can barely keep them in the mug. And I'll sit there and sit there and sit there."

We pass another billboard. This one for Waffle House.

In forty-four miles.

In around thirty minutes, we'll be in town.

"I'm gonna sit on the couch with my laptop, phone, tablet, and PlayStation and stuff my face with Spicy Doritos and Code Red Mountain Dew," Sheldon says. We've lived a lifetime since Theo took all our electronics during camp orientation.

At least it's nice and warm in the van.

"I'm gonna take a vacation," Steve says. "Go so far south that they've never heard of snow."

Vivian snorts. "If you keep going south, you'll end up at the South Pole. They have nothing but snow there."

My belly shakes with laughter, and it makes me ache even more.

"I'm going to . . . um . . . I'm going to . . ." Paul's answer goes unfinished. What is he going to do when the world finds out what his dad has been doing at the camp?

We're getting closer to town, and I'm starting to recognize a few of the small cabins located off the highway. Something is off though. It's been snowing here too. Of course it has. But the roads are empty and covered with thick white powder. The town is supposed to de-ice and cinder the roads when we get a certain amount of snow. A bunch of people at our church work for the town, and they often take care of the church parking lot when they are out on one of their runs.

This road is wild and abandoned.

I don't have much time to think about this as more contractions rock my belly.

In spite of myself, I let out a pained grunt.

"Try to stay as still as you can. And stay calm," Steve says.

We spent the night being chased by the victims of Fannon-Pharma's horrible medical experiments, almost freezing to death, destroying an industrial building, and I'm about to have a baby any second now. "You stay calm," I snap.

Steve puts a reassuring hand on my shoulder.

"I'm sorry," I say.

He smiles. "Don't worry about it. I know staying calm is easier said than done."

I close my eyes and try to relax. I'm able to manage my breathing, but the staying still part is harder. The snow and ice are uneven, and it's like we're driving on a very bumpy road. We make a series of turns, and I can tell the van is slowing down.

Suddenly the pain in my stomach becomes sharp, like jagged glass inside of me.

"Do you smell that?" Vivian asks.

"Yeah," Smentkowski says. "It's gas."

I can't pay any attention to that. I can tell that the baby is ready to come out.

"Steve?" I say. It's more of a pained moan.

I turn around in my seat. "Steve, we have a big problem."

"Hell yeah we do," he says in a tense whisper.

The way he says this makes the tiny hairs on the back of my neck stand up.

My eyes flutter open.

We're stopped at the Chevron. The first gas station you hit when you arrive in town.

I stare at it.

What's left of it.

The gas station would fit better in a war zone than a small mountain town.

The fuel pumps have been tossed every which way, and that smell has to be coming from gasoline gushing out of a large reservoir tank and into the snow. I glance over at the mini-mart behind the station. Glass glitters in the headlights. All the windows have been smashed. Part of a soda machine from the store sticks out of the snow. There's a pulverized police cruiser and a clump of cars that must have been in some kind of a crash.

"Don't look," Steve says, squeezing my shoulder again.

But it's too late.

I can see the body parts. I can see the blood.

I tense up again. "What's happened?" I ask. "What's happening?"

Even though I already know the answer, a terrible scream fills the empty road.

The baby is coming.

And the . . . zombies have taken control of the town.

VIVIAN ELLENSHAW

Welcome to Flagstaff.

The scene in front of us makes the world we left behind at Camp Featherlite seem downright calm and organized. We pass a coffee shop called Late for the Train. It's painted that weird Arizona beigey-orange color and in better times is probably a fun local hangout. But now its coffee roaster has been thrown into the middle of the parking lot. There's a table upside down on its flat roof.

Roger hits the gas again.

"The hospital is on Forest," Fannon says.

"It's faster to go around and up Columbus," Roger says through gritted teeth.

We pass several snow-covered abandoned cars.

"Maybe during Monday-morning traffic, but the roads are deserted. Turn on Forest!" Fannon tells him.

Perfect. It's the zombie apocalypse, and two guys are going to argue about directions.

One thing we don't see is any other people. Either they're hiding . . .

Or dead.

I scoot my hand closer to Miller's, but he's too busy pressing his face to the window and surveying the destruction to notice.

"Who's driving this car? You or me, boy?" Roger says.

What I need to do is stay busy. I press the camera close to my face and focus on getting a good shot.

Smentkowski turns around. "You're filming this?"

"I have to," I tell him. "We have to make sure the world knows what happened."

And knows about Allie.

We continue to speed along, and honestly I have no idea where we are. On Columbus. Or on Forest. Rachel calls Miller's name. He can't turn his eyes away from the blur of smashed-up cars and trashed buildings. She cries out.

Rachel is having the baby.

Soon.

The outline of a bloody severed arm appears on the camera's LCD screen. I turn off the camera. I've got way too many shots of horrible stuff.

I jump at the sound of a familiar scream. The monsters are nearby.

"Are we almost there?" I can't help but shiver.

"If we'd have taken Forest, we'd be there *already*," Fannon grouses.

This time, Miller does put his hand in mine. "We'll be fine. Everything will be fine."

Spoken like The Courageous Captain.

My blood runs so, so, so cold.

"Listen to me, Steve." When he doesn't look at me, I lean in front of his face and force him to see me. "You have to promise me that you won't do anything stupid."

Rachel moans again.

"I'm not stupid, Vivian," he says with a frown. He smells as good as he did when we kissed on the roof. I need him to be The Jock with a Heart of Gold. I need him to live.

I lean even closer. "I'm not saying you're stupid. I'm saying don't *do* anything stupid. You have to promise me."

"I promise," he says flatly.

This is a lie.

I don't know what Steve Miller was when he arrived at camp, but he's now The Courageous Captain.

I want to scream.

To scream like one of those creatures and have it echo all over and terrify people for miles and miles.

"How long is it to the hospital?" Miller asks.

We're coming up to an intersection. One of the traffic signals has been knocked all the way over and lies on the ground. Another sways from side to side, still standing, but only barely. On the plus side, its red light blinks over and over in emergency mode.

Smentkowski is thinking along these lines too. "The town has power," he says.

There's a large Bashas' grocery store on the corner with its neon sign lit. Were it not for the mess in the parking lot, the place might look almost cheerful. Roger slows down to make the turn onto Columbus.

We're hit hard on the passenger side.

Rachel and I scream in unison at the sound of bending, twisting metal, and a massive dent in the rear door pushes us toward the opposite side of the van.

My stomach lurches as the van spins around. Miller tries to steady both Rachel and me at the same time. Smentkowski's head smacks against the window. He's probably just had half his programming skills knocked out of him.

Roger is able to straighten us out but not to stop the skid.

We keep sliding into and through the Bashas' parking lot, and we don't stop until we sideswipe an abandoned truck and crash into one of the brick pillars in front of the store.

At first, I think we've been in some kind of a car accident. But we didn't pass a single car on the road. There probably isn't another vehicle on the road for miles and miles.

Smentkowski helps Rachel sit up. "What the hell happened?" he asks.

His question is answered a second later by the screech of one of the monsters, who lands on the roof of the van with a heavy thud. One of those things rammed the van. I scream again as I'm barely able to move out of the way before the dented, bent metal takes my eye out. Even still, a piece of jagged metal scrapes the side of my face.

Blood runs down my neck.

"Oh God. Vivian, are you okay?" Steve asks, swatting at my neck.

"I'm fine," I say, even though I feel like half my face has been torn off. "Roger! Can't you get us the hell out of here?"

As these words leave my mouth, I realize that I can barely hear anything over the sound of the revving engine. Roger is trying to move. But we're stuck.

He takes his foot off the gas. "I think all that spinning around took out the steering column or maybe tore the rear tires off their axles or—"

"We can't sit here and wait for the monsters to make an early breakfast of us," Fannon interrupts in a high-pitched voice.

"They're just hungry," Rachel pants. "They can't help it. Not their fault. Not . . ."

Her effort to make excuses for the creatures is interrupted

by another awful scream. The zombie jumps off the roof and lands on the hood of the van, sending us bouncing out of our seats. It punches a fist through the front windshield, hitting Roger smack in the chest.

Shit. We have to get out of here.

Right now.

I shove myself over Miller and rip the tie off the door. "We have to get out of here!"

"Let's get into the store," Fannon says. "The hospital is behind the store. There's a patch of trees, and then we can run across Forest. If we can get out the back door, we might make it!"

Smentkowski pushes and I pull, and somehow we get Rachel out of the van. Roger stumbles out of the driver's side, barely able to walk. Fannon has the best idea. He takes the shotgun and throws it as hard as he can right at the monster's head. The thing probably isn't seriously hurt, but it's enough of a distraction to allow us to get into the Bashas'.

Working together, Smentkowski and I are able to hobble along with Rachel. I knock over a rack of discounted Christmas stuff. Ornaments that nobody wanted. A stuffed animal chicken who sings "Jingle Bells." Leftover red and green Hershey's Kisses. A sign that reads NOW 70% OFF slides along the floor.

I'm out of breath.

We're inside.

The lights are on, so at least we can see.

Smentkowski gets Rachel loaded in a shopping cart, so at least the problem of how to move her has been resolved. But she's onto something about the eating. The monsters have clearly been inside the store.

Eaten everything in sight.

There are a few discarded containers on the tile floor of things like laundry detergent and dish soap that the monsters must have tried to eat before realizing that stuff is poison. Those aisles are mostly intact. The food aisles though.

Those have been torn apart.

We're standing in front of an aisle with a CRACKERS, COOKIES, & SNACKS sign overhead. Empty Cheez-It boxes and Oreo packages are strewn all over the floor, and the bare shelves are haphazard and broken.

What I wouldn't give to have my oar back right now. "We need a weapon."

"We need to get out of here," Fannon says.

"I . . . I agree," Roger says, not making it clear who he agrees with. Then he clarifies. "That girl is about to pop. We have to get her to a doctor."

Miller presses his lips together and nods. "Okay. We're going out the back door. When we get out there, get ready to run. Paul, Rachel is your responsibility. You know where the hospital is. Don't think about anything else. When you get outside, you run."

"Got it," Fannon says.

We follow behind Miller. He grabs a shopping cart and takes an odd route, leading us through the aisle where they keep the barbecue supplies. He loads his cart up with bags of charcoal, lighter fluid, several lighters, and packages of paper towels. He opens the lighter packages as we walk.

"Just in case," he says.

Every once in a while, we hear a series of snorts and crunches.

We all know.

We're not alone in the store.

Miller points to a green EMERGENCY EXIT sign near the back, to the right of the butcher counter. "Okay, there it is. Let's get ready to run. Paul. Now."

Roger casts a reluctant glance back at us. But he and Fannon both take a side of the shopping cart holding Rachel and make a break for the door.

I take off after Fannon even though I don't know why we have to run or where we're even running to, but when we come to the end of the aisle, it's clear what's happening.

And Miller must have expected it.

Whatever happened in that factory, he and Rachel understand those things better than I do. Three of the zombies are behind the smashed-in glass butcher's counter stuffing raw steak and hamburger into their monster mouths. It's the first time I've really been able to get a good look at them in the light. There are two small ones and a third that towers over the others by a foot or so. They all have the same bluish-green fishy skin, but the iridescent scales create different patterns, much like people would have freckles or sunspots.

The monsters freeze for a second and watch us with their black eyes.

The big one roars.

They're coming our way.

We're going to be chased by three of those monsters into the narrow hallway that leads to the store's rear exit. We'll never be able to fight off three of those things. There's an aluminum dolly near the hallway entrance, and Miller grabs it, dragging it with one hand and the shopping cart with the other.

This is it.

Miller pushes me down the hallway and blocks it with his shopping cart.

"Go! Go now!" he screams.

Oh God. I can see his plan.

He's going to stay and fight them.

He's going down with the ship.

He's going to try to buy us enough time to get away. Steve Miller plans to set the shopping cart on fire and stop the zombies from entering the hallway for as long as he can. Miller is basically going to be a one-man version of the Spartans at Thermopylae.

I grab his hand, and I squeeze it hard. I don't care if I hurt him. "No! No! I won't let you do this. I won't let you die for us." For me.

I make a grab for a bag of charcoal and one of the lighters. Maybe we could use the charcoal briquettes like cannonballs. Maybe we could set the things on fire. Maybe the two of us working together could successfully fight them. There have to be other things to use as weapons. This is Arizona. The land famous for no gun control. There has to be a rifle around here somewhere.

There has to be.

Miller blocks my access to the cart and pushes me back again. He hoists the silver dolly up, getting ready to use it like a battering ram. "Vivian! Those monsters are ten times as fast as we are, and they're getting smarter. There's *no way* we'll be able to stall them long enough for all of us to get away, and we can't fight three of them and win, especially without the gun. I'll buy you as much time as I can. You have to go. Now!"

Those things continue to watch us. Surveying our fight with almost amusement.

No. No. No. I stand my ground.

"Get the hell out of here, Vee," Miller screams so close to me that my ears start to ring.

"I won't! I won't!" I make another attempt to get to the shopping cart.

The zombies cock their heads while I scream.

"Smentkowski!" Miller yells.

Miller pushes me back one last time into Smentkowski's arms. Smentkowski presses himself flat against the wall of the narrow hallway, and I squeeze past him. Once I am in front of him in the hallway, he shoves me forward as hard as he can. But I don't want to go on. I really want to stay. I really want to go down with the ship too.

I can smell the lighter fluid and hear the sizzle of charcoal as we move down the hall.

The rear door opens to a narrow access road and a wide land bank full of red rocks and short pine trees. Smentkowski slams the door behind us. Fannon is already off in the distance. Working with Roger to get Rachel's shopping cart across the rocks. A second later we can't see them anymore. They've left the strip of brightness created by the store's parking lot lights.

Smentkowski grabs my hand and tries to pull me in that direction.

I yank my hand free.

I've never hated someone so much in my life as I hate Smentkowski.

He is going to let Steve die.

I make for the door. "Let me go! We have to go back. We have to—"

Smentkowski shoves me one last time. "No!" he says. "It's not what he wants. If you go back in there, it means he'll die for nothing. If you care about Steve Miller, do what he told you. Vivian, this one time. Listen to someone else."

Listen.

This one time.

This one time I let Smentkowski take my hand.

And together.

We run.

STEVE MILLER

Too late, I realize what I really am.

The Courageous Captain.

Or maybe I always knew.

There's something strangely reassuring about knowing who I am. What I am.

Like at least the events of my life make some kind of sense.

I hope my mom isn't gonna be too pissed. She didn't want me coming to camp. She wanted me home. At least when you're dead, people can't say, *I told you so*.

I might be going down with the ship.

But I'm making sure my crew gets off in the lifeboats first.

I glance back at the door behind me.

I'm half expecting the door to open and Vivian to burst through.

But it stays closed.

I've saved the girl.

My girl.

The creatures creep toward me.

Now I wait.

For the inevitable.

SHELDON SMENTKOWSKI

Thank God I'm able to get Vivian away from that damn door.

She finally follows me, and then *we* follow Paul and Roger.

Once we get into the trees it's kind of dark, but we still make pretty good time. The two of us don't have to push a shopping cart full of a pregnant girl, and Vivian is pretty athletic. I spend most of the time trying to run at the same pace.

We come out of the line of trees and stand facing a large complex of hospital buildings. I'm out of breath, so I point in the direction of the red EMERGENCY sign. Vivian nods, and we jog in that direction.

When we arrive at the main door, Roger leans against the wall, on the verge of collapse. The set of double glass doors has been boarded up with what look like tabletops. Paul beats his fists against the glass. But he, too, looks like he's ready to fall over, and his knocking doesn't seem to have accomplished much of anything. Rachel pants in a steady rhythm.

For all we know, there are more of those monsters out here.

We don't have time for this.

There's a large potted plant near the door.

Vivian gets the idea fast, and the two of us scramble around it. We each take a side. The thing is seriously heavy, and Vivian grunts as she lifts it. We're giving it a little bit of a swing, preparing to toss it into the hospital door, when the wood pieces are cautiously lifted. I spot two guards in Silverstone uniforms. They both have raised handguns pointed in our direction.

Behind them, a thin woman in blue scrubs peers through the gaps in their shoulders.

"Help," Vivian shouts. "We need help."

The men pry the glass doors open with their fingers. When it's open wide enough for Rachel to pass through, Fannon and Roger hurry her inside the building.

I push Vivian toward the door. "We made it," I say with an exhale.

On the opposite side of the door, two women in scrubs are already hustling Rachel onto a gurney and wheeling her away from us.

Vivian squeezes through the door. She turns around and glances over her shoulder at me.

I smile. It's meant to be reassuring.

We made it.

Her mouth opens into a terrible scream. She tumbles to the ground. Looks of panic overtake the faces of the guards. Something cold slithers around my arm. Warm breath on my ear and the smell of an aquarium that desperately needs to be cleaned.

The monster has come for me.

There's a snap as I'm jerked backward.

I'm pretty sure my arm is broken.

It feels like nails are being driven into my neck.

My feet fall slack as I'm dragged through the snow.

Vivian gets farther and farther away. She's up on her feet again, trying to get past the guards at the door. She'd probably come into the fucking street and try to fist-fight the thing if the guards would let her.

The space between us is filled with all the things I'll never get to do. The apologies I'll never make. Sights I'll never see. My potential, whatever it is, or was, dwindles away. Vanishes forever.

Gunfire breaks into the street. I spot the smallish zombie from the grocery store running in my direction. Steve was right. We couldn't kill those things. Only delay them for a while.

More guys in black Silverstone uniforms scramble around inside the hospital. They're shouting and firing in every direction and boarding up the windows again.

I close my eyes.

And then . . .

RACHEL BENEDICT

Push. Push. Push. *You have to stay with me. You're doing great. Just one more big push ought to do it. I know it hurts. Squeeze my hand, Rachel. You're doing great. You've come so far. You can do it. It's okay. It'll be okay. Breathe. I know it hurts. You're doing so good, sweetheart. Almost. Almost.*

Then.

The most gorgeous, deep, dark blue eyes I have ever seen.

Blue.

Like cobalt. Or the deepest ocean.

It's a girl.

And I love her more than anything.

PAUL FANNON

Stevie Allison Benedict is born at 4:47 a.m.

We weren't able to tell Rachel about Smentkowski until after she'd named the baby.

Roger has a broken arm and a huge gash on his stomach. He's in surgery for a while. They're able to fix Vivian's face with some surgical tape, but my arm needs stitches. I'm out for a while for a blood transfusion. Then they give me what seems like about a hundred shots.

My dad isn't here to make sense of it all for me.

As soon as Rachel and the baby are in stable condition, we're all moved into a quarantine unit at the hospital. Doctors and nurses in cartoonish hazmat suits come and go. We're not allowed to call our parents. We're not allowed to see each other. We're not allowed to watch the news or access a computer or use the phone.

We're given old stacks of magazines and told to be patient.

Then, we wait.

After an eternity, we're moved to Fort Huachuca, an army base close to the Mexican border. In some ways, this is better.

We're allowed to see each other and watch TV.

In some ways, it's worse.

We find out what the world thinks is going on.

And about how royally screwed we are.

The day after we're checked in at the base, we're more or less able to wander around our isolation barracks. The first time I see Vivian again is in the commissary. I'm sitting there with a plate full of cold chicken and an unopened container of green Jell-O.

She takes the chair across from me. She's wearing a pair of Silverstone blue sweats, same as me. No *hello* or *how have you been* or anything, just, "They took it. Those bastards took it."

When I stare back at her, she goes on. "The camera. Allie's camera. I thought they might try something, so I hid it under the mattress. I went out for a bunch of tests, and when I came back it was gone. We've got nothing. Allison and Steve and Sheldon died for nothing."

Vivian gets up and paces around the table.

"They died to save us. That's why they died," I say.

An expression of horror crosses her face, and she deflates, falling into her chair again. "I know," she says. "I know. But after everything that's happened, I was hoping that something good would come out of it."

I nod. It's easier to believe that our friends died to expose some big conspiracy instead of so that I could be sitting here, poking at my lunch.

"Have you heard anything about our parents?" she asks me.

I shake my head.

She leans forward. "I overheard one of the nurses saying that my mom has a lawyer and that Rachel's dad got the governor to call." She glances at the soldiers guarding the exit. "They have to let us out of here, right?"

I shrug. "I don't think they *have* to do anything."

Vivian's shoulders fall. "Have you seen the news?"

Oh yeah.

We're the Featherlite Four.

Three teenagers and a camp employee. The only survivors of

the worst blizzard in the history of the state of Arizona. An environmental disaster that killed over four hundred people.

Roger mostly stays in his room.

We're all listed as being in critical condition.

We learn that after the first monster broke loose, the afternoon we arrived at camp, Silverstone was able to evacuate most of Flagstaff, sending everyone who would go to Phoenix and rounding up everyone else and putting them in high school gyms and hospitals and churches. Flagstaff Medical Center was actually a safe haven site for locals.

I'm pretty sure this is what ended up saving our lives. That we saw hundreds of people at the hospital.

And *they* saw *us*.

The government can't deny we exist. And our parents are squawking enough that Silverstone can't just whack us.

They even show Rachel's dad several times on the news. He looks about like what you'd expect. Kind of bald and kind of cranky, and he takes turns offering up his church for anyone in need and asking everyone to pray for his daughter.

The worst of it though is when they show that actress Dorian Leigh DuMonde in a velvet dress, posed in front of some castle in Transylvania, with mascara running down her face. It takes all my strength to keep Vivian from kicking in the television.

Army people come and go.

Silverstone people come and go.

They don't introduce themselves.

We're interviewed separately.

We're interviewed together.

As the days stretch on, it's more like Vivian is interviewing them. One morning, I think it might be a Tuesday, we're in the interview room.

Vivian: What happened to Steve Miller?

Silverstone Man 1: This would be your boyfriend from camp?

Vivian: You know who he is! When are you letting us out of here?

Silverstone Man 2: When we believe that it will be safe.

Vivian: For whom?

Silverstone Man 2: We also need to make sure we understand what happened at camp.

Vivian: We've been over that. The zombies destroyed it.

Silverstone Man 1: Ah yes. Those would be the genetically engineered super soldiers.

Silverstone Man 2: (laughs) The fish men.

Vivian: I didn't say they were fish men. And you guys should know what they are. You created them.

Silverstone Man 1: I don't know anything. And neither do you.

Silverstone Man 2: The sooner you become part of the solution, the sooner you can go home, Miss Ellenshaw.

The room is suddenly even chillier.

The baby stops squirming around.

My blood runs cold. Rachel told me all about Silverstone and their threats against my father. That made me feel a little better. Like, it's a relief to know Dad isn't a cold-blooded killer. But my friends don't need their fatness "cured." They need people like me and my father to treat them with respect. If we make it out of this, it's gonna be on me to make sure that happens

And that was a big *if*. Because the Silverstone guys said that same thing to my father.

You're either part of the problem or you're part of the solution.

Before they killed Kaiser.

It was obviously meant to intimidate us.

If we want to go home, we have to convince them that we are part of a solution that doesn't include anyone from Silverstone being held accountable for their actions.

The only thing we've got going for us is that everyone really likes the baby. And the baby has great timing. When things are getting rough, little Stevie will let out the cutest yawn and everyone will settle down. Or when the interview goes on too long, she'll cry and the Silverstone guys will mumble something about coming back later.

The problem is.

They do keep coming back later.

That night we have dinner in the TV room. They seem to be on some kind of a schedule with the meals, and tonight is Salisbury steak with macaroni and cheese.

Yep. It's definitely Tuesday.

"All the interviews. I think they're a diversionary tactic,"

Vivian says as she makes herself a plate. "They're stalling. They're keeping us here while they clean everything up."

Rachel is distracted by the baby but nods along.

Sometimes it really sucks not being as smart as they are.

"I agree," she says. "They were mostly able to keep people in town from seeing what was going on. But given how many cell phones and cameras are out there, someone must have gotten footage of the campers who were turned into . . . well . . . you know. Silverstone is going around destroying everything. Getting to everybody. By the time they let us out of here, we'll be three hysterical kids trying to tell the world about monsters in the woods."

"And Roger," I add. I'm not sure how Silverstone is going to deal with him.

Vivian has finished eating, and she gets up and goes around to Rachel's side of the table. "Here, let me take the baby so you can eat." She thinks for a minute. "At least we know for sure that we're being punished by the government and not God."

Rachel smiles. "True," she says.

We've become an odd little family. Four strangers who now have nothing but each other.

Vivian scoops up little Stevie and walks slowly around the table. "Plus, they have to get to the first responders. That woman I spoke to when I dialed 911, for instance. She knew about the zombies even before I called."

Rachel chews a bite of pasta and nods again. "Fifty bucks says that lady has fallen down an open elevator shaft by now."

I shudder.

Rachel cuts up her steak and pours herself a cup of juice.

"The longer we're here, the more unreal everything seems. The more unreal it feels."

She's right.

Plus, despite everything, I miss my parents.

And my house.

And the feeling of sleeping in my own bed.

I can't help feeling that outside the barracks, life goes on for everyone else.

And we'll be stuck here forever.

"No matter what we do, we'll never be able to make them pay," Vivian says with a disgruntled huff. "And if we don't get out of here, it will have all been for nothing."

The three of us exchange a look.

No words are spoken, but we make a pact in silence.

CUT

VIVIAN ELLENSHAW

I still have nightmares.

I keep remembering Miller in that hallway.   .

Keep seeing his face.

He told me that he'd never let anything eat my heart out.

He kept his word. But sometimes, I feel like my heart has been destroyed anyway.

I wish I could go back to the beginning and do everything again.

I wish I could save Allie.

And Steve.

And Sheldon.

Of course, there were a lot of other victims too. All the kids at camp. The counselors. The employees. All that human potential was lost. Each person left behind a family and friends. Zombie Brian's mother will never be the same. Silverstone, and their fat-phobic plan that treated fat people like disposable property, hurt everyone. They left devastated communities and wounds that can never heal.

I post a Christmas card from Dad on my bulletin board and glance out the window of my room, peeking through the slats of the wooden blinds. Like always, there's a plain, generic black sedan parked across the street. Silverstone has been watching us for months. Making sure we don't say anything to anyone. Like anyone would believe us. But that's not what I'm looking for. I spot Fannon's Porsche taking the corner at Pembroke and pulling up fast to the curb in front of our house. A silver minivan is right behind the sports car.

"They're here!" I shout as I take the stairs as fast as I can.

On the way to the front door, I pass Coach—I mean Brad. He and Mom are putting a bow on the last package. We've finally found something we all agree on. That shopping for little baby Stevie is fun. They've stacked presents all around the Christmas tree and around the fireplace. Whatever else happens, Stevie is going to be one spoiled little girl.

I throw open the door in time to see Fannon escorting Rachel up the walk. Mrs. Fannon is here too, holding Rachel's other arm. I can't help but smile. Rachel is one of the most capable girls I know. But she's also patient with them and lets the Fannons believe they are helping her. Paul's dad has been missing since the disaster at camp.

It's one more thing we don't talk about.

Pastor Benedict follows behind, carrying little Stevie. She's in a fluffy red velvet dress and white stockings. The tiny amount of blonde hair she has is in a ponytail that sticks straight up.

I hug them all as they enter the house.

Mrs. Benedict is the spitting image of Rachel. She has a dress that matches the baby's and is the last to come inside. "Happy holidays, dear," she says as she hands me a huge tray of brownies.

Maria has put out an epic spread of roast beef and potato pancakes and green bean casserole. We sing carols and decorate cookies and open presents. It takes Stevie over an hour to get through all her gifts. Her favorite thing seems to be a tiny squeaky accordion from the Fannons that I am seriously glad will be going home with the Benedicts. After Stevie goes to sleep, we play a game of Monopoly that lasts late into the night.

When I'm in the kitchen clearing away the dishes, I stare out the patio door. Sometimes, after dark, I could swear that I see something moving a little too fast through the oleander bushes that surround the swimming pool.

But I don't want to think about that now.

Mom comes to wrap an arm around my shoulders. I give her hand a squeeze.

Tonight is about all we have left.

We may have our nightmares, but we also have each other.

For tonight, that's enough.

ACKNOWLEDGMENTS

Thank you so much for reading this book! I hope my spooky story kept you up just a tiny bit past your bedtime.

A million thanks to Alice Sutherland-Hawes, Chloe Seager, and the entire team at the Madeleine Milburn Agency. Alice, I am forever grateful to you for finding the perfect home for my zombie tale and quirky characters. Chloe, thank you for continuing to champion my work.

So much love and appreciation to the whole team at Razorbill Books—most especially to my wonderful editor, Julie Rosenberg, who provided invaluable guidance in polishing my pages and helped me make this story the very best I could. Thanks as well to Alex Sanchez for such insightful feedback, and to Krista Ahlberg and Kate Frentzel for incredible copyediting. I promise never to misspell "horde" again! I hope everyone loves the cover of this book as much as I do and I am so grateful to Samira Iravani for the cover design and to Ursula Decay for the fierce illustration of my girl, Vivian. Finally, thanks so much to Jayne Ziemba and Casey McIntyre for all their support of this book.

Thank you to my friends and family, especially my mom, May Porter, Cassidy Pavelich, and Amie Allor. As always, thank you to my BFF Riki Cleveland for friendship and always being willing to read my horrible first drafts, and to my trusted critique partner, Amy Trueblood, for wit, wisdom, and on-point notes.

To the Arizona YA/MG writer community. Thank you all, especially Dusti Bowling, Stephanie Elliot, and Lorri Phillips. I am so thankful for our research trips and writing dates. You know you've got a great group of friends when they are willing to spend their evenings tracking down zombie candy or debating what monsters sound like when they scream.

Thanks to my early readers, including Laurie Elizabeth Flynn and Nancy Richardson Fischer. Any mistakes are my own.

To my wonderful husband, Jim, thank you for your tireless support, for always being willing to go on coffee runs, and for sticking with me for almost twenty years. To my Evelyn, I am so proud of you. I can't wait to see what comes next in your story!